SHADOW BORN

By Jasmine Walt & Rebecca Hamilton

SHADOWS of SALEM

SHADOW BORN

Chicago Police Detective Brooke Chandler is keeping a secret...and if she's not careful, it could get her killed.

Brooke is no stranger to the supernatural. In Chicago, vampires are just as prevalent as drug lords, and infinitely more bloodthirsty. So when her partner and fiancé dies in a mysterious fire while chasing down a lead in Salem, she suspects something dark and otherworldly is at play.

Blessed with the ability to see into the past by touching inanimate objects, Brooke transfers to the Salem PD, hoping her talent will help her get to the bottom of things. Between dodging assassination attempts and being stonewalled at every turn, the going is tough. Add in a mysterious fae club owner with secrets of his own and a personal grudge against her, and it becomes nearly impossible.

If Brooke wants to play in the supernatural sandbox, she's going to have to roll up her sleeves and get dirty. But how many people will have to die for Brooke to discover the truth?

one

Wallet. Check.
Toothbrush. Check.
.1911 pistol. Check.
Vampire bullets.

I paused at the last one, my fingers curled around the small steel case tucked into my duffel bag full of essentials. Standing at the edge of my crappy motel bed in Buffalo, I lifted the box to the dusty shaft of light filtering in through the window and cracked open the box to peer down at the hand-crafted wooden bullets inside. They were each filed to sharp points, mimicking stakes, and worked just as well as the real thing—provided you were a good enough shot to take out a fast-moving vampire.

I was a good enough shot.

Thank you, Uncle Oscar, I thought, closing the box and tucking it back into my duffel. Shooting wasn't the only thing he'd taught me; my uncle had also taught me how to make these bullets. And while he wasn't actually my uncle, he was still the only family I knew. Raised me since the day my parents dumped me on his doorstep at six years old.

Oscar had kept me on a tight leash as far as the supernatural were concerned, refusing to let me anywhere near anything that even hinted at magic. But Chicago was infested with vampires, so rather than trying to fight a losing battle on that front, he'd trained me to protect myself. I was leaving Chicago behind now, true, but I'd been using these bullets all my life. I wouldn't feel safe without them.

Besides, who was to say the place I was going didn't have vampires, too? Salem had so much supernatural folklore surrounding it that I couldn't rule anything out.

I zipped up my duffel, did a quick check around the motel room to make sure I hadn't forgotten anything, then grabbed my luggage and headed outside. Between the vampire gun strapped beneath my jacket, the police-issue S&W .40 at my hip, and the detective's shield hooked through my belt, I felt pretty comfortable about my safety. Even so, I took a good look around the parking lot as I made my way to my Jeep. It didn't pay to be off-guard, and I was in new territory.

I made a pit-stop at a Dunkin' Donuts for coffee and a breakfast sandwich, then headed onto the I-90 to finish the last leg of my journey. The Chief of the Salem PD had approved my request to come out there on loan from Chicago PD a week ago, and I'd wasted no time packing my stuff up, getting someone to sublet my apartment, and finding a place to stay in Salem before hitting the road. If not for the fourteen-hour trip, I would have done the whole drive in one shot, but I wanted to arrive at the station to meet my new teammates as alert and fresh as possible.

Unfortunately, the Chief wouldn't be there herself, as she left town just two days ago due to a family death, but she assured me that the captain of the department handling Tom's case would roll out the welcome mat for me in her stead.

A pang hit my chest at the idea of having to work without my partner, and I tightened my grip on the steering wheel. Of course, Tom Garrison, had been more than just my partner—he'd also been my fiancé. The love of my life, the first man who'd understood my needs and desires and accepted me for who I was.

Well, at least who he figured I was.

Tom knew about my vampire-staking ways, but he didn't know about my strange ability. I'd been holding off on telling him because Uncle Oscar had instilled in me from a young age that revealing my talent would put me and those around me in grave danger. I didn't want to put Tom in danger.

Yeah, and look how that turned out.

Maybe if Tom had known what I could do, he would have taken me with him to Salem when he'd gone back to check into that missing person's case. If he hadn't left me behind, then maybe, just maybe, he'd still be alive.

"Stop that," I muttered, placing my breakfast sandwich on the passenger's seat so I could swipe at the stray tear trailing down my cheek. My fingers left a greasy streak across my skin as I wiped away the drop of moisture, and I blinked back the rest of my tears. It wouldn't do to arrive at my new precinct looking as if I'd just finished watching *Titanic* or something. If I showed up looking like a pitiful damsel in distress, they'd put me on traffic duty, which was *not* what I wanted.

I wasn't going to Salem to get away from Chicago or the specter of my dead fiancé. I was going to find out what had happened to him. And *why*. I'd been told the motel room he'd been staying in had caught fire and that no evidence had survived the blaze, but that wasn't good enough. I was going to hunt down the truth, and when I found out who killed my fiancé, I would make sure they were brought to justice.

I still didn't understand how Tom could be gone. My fiancé wasn't a weakling. He'd gone up against his fair share of vampires, just like me. Whoever killed him had to be at least as strong as a vamp, but possibly even stronger…somehow. The best place to start would be with finding Salem's supernatural pulse.

Sighing, I took in the world outside my window, hoping its beauty would temporarily relieve me from my dark memories. The early fall hillsides were bursting with color from the turning oak and maple leaves that surrounded me from either side of the highway as well as the rolling hills up ahead. The wind caught at my silver curls, tugging them free from their pins so that the strands whipped around my face.

Hmm. How was my new precinct going to react to *that*? My mercury-colored hair always drew strange looks, though no-one really ever said anything about it by the time I'd graduated grade school. As a freshman, they'd teased me for having the hair of an old lady and strange lavender-blue eyes, but I'd shown them I wasn't afraid to sock them in their teeth, and they'd kept their mouths shut after that.

Adults, on the other hand, knew better than to say anything in the first place—at least most of them. But that didn't mean I wouldn't be subject to their stares, and I would walk around knowing that they were dying to ask me about my unusual coloring.

Strange how, as an adult, I almost missed the forthrightness of the peers from my childhood.

Letting out a contented sigh, I tilted my head, enjoying the nip of winter that kissed my cheeks. I'd been born in Nevada, or so Oscar told me, but after being raised in Chicago, I was a winter girl through and through. I loved the cold weather, and I was looking forward to the snowfall in a more rural area, instead of watching it get stomped to a muddy slush in the big city.

Just as I was passing the sign for Wakefield, I caught sight of a woman kneeling next to a beat-up Crown Victoria, struggling to change a flat tire. It was still daylight, but sunset streaked the sky with brilliant reds and golds, and I didn't feel right about leaving her alone on the highway when I knew night would fall soon. So I pulled over to the shoulder, parked my car at a respectable distance behind hers, then went over to help.

"Hey there," I said with a friendly smile. "Need a hand?"

"Oh yes, please!" the woman cried, a southern twang evident in her voice as she flashed me a grateful, if harried, smile. She looked to be in her thirties, wearing a plain white tee shirt and faded jeans, and her dark brown hair was pulled back into a messy bun that was halfway unraveled by the wind. Frustration sparked in her brown eyes as she glared at the wrench, which didn't seem to be cooperating with her efforts to unscrew the bolts on the tire. "I know I should be able to use a wrench at my age, but I can't get this to work."

"No worries," I said, kneeling beside her. "I've changed a few of these in my time." I took the wrench from her, then set to work on the first rusty bolt. "Oof," I grunted. "No wonder you're having trouble. This thing doesn't want to give."

Truthfully, it wasn't hard to remove the bolts, even if they were rusty, but I played it up because I could tell she was embarrassed that another woman, a *younger* woman, was doing this for her. As a cop, I was pretty good at reading emotions, and I could tell by the strain behind her smile and the way she fidgeted that she was a little uncomfortable about the situation. Judging by the lack of a ring on her finger and the fresh-looking Salem High School bumper sticker on the back of her car, I figured she was a single mother, and likely prided herself on being independent.

"So, you're from Salem, are you?" I asked.

"Not a native, but I've lived there a few years now." The woman relaxed a little, comfortable with the idea of conversing over sitting around and watching me work. "It's a nice town."

"That's great to hear. I'm actually moving there."

"Are you really?" The woman's tone became friendlier. "Where from?"

I opened my mouth to answer, but just as I touched the final bolt, a flash came to me. Suddenly, I was crouched in a driveway on a moonlight night, watching the woman fight with a man.

"You're not leaving me, Shelley!" the man shouted. Both of the woman's arms were caught up tightly in his meaty fists, and their wedding rings flashed in the moonlight.

"Yes, I am!" The woman struggled against his grip. Her dark hair whipped to the side, revealing a black eye and bruising on her cheekbone. "I'm taking Jason, and we're leaving! I can't deal with this anymore!"

"Like hell you are!" The man let go of one of her wrists, and the woman cried out as he punched her in the face. There was a loud crunch as her nose broke. "The only way you're leaving me is in a body bag, bitch."

"Are you okay?"

I blinked as the scene fell away, Shelley's voice drawing me back to the real world. Turning my head, I looked into dark brown eyes that were round with concern.

"Yeah, I'm fine, sorry." I wiped a hand across my face, then cursed inwardly as black grime from my fingers streaked across my nose. "I'm just really tired from all the driving."

"Oh, I'm sure you are." Shelley laughed, perhaps at the scrunched up look on my face, then stood. "Here, let me get you some of Tyler's baby-wipes from the car."

While she rummaged in the back seat for baby wipes, I finished changing the tire. Judging by the fussy baby sounds and mommy's subsequent cooing, Tyler must have been the owner of that car seat. By the time she calmed him down and retrieved the wipes, I was done with the tire.

"Thanks so much," she said as I stood. "I really don't know what I would have done without you."

"No problem." I smiled, reaching for the baby wipes in her hand. The silver ring on her middle finger brushed my skin, and I stiffened as another vision swept over me, this one of a shadowy figure with glowing red eyes standing in a darkened alley. He opened his mouth, and I caught a flash of white fang.

Vampire.

"Are you sure you're all right?" Shelley asked, breaking through the vision. "Maybe you should sleep for a few hours."

"No, no, I'm fine." I shook my head to clear it, then took the wipe and cleaned my face and then my hands. "I've got coffee in the car." I hesitated, then decided to go for it. "I should have introduced myself. My name is Brooke Chandler, and I'm the new detective in Salem. If you ever need any help, please don't hesitate to come to me."

Her eyes widened. "I'm Shelley Williams, and I appreciate the offer. That'd be great."

I scribbled my address on a diner-quality napkin she dug from her purse, then pressed it into her hand. She bit her lip, and by the glimmer in her eyes, I could tell she was considering whether to tell me about her troubles. But in the end, she only smiled. "Maybe I'll come by with cookies some time."

"You're more than welcome to. Have a nice day."

But as I walked back to my car, I wasn't thinking about cookies. I was thinking about vampires. And about how nice it was that I'd chosen to pack my wooden stake bullets after all.

two

*F*uck *going down to the station,* I thought, collapsing onto my bed with a groan.

By the time I'd finished unpacking, I was so exhausted I barely had the strength to pull my cellphone out of my jean pocket and order pizza. The long drive, plus my lack of sleep, had well and truly tuckered me out.

Thank God I've got a place to live, I told myself as I stared up at the peeling paint on the popcorn ceiling of my new bedroom. The walls weren't a hell of a lot better, and the linoleum in the kitchen needed redoing, but I couldn't really complain since this wasn't my apartment.

Since I wasn't staying in Salem permanently, I'd chosen to sublet a rental on Airbnb instead of paying through the nose for a motel room for who knew how long. The peeling paint and outdated kitchen was what I got for going cheap, and truthfully, it wasn't as if I needed fancy digs. I wasn't planning on spending a lot of time in the apartment, and as soon as I accomplished what I came here for, I was going back home.

I probably would have stared up at the ceiling all night if the pizza delivery guy hadn't decided to lean on my doorbell. If not for the smell of hot mozzarella and yeast, I might have let him stand out there all evening, but the allure of thin-crust, tomato-basil pizza pulled me from the bed and into the living room.

I paid for the pizza, and my suddenly growling stomach prompted me to grab one of my host's blue-and-white ceramic plates from the yellowed cupboards and plop down on the faux leather couch with my dinner. A couple of slices later, my back pain had receded and my energy was up. Knowing I wouldn't be able to pass out on my new mattress now, I sucked the pizza grease off my fingers and grabbed my laptop so I could continue investigating the rash of disappearances that Tom had come out here to investigate.

According to the letter sent to him by Devon Randall, one of the captains at the Salem PD precinct, kids were going missing from the orphanage that Tom had grown up in, which was why he'd come back. His close ties to the place pulled at his heartstring, and he'd wanted to help. The fact that he'd wound up dead just a week after couldn't be a coincidence, and I was sure whoever was responsible for the kidnappings was also responsible for Tom's death.

The problem was, the only article I could find about the kidnappings was the one I'd found when hacking into Tom's email address, and it didn't say a lot.

Sighing, I pulled up the piece, which had been shoved into a tiny corner on the Boston Herald's website, and read it again. Featured at the top of the article was a photo of two Asian boys, brothers that had been left at the New Advent Home for Children, Boston's orphanage, when they were only two years old. A statement from the Haven had said the two boys had been put to bed with the rest of the children, and the next day they were gone. There was absolutely no trace of them, and no clues as where they might have ended up since their parentage was unknown.

Scowling, I chewed my bottom lip and tried for the billionth time to figure out how that made any sense. Children didn't just up and disappear—either someone had crept into the orphanage and stolen them, or someone from the inside had done it. Tom must have questioned the orphanage staff, because that was the logical place to start. I would have to do the same, once Captain Randall handed over the case file to me.

God, I wished Tom would have given me more details about the kidnappings. But the few times I'd spoken to him on the phone, he hadn't wanted to talk about it. I'd found that strange— we were partners and discussed cases all the time—but I'd let him have his space. After all, I figured he'd be home soon.

If only I'd pushed harder, demanded some details, I'd have been able to help him somehow. Hell, I should have just hopped on a plane and flown out here the moment I felt something was off.

Pulling out my cell phone, I dialed my own voicemail, then sorted through the messages until I found the one from Tom. Taking a breath, I ordered the voicemail to play, then waited for my heart to break all over again.

"Hey baby." His voice was hushed and full of strain, as if he was

in dangerous environment and didn't want to be overheard. *"I know you're sleeping now, but I just wanted to call you and tell you that I'm sorry. I know I fucked up, but I was just trying to do what I needed to. I don't know what's going to happen when I hang up this phone, but I love you. I love you so much, and I know you love me, too. But whatever you do, don't come looking for me. It's not safe."*

The clip ended, and tears slipped down my cheeks as a cool female voice asked me if I wanted to replay the message again. I jabbed the END button on my cellphone with an angry finger, then tossed it back onto the bed as rage burned in my chest.

Just what, exactly, had he meant? Whatever was going on here, it was way bigger than a case of a couple missing kids. Especially if Tom was telling *me* it wasn't safe here. For fuck's sake, we lived in vampire-infested Chicago. For Tom to tell me a small town like Salem wasn't safe meant that something big was going on here.

And damned if I wasn't going to find out what.

The next day started off well enough. I woke up bright and early, made myself an onion and mushroom omelet, and had enough time after that to put some work into my appearance, which was important since this was my first day on the job. I didn't really know what was considered business casual in Salem, but I dressed as if I was heading into work at Chicago PD on my first day as a detective—sensible black flats, crisp grey slacks, a black turtleneck, and one of three special blazers that I never left for work without.

I loaded my 1911 with the wooden vampire bullets I brought along, then tucked it into the concealed carry pocket built into the left side of my blazer. Since I couldn't officially carry a non-police issue firearm while on the job, and there was no way I could explain firing wooden bullets anyway, I had to take extra measures to keep myself armed and dangerous against vampires, but it was worth it. No way was I going out, even in broad daylight, without my gun. Not after that vision I'd seen when touching Shelley's ring.

I wonder if she made it back to town, and if she's coming by with those cookies, I thought as I trotted down the stairs and headed out into the early morning sunshine. There were definitely secrets lurking behind those shadowed eyes of hers, and if she was tangled up with vampires in any kind of way, I was sure she was going to need my help eventually.

I just hoped that when she came knocking on my door, she wouldn't be bringing a horde of the undead with her.

Since the station was only a ten-minute walk from my apartment, I hoofed it so I could get a feel for the town. The chill wind ruffled my loose curls as I traversed the sidewalks, passing by colonial-style houses and brick storefronts. There were plenty of people out and about, rushing their kids off to school or heading for work themselves, and I exchanged smiles and nods with them as I passed. Salem was definitely a small town compared to Chicago, but it wasn't so small that a newcomer would stand out.

The station was a two-story brick building off Margin Street, and I had to say it looked a hell of a lot smaller than my precinct back in Chicago. Hell, I didn't think it could fit more than our homicide detective division. But then again, there was only about one homicide a year in this small town, so it wasn't like they needed a lot of cops.

I let myself in through the front door, then glanced around at the white walls, reddish brown floor tile, and boring black carpet. To my left were the bathrooms and some waiting chairs, and in front of me and to the right were greeting stations that were walled off and protected by bullet proof glass. Most of the different department windows had their shades drawn, but the one in front of me was open, and someone was sitting behind it, tapping away at their keyboard.

"Good morning," a uniformed brunette greeted me as I approached the window, a Bostonian accent evident in her brisk voice. "Can I help you?"

"I'm Detective Brooke Chandler, on loan from Chicago PD." I flashed her a friendly smile. "I'm reporting to Captain Randall."

"Ah! Yes, he said to expect you." The uniform snatched up the phone on her desk. "Just a moment."

A couple of minutes later, the uniform cleared me, then gave me the passcode to enter the doorway that led to the rest of the precinct. I punched in the code, then followed her directions, trotting up the stairs to the second floor. I went down a hall, into a room marked 'support services division', then stopped outside a closed door on the opposite side. I eyed the brass placard on the door that said 'Captain's Office', then glanced around the room to make sure I had the right place. If not for the uniform jackets draped on the backs of chairs, and the map on the far wall stuck with pins and riddled with pictures of suspects, I would have thought nobody worked here. But then again, they might all be off doing something.

Never mind that, I scolded myself, knocking on the door. *You're not here to criticize the precinct. You're here to look into Tom's case.*

"Come in," called a deep, male voice.

I pushed open the door and stepped into a rectangular office that was half the size of my bedroom. Maps, artwork, and certificates of achievement hung on the walls above file cabinets and shelves, and the majority of the space was dominated by a cherry-wood L-shaped desk. Behind the desk sat a large, broad-shouldered man in uniform with blocky features, a crew cut, and a stern, unfriendly expression on his face.

"Detective Chandler." He jerked his head down once in what I imagined was an acknowledgement of my presence. "You're late."

"Sorry, sir." My spine stiffened, but I forced myself not to sound defensive. "It was a long trip."

"Maybe, but I was expecting you last night, and I don't appreciate having my time wasted." He gestured to the blue visitors' chairs impatiently. "Have a seat."

I did as instructed, resisting the urge to grit my teeth. The Chief of the Salem PD, Mary Spencer, had been more than friendly on the phone, and I'd assumed Captain Randall would be the same, especially since he'd been friends with Tom. But there was no such luck on my part, and if the way the skin around his mouth tightened was any indication, he looked as though he wasn't very happy to see me.

So much for rolling out the welcome mat.

"All right, well now that we're here, let's get this over with." The Captain reached into a drawer and drew out a substantial stack of forms. "These are from HR. You're to fill them out and turn them in before you're allowed access to anything in this precinct. I'm assigning Detective Guy Baxter as your buddy, so you can go on and get cozy with him in the bullpen. He'll answer any questions you have and show you around the building."

He pushed the papers at me, then turned back to his computer, fingers already poised over the keyboard as if there was a burningly urgent email he just couldn't *wait* to reply to. I stared at him in disbelief, unable to fathom how casually he'd dismissed me.

"Excuse me, sir, but this isn't right." I straightened in my seat. "You can't just drop this on me and then toss me into the bullpen."

Captain Randall scowled, turning his attention back to me. "Are you telling me what I can and can't do, Detective?"

I bit back the retort that sprang to my lips—the look in his dark eyes was growing dangerous, and I was trying to get things back on track, not make them worse. "No, sir, it's just that this is my first day here. I expected a little more from our first meeting."

The Captain fully turned his body toward mine now, swiveling his chair around. "What, did you want a pep talk? Because the last time I checked, nobody was forcing you to come out here. I didn't think I'd need to hold your hand since you're an experienced detective."

"No, you don't," I agreed, my voice growing tight despite my efforts to rein in my temper. "I'm an excellent detective, which is why I came here. I want to find out what happened to Tom, and I also want to take over the kidnapping case he was working on for you."

Captain Randall blinked. "Kidnapping case? What the hell are you talking about?"

"The missing kids from the orphanage Tom grew up in." Incredulity crept into my voice. "He said a couple of the cases were connected to Salem, which was why you called him, and that he came out because he felt personally connected. And now he's dead, and *I* feel personally responsible for letting him come out here by himself. I want to take over his case and find some answers."

Captain Randall shook his head, looking at me as though I'd grown a second set of eyes. "Look, Detective Chandler, I don't know what kind of problems you and Tom were having where he felt like he couldn't be honest with you, but he didn't come out here to look for any missing kids. I called him up to help me with an old murder investigation he'd been working on years ago. There were no kids involved, and no orphanage, either."

"W-what?" I gripped the arms of my chair so hard that my fingernails scratched the wood. "That's ridiculous. Tom wouldn't lie to me."

Annoyance flashed in Captain Randall's eyes, and he bared his teeth at me. "Again, I don't know what kind of relationship the two of you had—"

"We were getting *married*." I surged to my feet, unable to hold my anger in any longer. "That's what kind of relationship we had. Tom was my fiancé, and we told each other *everything*. If he said there was a kidnapping case, then there was."

"Look, Detective," the Captain said, his voice hard. "Tom was a good man and a good detective. Unfortunately, we can't ask him why he told you what he did, but I'm sure he had his reasons."

"I can't accept this." Anxious now, I yanked my phone from my pocket and pulled up the article I'd found in Tom's email. "Look, here's an article on two of the missing kids. You can't tell me that's not real." I shoved the screen in Captain Randall's face.

The Captain's eyes narrowed, eyebrows furrowing in concentration as he read the article. He shook his head. "I don't know where you got this article, but your information is wrong. I've never even heard of those two boys."

"This article is from the Boston Herald," I said, though my determination was starting to waver. "Are you saying it's a lie?"

"I'm saying I've never heard of those boys, and that Tom wasn't working on a kidnapping case with me." Captain Randall's voice was firm. "Look, Chandler, I know you're upset that he's gone, but there's nothing more to do than move on. If you're not going to do your job, the door's there. Otherwise, take your paperwork and get out of my office."

"I—" I clamped my lips together, choosing my words carefully before the Captain really did give me the boot. "Sir, I would appreciate it if I could at least take a look at the file regarding Tom's death. I just don't believe he died in a fire."

"You'll get your files tomorrow," he said. "Today, you're to finish that paperwork and get familiar with the way we do things around here. Just because you're here to work on Tom's case—a case which I don't believe needs further investigating, by the way—doesn't mean you won't be expected to help out the department as needed. Have I made myself clear?"

"Crystal," I bit out.

He turned back to his computer. "Good. You're dismissed."

I gnashed my teeth against the protest bubbling up in my throat, knowing that if he turned back to look at me again, it would be the last time he ever did. So instead of pushing the matter, I grabbed my stack of paperwork, then headed out into the bullpen to find a seat.

The sooner I did that, the sooner I could figure out why Captain Randall was lying to me, and what *really* happened to my fiancé and those missing kids.

three

The bullpen here was a quarter of the size of the one back at my old precinct in Chicago. It was a rectangular space separated from the sergeants' offices by a wall that was high enough to shield the cops that sat at their desks typing reports, but low enough that you could easily peer over the top to check on them if you wanted to.

As I walked through the area, searching for my desk, I caught sight of a man on his hands and knees next to his desk, muttering curses under his breath as he pawed at the scratched tile floor. He was a stocky guy with short, wavy brown hair, dressed in a pair of black slacks and a button-down blue shirt. I could tell he was a detective by the shiny detective's shield winking at his belt, not far from the gun holstered at his side.

"Hey there," I said, approaching him cautiously so as not to startle him. I didn't need him banging his head on the desk or something. "Need some help?"

The man raised his head, his dark eyes narrowing as he took me in. I pegged his age at around forty from the weathered lines in his square face. "You're Brooke Chandler?"

"Yeah. You know my name?"

"Of course. I'm Guy Baxter." He gestured to the tile. "One of my contact lenses popped out, so if you wouldn't mind helping me look for it…"

"Sure, of course." I crouched beside him, then carefully began scanning the area.

"While we're here, guess I'd better give you the basics about me," he said as he resumed hunting for his contact lens. "I'm forty-two, twice-divorced, no kids, and a workaholic. There might not be as much crime here in Salem as there is in Chicago, but I've been working at this precinct for ten years now, and anybody here can tell you, I prefer to burn the midnight oil. I hope you can keep up with that."

"Sounds perfect," I said, shrugging my shoulders. I was going to need him to help me out since I technically didn't have any jurisdiction here, so the more available he was, the better.

"You Catholic?" Baxter asked.

"Huh?" I turned to look at him with a frown.

"The cross on your neck." Baxter's eyes fixed on my chest, and I realized the chain I'd tucked beneath my turtleneck had somehow slipped out and was dangling forward. "I assumed you were religious."

"Oh." I touched the tiny silver cross, and emotion welled up in my chest so fast that tears actually sprang to my eyes. I pushed them back, along with my feelings, and returned my hand to the ground. "It was my fiancé's. He gave it to me a few months before he came out here."

"Oh, yeah. Tom Garrison." Baxter's tough-guy face softened a little with sympathy, and he nodded. "I never got to meet him, but I heard he was a good cop. Anyway, my brother is a priest, and he runs the Gateway Church off Liberty Street, so I figured I'd say you should stop by there."

"Oh, well, thank you." I smiled. "Maybe I will sometime."

My hand brushed against the sticky plastic of the contact lens, and triumph rushed through me. But before I could say anything, a vision burst into my mind, and I sucked in a breath.

Standing right here, just on the other side of this desk, was my fiancé. And he was talking to Detective Baxter.

The vision was gone as quickly as it came. Anger rushed through me, and I whipped my head to the side to confront Baxter. "Are you *sure* you've never met Tom?"

"Sure as the ground beneath my feet." Confusion filled Baxter's eyes as he narrowed them. "Why?"

"I—" The words caught in my throat, and I pressed my lips together. What was I going to tell him, that I'd just seen a vision of him and Tom talking together? He'd say I was crazy, and anyone else would believe the same. My ability wasn't normal, and as far as I could tell, Baxter was a regular guy.

But if that was the case, then why was he telling me he'd never met Tom when the vision I'd had clearly indicated otherwise?

"Never mind," I said quickly, then plucked the lens from the tile and held it out to him. "Here's your contact."

"Great. Thanks." Confusion morphed into relief as he took it from me, then rose. "I'd better go and wash this off."

I stood with him, and just as I got to my feet, another detective passed by us on the way to his desk. On a hunch, I reached out and snagged him by the elbow, pulling him to a stop.

"Hi," I said, flashing him a smile. "I'm Brooke Chandler, the new detective in town."

He smiled back, the annoyance melting from his oriental features. "Bobby Yan. Nice to see a new face here."

"Yeah. You know, I was wondering, did you know my fiancé, Tom? He worked here about ten years ago, came back here recently to help out with a case."

The smile flitted from Bobby's face, replaced by a more serious look. "Oh, yeah, I knew Tom. Everybody who was here around that time did. He's a hard man to forget, and it's a damn shame we lost him to that fire. I'm very sorry for your loss."

"Yeah, that's what everyone says," Baxter agreed. "I wish I'd known him."

"Very funny, Baxter." Bobby scowled. "You shouldn't be making jokes like that under these circumstances."

"What are you talking about?" Baxter asked, his eyebrows pulling together, but Bobby only shook his head. "Whatever, I don't have time for this. I need to fix my contact." He brushed past us.

"Don't mind Baxter," Bobby told me. "He's got his moments, but he's a great detective."

"I hope you're right," I said as Bobby continued onto his desk.

I looked over my shoulder to watch Baxter as he disappeared down the hall. If Baxter wasn't lying, that meant there was something wrong with his memory, and an addled mind did *not* a good detective make.

It took me most of the day to finish filling out the paperwork and go through the mandatory orientation course that HR required. I was hoping I could get my hands on Tom's file before it was time to go home, but as luck would have it, Baxter caught a case, and the captain ordered me to go with him.

God, but part of me wished I'd waited until the Chief had come back in town before coming to Salem. If she was here, she could help me cut through Captain Randall's wall of bullshit and get to the bottom of things. Now I'd have to deal until she was back.

I reviewed the notes I'd taken as Baxter drove us to the suspect's office in his white Chevy Impala. We were going after an accountant named Remy Vox who was suspected of running a drug-trafficking operation under the table. "So…what's the plan?"

"We're going to ask the man some questions, for starters." Baxter kept his gaze fixated on the road as he headed toward downtown Salem. This was the touristy section of town, lined with small brick buildings and Georgian and Italianate style homes that were interspersed with museums and witch shops. "Hopefully we'll either get something out of him or see something in plain sight that's enough to squeeze a warrant out of the judge."

"Right." I sighed a little, trying to keep the annoyance out of my voice and expression. I didn't need Baxter to explain to me the purpose of an interview. "Do you think he's even going to be at the office at this hour?" We'd spent quite a bit of time studying the case files, and the sun was starting to set now.

"If he's not, we'll catch him first thing tomorrow," Baxter said. "But in the meantime, we might as well try."

I slanted a look at him, trying to figure out my new partner. Everything I'd seen so far—from the methodical way he'd studied the case file to the laser-focus in his eyes when he drove—indicated a man fully possessed of his wits. So how was it that he couldn't remember my fiancé?

He has to be lying, I thought, my stomach tightening. But why? Why would Baxter lie about something like this, when Bobby had made it clear that Baxter was around at the same time Tom was? I bet that if I asked the other detectives, they would all say the same thing, so what did Baxter have to gain by pretending he didn't know my fiancé? Whatever the reason, I bet that if I could uncover it, I would be one step closer to discovering what had really happened to Tom.

Baxter parked us illegally outside a Dunkin' Donuts off Washington and Essex, and I blinked as he reached for the door handle. "Where are you going?"

He turned back and looked at me as though I were an idiot. "We're going on foot from here. In case you haven't noticed, the streets here are small and crowded."

"Oh." I let out a breath, then followed Baxter out of the car. I'd thought we were making a pit stop at Dunkin' Donuts, and while that was stereotypical of a cop, it was also pretty unprofessional considering we were on our way to an interview.

I followed Baxter up Washington and around the corner to Essex Street, passing a burbling fountain along the way. Men and women stood in the middle of the cobblestoned street or at tables, flagging down passersby and getting them to sign up for their ghost tours.

My nose twitched at the scent of burning incense drifting from the open door of a witch shop, and I turned, gazing curiously at the bundles of herbs hanging inside the storefront windows. How many of these people were charlatans, and how many had real power?

If I could find a real witch here, and befriend them, perhaps I could get them to lead me to the *real* supernatural hotspot in this town. Because even though this was where all the paranormal-*looking* stuff was in Salem, at the end of the day, it was still just a tourist trap. I didn't need a tarot reading, or a guide to tell me how to photograph ghosts. I needed real answers.

"Here we are." Baxter stopped in front of a glass door next to the Salem Five Bank. From a quick glance at the signage, I figured out that this was an office rental space. "Let's see what Mr. Vox has to say for himself."

He pushed through the glass door, and I followed. A blonde receptionist in her late thirties glanced up from behind her desk, and offered a friendly smile.

"Good evening," she said. "How can I help you?"

Baxter unhooked his badge and placed it on the desk. "I'm Detective Guy Baxter, and this is Detective Chandler." He tilted his head in my direction in the briefest of acknowledgements. "We're looking for Remy Vox."

"Oh." The receptionist blinked, then glanced down at her log. "I'm afraid Mr. Vox isn't here right now. He left just a few minutes ago."

"I see." Baxter's expression didn't change, but his eyes darkened. "Do you know when he'll be back in, ma'am?"

"At this hour, he's gone for the day. I expect he'll be back in at his usual time tomorrow. Nine a.m. Would you like to leave a message for him?"

"Sure." Baxter dug out a card from his pocket and passed it to the receptionist. "Tell him I need to ask him a few questions about an important matter. Appreciate your time."

"Well, that sucks," I said as we walked back outside. And it really did, because I'd been hoping to get this over with so I could go home. But as I glanced up the street, I noticed a man with dark blond hair wearing a charcoal grey woolen coat walking briskly up away from us. From the back, he looked a lot like our guy.

"Hey, Baxter...I think that's Vox."

"Oh, yeah?" Baxter followed my gaze, and a smile curled his lips. "Sure looks like it. Let's see if we can flag him down."

I arched an eyebrow as Baxter immediately began heading up the street. "You're going to have to move a little faster than that if you want to catch up to him."

Baxter snorted. "I'm not an idiot, Chandler," he said irritably. "I'm not in the habit of accosting citizens on the sidewalk. We'll follow him to wherever he's headed, then take him aside for a quick conversation."

My lips curled into a smile despite myself. "All right, if you say—"

A muffled shriek cut my words off, and I jerked my head to the left just in time to see a guy in a ski mask burst out of the CVS, clutching a knife in one hand and a bulging paper bag in the other that I was willing to bet wasn't filled with Slim Jims and Cheetos.

"Dammit." Baxter snarled under his breath as I rushed forward, probably because we were letting our drug-dealing accountant get away. But there was no way I was letting this guy rob a store right in front of our eyes.

"Stop!" I shouted as my flats slapped against the cobblestones.

Shit, that was uncomfortable. I was going to need to wear better shoes next time if I planned on making a habit of this. "Stop, police!"

The guy briefly glanced over his shoulder, eyes wide with fear, which turned out to be a mistake. The epitome of grace, he tripped on one of the cobblestones and crashed face-first into the hard ground. The paper bag flew from his hand, and I grinned triumphantly as cash spilled onto the street.

"Oh, no you don't!" I shouted as he began to get onto his knees. I tackled him, then grabbed and twisted the wrist of the hand still clutching the knife. Yelping, his grip loosened, and the knife clattered to the ground, safely out of reach.

"Police brutality!" he yelled as I yanked both his wrists behind his back, digging my knee into his sacrum to ensure he didn't get up.

"Yeah, yeah," I muttered as I cuffed his wrists. "Tell it to someone who cares."

"I guess you didn't need my help." Baxter's voice came from my right, and I looked up to see him standing there, both his eyebrows raised approvingly. The sight almost mollified me, until I remembered that he was a liar and was keeping secrets from me about my fiancé.

"Yeah, well, just because I did the hard part doesn't mean you get to put up your feet." I yanked the perp to standing, then shoved him toward Baxter. "Read him his rights and take care of the paperwork. I'll see if I can catch up with Vox."

"Wait!" Baxter called as I spun away. "You can't just go walking off! You don't have jurisdiction!"

I ignored him, pushing through the crowd of gawkers and

headed after our suspect before Baxter could say another word. Maybe I didn't have jurisdiction, but I didn't trust him, and I was better off working without him. Vox might not have anything to do with Tom's death, but I had a sudden urge to go after him, and I didn't need Baxter to take a single guy like him down.

four

Knowing that Baxter couldn't very well stop me with his hands full of criminal, I hurried onward. I couldn't tell you why, but something urged me to catch up with our original suspect despite the fact I hadn't wanted to take this case in the first place. Call it Detective's Intuition.

As I walked, I touched lamp posts and shop windows, catching little glimpses of him here and there to make sure I was on the right track. These little visions had me take two right turns and then a left, and then I caught sight of Vox turning the corner. His disappearance from my view once again galvanized me into action, and I stepped off the sidewalk and onto the street so I could hurry after him without having to push through the crowded sidewalk.

I rounded another corner just as Vox stepped into the parking lot in front of a high-end club. The stacked stone exterior of the building was awash in purple light, no doubt coming from the bulbs recessed into the rooftop ledge, and above the chrome double doors, huge metal letters spelled ENVY Nightlife. Judging by the full parking lot and the line of people spilling out onto the sidewalk, this was a popular joint. It also looked completely out of place amongst the little red brick buildings smooshed close together.

Unfortunately for me, Vox was apparently high enough on the food chain to bypass the line. He went straight up to the biggest bouncer I'd ever seen in my life. Seriously, if mountains wore suits, that's what this guy looked like, right down to his craggy dark face and plate-sized hands that probably looked like obsidian boulders when they were clenched.

And the worst thing was, he wasn't even the only one out there. I counted three other enormous men in suits patrolling the outside of the club, all fitted with black shades and earpieces, and the bulges beneath their suit jackets suggested they were packing heat.

Just what the hell kind of club was this, that the owner felt the need to have armed security guards around?

Mountain Man seemed to recognize Vox on the spot, because he inclined his massive head, then stepped aside to allow him entry. Dance music, heavy on the bass, spilled into the crisp air as the bouncer opened the door, but as soon as Vox was inside, the door shut and the sound abruptly cut off.

So, they'd soundproofed the building, too. Yeah, that wasn't weird at all.

I had half a mind to march up to the bouncer and flash my badge, but the idea of doing so made the hairs on the back of my neck crackle. I had the feeling these men wouldn't take kindly to being heckled by a cop the size of their pinky toes, and even if I did manage to muscle my way into the club, the commotion would likely alert my suspect, which was the last thing I wanted.

But how to bypass the line? At least as a detective I got to wear plain clothes. They wouldn't be able to tell I was a cop. Slacks and a black blazer didn't exactly scream detective to most people. But being a nobody wasn't going to get me inside, either.

A car door slammed nearby, and I turned toward the sound to see a man in a steel suit walking away from a red Lamborghini. I figured a guy like him wasn't going to be waiting in line, so I turned toward him, then allowed my wrist to brush against his platinum cufflink.

I got a flash of the outside of a hotel called *The White Stag*, and then another one of a girl beneath him, her cheeks flushed and her blonde hair spread across the snowy white sheets as she moved with him.

"Oh, Vance," she moaned, arching her back. "Fuck me. Fuck me harder."

Money left on the dresser had me thinking she wasn't the first woman he'd brought to that hotel, and that she likely wouldn't be the last.

Perfect.

The vision broke, and I snagged his wrist before he could get away. "Hey, Vance," I purred, giving him my best seductive smile. "Remember me? From the White Stag?"

His eyebrows furrowed together as he came to a halt. After a long pause and an uneasy expression, he offered, "Natasha?"

"I knew you would remember me." My smile widened as I curled my hand around his arm and pressed myself against him. Yeah, so I didn't exactly look like I was dressed for the club, but that wasn't going to stop me. "I'm here to meet a friend, but I got here late and I don't want to make her wait an hour while I stand in this stupid line. Do you think you could be a doll and help me out?" I reached up and pressed my lips against his cheek.

"For you, anything." His lips curled into a smile, but though the words oozed charm, they were perfunctory—something he said to all the girls, I'd bet.

Oh, well, I'd take it. I allowed him to lead me to the doors, and the way the Mountain Man moved aside for us without hesitation confirmed my suspicion that Vance, whoever he was, was a regular.

"Thanks, doll." I disentangled myself from Vance, then disappeared into the crowd before he could say anything more. I might have been one in a long line of girls, but the hunger I'd glimpsed in his eyes told me he was willing to take me for a second ride.

Not that there had ever been a first, or that there ever would be, but he didn't need to know that.

Once I was sure I'd lost Vance, I leaned up against a wall and looked around. The club was huge—a two-story affair with posh furniture, crystal chandeliers, and a dance floor packed with clubbers bumping and grinding to the music. The walls were mirrored, and my eyes narrowed as I noticed quite a few pale-skinned patrons who weren't showing up in the reflections.

Vampires.

My heart skipped a beat, and I was suddenly very happy to feel the weight of my vampire gun pressing against my side. But as I continued scanning the room, I noticed the vamps weren't the only odd things here. At first glance, everyone *seemed* human, but as I looked closer, I noticed some of these people were very *off.*

A woman wearing long evening dress with a high slit in the skirt lounged on an overstuffed couch with a long-haired man. Though the pair looked normal-enough, when I glanced at them out of the corner of my eye, I swore they had scaly golden skin.

Across the room from where I stood, a wiry man dressed in suspenders, slacks, and a tank top sipped from a wine glass as he glanced at me from beneath his fedora, and I had to fight against the urge to flinch as I met his neon-green, vertically pupiled eyes.

And then there was the matter of the trio of slender, diminutive girls that looked barely old enough to be legal, giggling and gliding through the room. Their sparkly dresses would have been enough to catch attention on their own, but every time they passed beneath the chandeliers, I caught glimpses of gossamer wings streaming from their delicate shoulder blades.

Excitement burst through my veins as I realized that I'd stumbled upon the exact place I'd set out for. *The supernatural pulse of Salem.* And now that I was here, I was seeing *way* more otherworldly stuff than my Uncle Oscar had ever let on existed back in Chicago. I always suspected there were more than just vampires out in the world *somewhere*, but this was my first visual confirmation, and I was eager to see more.

Down girl.

I schooled my expression into one of boredom. If I started looking around the place like a kid in the candy store, people would get suspicious. After all, I'd come in here with a regular, so they probably assumed I was either a supernatural or genned in with the community. If they discovered otherwise, I was going to be tossed out on my ass faster than I could say "Mountain Man."

I ordered a dirty martini from the bar, then casually sipped at it while running my free hand across the bar top, railings, backs of couches, and any other surfaces I could touch without looking suspicious.

Normally I would have caught a flash of something, but the objects in this place were being particularly stubborn, the smooth, glassy surfaces telling me nothing. I'd come across this phenomenon before—the place had been "swept," the memories cleared from the surfaces so that I couldn't use my talent against them.

I'd always figured that sweeping was some kind of vampire talent, but considering the number of other supernaturals here, I wasn't so sure now. Just how did it work, anyway? I'd thought that sweeping meant the memories were literally being swept away from the surface, but with the number of patrons frequenting this space, I was pretty sure that was impossible. Maybe the furniture was spelled to keep memories from imprinting on it, which was why I wasn't getting any flashes. Or maybe there was something else about this that I just didn't understand.

I snorted at that. There was a *lot* about the supernatural world that I didn't understand, which was something I planned to remedy as quickly as possible. I might not be able to use my talent on the club itself, but I was reasonably sure it would still work on the people. And the thing about clubs was that you could brush against numerous bodies and no one would ever know you were secretly looking into their pasts.

Out of the corner of my eye, I caught a flash of dark blond hair—Vox, heading up the wraparound staircase that led to the mezzanine.

I followed, giving him a little bit of a lead so that he didn't notice me. I suppose I could have just grabbed him, but I didn't want to cause a scene in a place like this. Besides, I was curious to see where he was headed.

The mezzanine was a kind of lounge-slash-gaming area, with several pool tables set up as well as two dart boards, all of which were in full use. Green lamps suspended from the ceiling shed soft light over round dark wooden tables, and at these sat patrons, sipping drinks and talking quietly.

I spotted Vance in a corner, his head bent low as he discussed something with a woman in a silver dress whose skin turned the color and texture of bark when I looked at her out of the corner of my eye.

Despite the pool tables and dart boards, I had a feeling this section of the club was where supernaturals came to talk business. But as much as I wanted to strain my ears and listen to their conversations, I couldn't, because Vox was continuing down a shadowed corridor.

Casting one last glance at the tables, I hurried after Vox. The dance music receded as I headed deeper into the dark hall with velvet tufted walls the color of wine. The whole place was a bit much, but I guess it was standard for a fancy club.

Vox had already disappeared, presumably through one of the many brass doors lining the walls. Rather than try each one, I headed for the one that was cracked open and spilling soft light into the hall that was otherwise only illuminated by the faintly lit wall sconces.

"I see," a deep, Scottish voice said as I peered in through the crack.

I could make out the silhouette of Vox bowing before a man

seated behind a grand mahogany desk. The man wore a dark suit with a blood-red tie, and judging by the breadth of his shoulders, I didn't think he was small. Thick, inky hair framed his face, and while the angle and the lack of light made it hard to get more specific details, I got the impression of aristocratic and handsome features.

"And so you've come to beg another boon of me?" the man continued.

"Please, Lord Tremaine." Vox seemed to bow even lower. A visible tremor went through his spine, something I found interesting because he didn't seem like the type of man to cower. Whoever this "Lord Tremaine" was, he was powerful. "It's my only hope."

I leaned in a little closer, pushing the crack infinitesimally wider so that I could try to hear more. But just as Tremaine opened his mouth to speak again, a vice-like grip clamped around my arm and yanked me away.

"Hey!" I yelped as my assailant swung me around. I reached for my badge instinctively, then swallowed hard at the sight of another Mountain Man. This one had white hair cropped close to his skull and eerie eyes the color of winter frost. There was something ancient and alien in those eyes that sent a shiver crawling up my spine.

"We don't take kindly to eavesdroppers," the Mountain Man growled as he spun me around. He secured my wrists behind my back with a zip-tie, then grabbed them with one hand while clamping down on my shoulder with his other hand.

"Let me go!" I stomped on his foot, hoping to dislodge his grip. Unfortunately, my attack was about as effective as, well, stomping on a mountain, and only resulted in a bolt of pain shooting up my ankle.

"Not a chance. You're coming with me, and if you even *think* about screaming, I'll cut your tongue out and feed it to the selkies."

five

I kept my mouth shut and gritted my teeth as the security guard perp-walked me to the end of the hall as if *I* was the fucking criminal. The audacity of it set my teeth on edge, but even if I didn't believe his threat to cut out my tongue, I doubted that saying anything would do any good in a place like this. In fact, it might just draw a couple of vampires up here, and that was the last thing I wanted to deal with.

As we came to a stop, the guard released my shoulder, then used his free hand to wrench open a door to my left. He confiscated my glock, then shoved me unceremoniously into the room and slammed the door behind me.

I twisted to the side, saving myself from the oncoming face-plant and smashing my shoulder into the cement floor instead. Pain radiated through my body, and I grunted, shoving myself up onto my knees just as the door bolt slid home with a loud click.

Fuck.

I glanced around, trying to determine if there was any means of escape, or at least a weapon I could use to free my wrists or defend myself. But the room was completely empty and devoid of windows. All I had was a lone caged lightbulb flickering overhead. I was in a concrete cage, and with my hands tied behind my back, I couldn't even reach for my cellphone to call for help or grab for the vampire gun pressing unhelpfully up against my rib cage.

My heartbeat ratcheted up, and I had to take deep breaths to calm myself. *Think, Brooke, think.* I had to keep my mind occupied, or I was going to lose it in here. What new information could I glean from my latest predicament?

The empty room was one thing, I mused, glancing around the space. Aside from the overhead light, there wasn't a single thing in the space. And from my experience, businesses rarely had empty rooms in their buildings. A good business used every inch of available space as efficiently as possible, so if this room was being kept empty, it was for a reason.

With the thick cement walls and reinforced door, I was beginning to suspect that *this* was exactly that reason: a holding cell for people like me who they caught snooping around where they shouldn't be.

What the hell kind of club needs a holding cell, though? Then again, this kind of club catered to a unique clientele. I could all too easily see security needing a place to temporarily hold a supernatural that got too out of control or broke the club rules in some way. I mean, the logical thing to do would be to toss them out on their asses, but maybe there were circumstances where that would be unwise.

Speaking of supernaturals, the guard had threatened to feed my tongue to a selkie. Did that mean selkies were a thing, or was that some kind of joke? After what I'd seen tonight, it wouldn't surprise me if selkies did exist.

I was dying to know what kinds of supernaturals *did* exist. I'd tried to learn when I was younger. As a teen, I'd picked up a dusty tome in a thrift store once about mythical beasts and took it home to study, but Uncle Oscar burned it the second he caught wind of it. Of course, I'd gotten to glimpse a couple of the pages inside first, and they spoke of shapeshifters and witches and elementals and all sorts of things—but that was just a book.

Right?

And nothing in that book that I'd gotten around to reading had spoken of large men with limbs as hard as rock. What kind of supernatural were the security guards here? If World of Warcraft could be considered a source for supernatural creatures, their hulking forms and eerie eyes would indicate they were giants or orcs or trolls.

But that was video game, and this was the world I lived in. I needed a way to separate fantasy from reality. A way to know just as much as the creatures who frequented this club knew. Somehow, I had a feeling I couldn't just up and ask the security guards when they came back.

If they came back…

Focus, Brooke. You're trying not to die.

Right. The reason I was in this whole mess in the first place was because they'd caught me snooping around. Of course they weren't going to take kindly to my questions. If I wanted answers, I was going to have to survive this place.

There was a jangle of keys, and I turned my head back to the door just in time to see it open. My heart stopped as Tremaine stepped into the room, along with the guard who'd manhandled me earlier as well as a second one. The two hulking men flanked him, and though they were a good foot taller, there was something about the aura radiating off Tremaine's tall, muscular frame that told me he was the most dangerous of the three.

A moment later, as he stepped into the light and I got my first real look at his face, my heart stuttered back to life.

If God and Satan got together on a sunny day to create something, I imagine they would have come up with something similar to the savage perfection that was Lord Tremaine's face. My gaze traveled across high, broad cheekbones that looked as though they could slice steel, down the length of a straight, Roman nose, and paused at cruel, sensual lips that were pressed into a straight line. His triangular jaw was strong, his skin tanned and glowing ever so slightly in the lamplight.

He was, in a word, otherworldly, but it was his eyes that captured my attention most. They were a brilliant green, the color of new leaves, and though they appeared human at a glance, there was something more ancient and alien about them than even the arctic stares of his security guards. Those eyes, framed by thick black lashes, widened as green fire sprang to life inside them.

"It's you again!" he growled, his Scottish burr growing thick with anger. I stumbled back instinctively as he took an angry step toward me.

"Me again?" I dug my heels into the ground to keep myself from scurrying away from Tremaine's menacing presence. Sure, he might be scary enough to send the monsters beneath my bed running for cover, but that didn't mean I had to let him see it.

"What the hell are you talking about?" I pressed.

"Dinnae give me that," he snarled, his Italian leather dress shoes clicking across the concrete as he closed the distance between us. "I'd recognize yer silver hair and witchy eyes from ten thousand leagues away. I dinnae know why ye've come back again, but I wilna let ye sink your meddling claws into my affairs anymore."

"Dude." It took a lot of effort for me to keep my voice even— Tremaine was less than a foot away, and the anger radiating from his big body was so palpable I swore it was singeing the tip of my nose. "I don't know what you've been smoking, but I've never laid eyes on you in my life. Believe me, I would know if I'd run across someone like you before."

Heat suffused my cheeks at that little slip, and I straightened as best I could with my hands still zip-tied behind my back.

Some of the anger left Tremaine's eyes, and his green glare grew cold, calculating. "Yer telling the truth, or at least you believe yerself to be." His gaze raked me up and down, sending a tremor through my spine, and his eyes lingered at the detective's shield winking at my belt. "A cop now, are ya?" he asked, disbelief ringing in his voice.

"Yes, I am," I said tightly. "And with the way your man over there manhandled me and took my gun, I'm well within my rights to charge him for assaulting an officer." I glared at the guard in question, but if he was the least bit intimidated by my threat, he didn't let it show.

"I know all of the police in this town," Tremaine murmured, his eyes still studying me as though I were a particularly vexing puzzle. "I would know if you'd been hiding under my nose as a member of the force."

"I'm a new transfer," I snapped, scowling. Not exactly the truth, but he didn't need to know that. "Not that I need to explain myself to you. Now why don't you untie me and give me my damned gun back? I came in here after a suspect, but if you don't let me loose now, I sure as hell will come back here with a task force and a warrant to scour this place top to bottom. I'm sure we'll be able to find something dirty enough to get your panties in a twist."

Tremaine laughed. "The police dinnae scare me." He scoffed. The sparkle of amusement in his eye sent a flush through my body, and I gritted my teeth against his asinine response. "But while we're on the subject, who's yer suspect? I cannae imagine it's me, or ye would have said so already, aye? Yet, that's the logical conclusion since ye were eavesdropping outside my door."

"That's none of your damn business."

"It is if yer in my club," Tremaine said, his voice softly menacing.

I was going in circles here. "Fine, then. Remy Vox," I snapped. "My partner and I are looking into an alleged drug-dealing operation he's got on the side. Now I gave you something. Tell me something."

Tremaine's eyes narrowed, and he turned away. I watched as he spoke quietly to one of the guards, and though I strained my ears to catch what they were saying, I couldn't hear a single word. *Dammit.* Why couldn't I have been born with super-hearing?

"Yes, sir," the guard said. "I'll take care of it."

"Good." Tremaine straightened. "Take care of her, too."

He turned and headed toward the exit.

"Wait...what?" I cried as fear ballooned in my chest. "You

can't kill me. I'm a fucking police officer!"

Tremaine didn't even bother to glance my way, and as the guard who'd originally brought me here closed in on me, I lost sight of Tremaine's retreating back. Cursing, I tried to fight against the guard as he grabbed my shoulder and wrists, but it was impossible with my hands tied behind my back. Besides, if the kick I'd given him earlier was any indication, I doubt that I'd be able to make a dent in him with brute force. I wondered if either of my guns would work on any of these guys.

"Your boss is gonna land your ass in jail," I warned. "You would be better served to let me go and return my firearm."

No response.

I growled as the guard dragged me down the stairs and past the dancing and drinking patrons. A few of them glanced my way as we passed, but for the most part, we were largely ignored. Was this a fairly normal sight for them? Ugh. That thought didn't make me feel at all better.

"You're gonna end up with a whole police force snooping around here, and you can't disappear them all," I tried again. "Don't take the fall for this one. Jail isn't a pretty place, even for a tough guy like you."

"Not worried about it," he said, voice void of any emotion.

He dragged me through the kitchen, a large area behind the bar full of stainless steel appliances and white tile. The air was heavy with the smell of fried food and the sound of sizzling meat; my stomach would have growled had the situation not been so dire. Despite my struggling and shouts, the kitchen staff didn't spare more than a cursory glance our way.

The guard shoved me through the back door, and I stumbled

into the dimly lit back alley. I would have tripped over the cobblestones if the guard hadn't snagged me by the arm...not that I was thanking him or anything, since they clearly meant to kill me.

"Let me go!" I shrieked as loudly as I could, hoping that someone outside the club—someone who might give a damn—would hear me and come running.

Except my screams seemed to die as they fell off my lips. No echoing off the walls, nothing. The alley was eerily silent; I couldn't even hear traffic whizzing by in the distance. It was like we were in a bubble.

And yet, I tried again, because it was all I could do at this point.

"Scream all you want, love. Nobody's going to hear you back here." A nasally voice caught my attention, and the guard hauled me around, bringing me face to face with a short, bald man sitting on a trash can. He looked me up and down, his mud-brown eyes gleaming with interest as he swung his short legs back and forth over the edge of the can. The guy focused his gaze on my assailant. "Another one, eh?" he asked. "You guys sure seem to be into 'taking care of business' lately."

"Just shut up and deal with her already," the guard growled.

The guy lifted a stubby hand, and wild fear raced through me as I realized that this little man was somehow going to kill me. Something icy burned around my wrists, and a loud crack split the air as my restraints fell away. The guard holding me startled, and he loosened his grip just enough for me to tear myself away.

"Don't move!" I shouted, pulling my vampire gun from its holster. I backed away, alternating the barrel of my gun between both men. "I'll shoot!"

The guard looked at me as though I were a mild annoyance, and the bald man laughed. "Just what do you think you're gonna do with that, kid?"

I hesitated, thrown off by how blasé the two of them were about my gun. Would my bullets even affect them? "You're both under arrest for assaulting a police officer. Put your hands up."

The bald guy shook his head. "It's no wonder the bossman wants you taken care of," he said ruefully. "If you're stupid enough to think that prison cells can hold us, then you don't belong here."

He lifted his hand and wiggled his fingers in my direction. Glowing green sparks drifted from his fingers, and I squeezed the trigger reflexively against the attack. Not exactly the reaction I would have to a human suspect wiggling fingers at me, but I learned a long time ago that you don't give supernaturals the same courtesy if you want to live.

"Oww!" The bald man cried as the wooden bullet ripped through his shoulder. His mud-brown eyes flashed an eerie yellow as he slapped his hand against the wound, and I gaped as golden liquid, rather than blood, stained his fingers. "Damn, lady, just what *are you?*"

"I'm pissed, and if you guys don't give me back my other gun, I'm going to—"

I stopped and blinked. The bald man was gone, and so was the hulking guard who'd been standing right next to him. What the fuck? They'd just been standing right in front of me! How could they be gone?

I rushed back inside the building, then skidded to a halt. The kitchen was completely empty. No cooks frying food, no pots and pans hanging from the walls...even the white tile was gone, replaced by stained concrete.

"No, this isn't right," I muttered, pushing my way past the double doors and into the club itself.

But the place was just as empty as the kitchen. The glossy bar and tables were gone, as were all the patrons. There was nothing here but concrete, dust, and some small piles of refuse.

I stood there in the middle of the room, completely stunned. I'd never come across anything like this in my life. How had an entire club full of people disappeared between one second and the next?

Wiping memories from objects was one thing, but wiping an entire place from existence was another. Even the building itself didn't seem the same…the ceiling was lower, and the mezzanine was completely gone.

My cellphone rang, and I jumped as the shrill tone echoed in the empty space. Heart hammering, I pulled it out and answered without looking at the caller ID.

"Brooke Chandler," I snapped.

"No need to take that snippy tone with me, Chandler," Detective Baxter scolded. "I've had my hands full dragging that perp back to the station without your help, but I thought I'd call you and let you know that we apprehended the suspect. So if you're still looking for him, you can go home."

"What?" I gripped the cellphone so hard I was surprised my fingers didn't leave dents in the plastic. "How is that possible? I just saw Vox a couple of minutes ago."

"Turns out we had the wrong guy," Baxter said, and I could hear the shrug in his voice. "Captain Randall said that he'd gotten a phone call with new information that put Vox in the clear, and one of the other detectives was already looking into the new suspect and nabbed him. Kind of sucks that we didn't get the collar, but what can you do?"

"What can you do," I echoed, my mind spinning back to the conversation I'd had with Tremaine. He'd stepped away and had a conversation with one of his guards after I'd mentioned Vox was my suspect, and the guard had said he would 'take care of it.' Was that what had happened? Had they somehow put Captain Randall onto a different suspect? Anger tightened my chest at the idea.

"You okay, Chandler?" Baxter asked, concern in his voice. "You seem kind of down."

I let out a breath. "I'm fine, Detective Baxter. It's just been a long day."

"Yeah, no kidding. Why don't you go home and take a load off? I'll see you in the morning."

"Sounds good." I clicked off, then took one last look around the room before exiting through the back alley and making my way toward home.

But not to relax.

No, after tonight there was no way I could put up my feet and chill. I didn't know who the hell this Tremaine guy thought he was, but I fully intended to tear apart this town until I found him.

six

By the time I got home, I'd worked myself up into a righteous fury. Somehow I'd gone from chasing down a drug dealer to being tied up and nearly killed by a pompous supernatural club owner with a stick up his ass.

It irked me to no end that I didn't know who or what Lord Tremaine was, so instead of eating the Chinese takeout I'd picked up on the way home, I snatched up my laptop, plopped down onto the couch, and settled in to do some serious Googling.

Since the only lead I had was the building, I started there. I'd noted the address before I left, so I plugged it in now, then did a search through county records to find out who owned it.

Turned out that it belonged to one Maddock Tremaine, purchased over five years ago. A little more digging revealed that he'd intended to turn it into a club, but due to unknown reasons, the building continued to sit empty.

Well, they're wrong about that.

I scoffed, saving the article to a bookmark folder before I closed it. Maddock Tremaine certainly had built a club inside the building. He'd just done it in such a way that he could make it vanish from the naked eye at will.

Just how powerful did someone have to be in order to do that?

A little shiver crawled along my spine at the thought of being face-to-face with a supernatural that potent. I was surprised he hadn't killed me himself—surely if he could make an entire club disappear, he had enough power in his pinky finger to end me. But he'd had his guards take me out back so a little bald man could do it instead.

What if he wasn't trying to kill you?

The thought popped into my head so suddenly that my fingers froze on the keyboard. I cast my thoughts back to that moment in the alley, searching for any context clues that indicated they were planning something else. Although they'd liberally flung around the phrase "take care of her," nobody had actually specified what that was supposed to mean. And in the end, all Mr. Trash Can had managed to do was wiggle his fingers and send a couple of sparks my way.

I mean, really, if they'd wanted to kill me, the guard that had hauled me out there could have done that easily enough. He could have snapped my neck between his thumb and forefinger, and there wouldn't have been a damn thing I could do about it. There was no need for that hocus pocus...unless they were trying to put some kind of spell on me instead.

Maybe they just wanted to make me forget what I saw, I mused. That theory certainly made sense. Take the human out back, wiggle your fingers at her until she sees stars in her eyes, then send her on her way with a slight case of amnesia. Easy enough.

The only problem was, I wasn't human. Or at least not a regular human anyway. I had a feeling that even if the guards and Mr. Trash Can didn't know that, Lord Tremaine did. The look in his eyes when he'd caught sight of me, coupled with what he'd said, was more than enough to suggest that he'd met me before.

Thing was, I was one-hundred percent sure *I* had never met *him*.

So how did he know me then?

I rose from the couch to collect my Chinese food. Now that some of the anger had worn off, my stomach was making its needs known. I cracked open my box of chicken lo mein and shoveled a few bites into my mouth using chopsticks.

Maybe he met you as a kid.

I chewed on a snow pea from my lo mein as I considered that. It was entirely plausible that he'd met me as a kid and I just didn't remember, as my life before Uncle Oscar was pretty fuzzy on the details. But what would I have done as a child that would have pissed him off so much that he'd thrown me out of his club without a second thought?

"I dinnae know why ye've come back again, but I wilna let you sink yer meddling claws into my affairs anymore."

His thick, Scottish burr echoed in my head as I swallowed. Come back *again*? Meddling in his affairs? No. My childhood memory might not be crystal clear, but I'd remember if I'd come to Salem at six years old and stuck my nose into Maddock's business.

Then again, he might not have been living in Salem when I was six years old. He'd only owned the club for the last five years. There was no way he and I had crossed paths when I was a kid, but the idea did make me wonder exactly what Mr. Tremaine *had* meant by his comment.

I set my box of half-eaten lo mein on the counter, then sat on the couch with my laptop again and Googled Maddock Tremaine's name.

A website for Tremaine Enterprises popped up, and next to it was a strange golden logo that at first glance looked like a badly drawn Nazi symbol. Upon closer inspection, I realized it was actually three arms bent at the elbows and connected at the shoulder joint. A quick search through images showed that symbol was actually part of the Tremaine family crest.

I opened up the website and had a look around. Tremaine Enterprises seemed to have its fingers in a lot of pies, everywhere from real estate to solar power to the automotive industry. That was a lot of ground to cover, and while I could spend plenty of time doing that, I didn't think I was going to find what I needed to know from his outside investments.

No, what I wanted to know was why a man—or whatever he was—with so many holdings spread across the planet was investing his time in running a supernatural club in small-town Salem. Too bad I couldn't Google *that*.

Instead, I navigated to the company bio, hoping to find something useful. According to the summary, Tremaine Enterprises had been around for the last two hundred years, and had been founded by Dougall Tremaine on the family's ancestral lands in Scotland. A small paragraph about Maddock himself told me that he'd inherited the company in full about ten years ago but had been working in it almost his whole life, already a savvy investor by the age of sixteen.

I wonder just how much of this bio is complete and utter bullshit.

I stared at the small photograph of Maddock Tremaine that took up a portion of my laptop screen. I mean, it all sounded good on paper, and I had no reason on the surface to think that any of it wasn't true. But I'd stared into Maddock's ancient eyes myself, and even though I didn't know much about supernaturals, I was willing to bet good money that it had been a very, very long time since Maddock Tremaine had been sixteen years old.

Sighing, I closed my laptop, then cleaned up my takeout and headed back to my bedroom. I was going to have to rummage through the precinct's database to see if I could glean any helpful information about Maddock. At the very least, I could dig out an address and see what my chances were that he actually lived at it.

Yeah, and while you're at it, you'd better have a good cover story for why you've lost your gun, and hope that they're willing to loan you one.

I groaned at the very thought, then froze as I caught sight of something resting on my pillow while reaching to turn out my light.

Something that looked very much like my S&W .40.

"Holy shit," I muttered as I approached the gun. It was sitting, along with a small bouquet of white roses, on top of a card the color of yellow custard. As I carefully lifted the gun out of the way, I saw that the center of the stationary was stamped with a relief of the Tremaine Enterprise logo.

My fingers itched to open it, but before I did that, I sat down and took the gun apart, making sure that it hadn't been tampered with in any way. It seemed fine, all parts accounted for, not even a single round missing from the magazine. So I put it back together, carefully returned it to my hip holster, and then reached for the card.

Welcome to Salem, the card read. *Stay out of my business, stay out of my club, and if you're lucky, you just might stay alive.*

seven

I'm not even remotely ashamed to admit that I spent an hour inspecting every nook and cranny of my apartment before going to bed, or that I jumped and twitched at every creak and whisper of wind I heard for another hour as I lay in bed trying to sleep. You would too, if someone had broken into your place and left a gun and a note on your bed without a single trace of other evidence to indicate that they'd been there.

It took me two more cups of coffee than usual to muster up the energy to walk into the precinct without a cloud of grumpiness hanging over my head, and even then, it was a near thing. But I smiled and greeted everyone I met, then braced myself for a scolding from my partner or the Captain for ditching him in the middle of an arrest.

Strangely, I got no complaints from either man. I wondered if someone upstairs was looking out for me…or if Maddock's orders for his guard to "take care of it" had anything to do with the distinct lack of consequences.

Unsettled, I went to knock on Captain Randall's door. Maybe I could coax some answers out of him that would help me determine whether he'd been bribed or magicked in any way.

"What is it, Chandler?" the Captain asked after he'd given me permission to enter. Annoyance rang clear in his tone as he looked up from the report he was reading. "I don't have time to hold your hand today."

It took great effort not to react to the barb. "I'm not here for hand-holding," I said, folding my hands behind my back as I came to stand in front of his desk. "I just came to check in on that drug-dealing case that Detective Baxter and I caught yesterday."

Captain Randall frowned. "The perpetrator was sent to booking last night and is currently awaiting arraignment. You don't need to concern yourself further."

I straightened my shoulders. "I appreciate that, Captain, but after the amount of time Detective Baxter and I put into the case, I'd like to know what happened. We hadn't even had a chance to question Remy Vox, so I don't have a lot to—"

"This sounds a lot like hand-holding, Chandler," Captain Randall interrupted. "And I'm not interested in hand-holding. If you want to know about the particulars, look it up in the database."

"I tried," I said as calmly as I could. "But the case file was locked."

Captain Randall arched an eyebrow. "Is that so? Well, then, I imagine that means it's above your clearance level."

Heat flushed my cheeks, and my hands tightened into fists

behind my back. The bastard was hiding something; I just *knew* it. His expression was hard as ever, but there was just the slightest hint of smugness in his eyes. I didn't know why, but Captain Randall was playing with me. And it was really pissing me off.

"I realize that, Captain," I said tightly. "But I don't understand why a simple drug-dealing case that I was assigned to *yesterday* is suddenly too high above my clearance level now."

Captain Randall's face turned ugly. "It's not your job to understand, Detective Chandler. Your job is to work on open cases, and right now, it sounds a lot like you're pestering me about a case that's already been closed. Does the Chicago PD usually pay you to work on closed cases??"

"No, but—"

"Then stop worrying about it." The Captain slammed an open palm on his desk, and if I were a lesser detective, I would have flinched. His dark eyes glittered with barely restrained fury. "I feel like we're having the same conversation we had yesterday, Detective, and that's not a good sign. You told me that you're an excellent detective, and I expect my detectives to understand the pecking order around here. This precinct doesn't have the manpower or the resources for me to allow detectives to pick at and fuss over cases that have already been closed. If you can't understand that, then you'd better hop onto a plane back to Chicago because I'm not interested in helping you if you're going to waste my time. Is that understood?"

"Yes, sir," I said through gritted teeth, and I really did. It meant that Captain Randall didn't want me poking around closed cases because he didn't want me to expose whatever he was trying to cover up.

But if I couldn't tackle him head on about this matter, I was just going to have to dig around behind his back until I exposed the truth.

The rest of the morning proved just as frustrating as my conversation with Captain Randall. He'd given me Tom's file, but it was full of dead-ends. There were notes on witnesses who had been spoken to, all of whom had claimed to see nothing, and I spent the morning making phone calls.

Since Tom had died at a motel, all of the people who'd been interviewed were long gone, and I was stuck trying to squeeze information out of them by phone. By the time lunch rolled around, I'd gotten absolutely nowhere and was so antsy for progress that it was all I could do not to jump out of my chair and race for the exit.

"Hey," Baxter said as I shrugged on my jacket. "You wanna go grab a bite? The Lobster Shanty serves some pretty great clam chowder." He pronounced the word 'chowdah', in true New England fashion. Just like Tom would have done.

My stomach perked up at the idea, and I told it to pipe down. "Thanks, but maybe next time. I'm still settling in at my apartment, and I thought I'd use my lunch break to catch up on things."

"All right." Baxter shrugged, but there was a hint of disappointment in his voice that made me frown. I couldn't imagine that the stalwart detective actually *wanted* to hang out with me—he was all business and no pleasure as far as I could see. Besides, I didn't trust him enough to have anything beyond a professional relationship with him, and even that was pushing it. "I'll see you in an hour."

"Yep." I slung my purse over my shoulder, then headed out to where I'd parked my jeep. I'd opted not to walk today, not because I was lazy, but because I planned on using my lunch break for some more investigative work.

I munched on the turkey sandwich I'd packed this morning as I drove to the Black Bear Inn. It had been a few weeks since Tom had reportedly burned to death there, but I was hoping I might still be able to find something of use amongst the ruins that could tell me more about how he'd died. And if not, maybe the staff could tell me something.

I pulled up in front of the inn, which didn't sound nearly as impressive as it was. It was a single story building a few blocks from Derby Road that wrapped around the lot in a boxy U-shape, with parking spots in front of each room. A small building stood in the center of the lot, with a service window that likely served as the check-in counter.

I parked my car next to the little shack, then approached the window. A fat man in a white button-up shirt sat there, his large thumbs a blur over his phone's screen. Either he was having a texting marathon, or he was playing some kind of video game, but whatever it was, he was so riveted that he didn't even glance up.

Annoyed, I rapped on the window with my knuckles. "Hello?"

He jumped, and the fat rolls beneath his shirt rippled as he nearly fell off his chair.

"Jesus!" he cried, grabbing onto the counter for support. His eyes went wide as they took me in. "Couldn't you give a man a little warning?"

I lifted an eyebrow. "Good afternoon, Mister…" I leaned in to read his name tag. "Jenkins. I'm Detective Brooke Chandler. I'm here following up on the death of Thomas Garrison." My throat tightened a little, but I forced myself to remain coolly professional. I was here as a detective, not as a grieving fiancée.

"Thomas Garrison?" The man scrunched up his face, and his beady eyes just about disappeared behind his pudgy cheeks. "I don't know anything about that."

I frowned. "You don't remember one of your hotel rooms catching fire a couple weeks ago?"

Jenkins's chins wagged as he laughed. "Ma'am, I think I would have remembered if one of our rooms burned down. You don't see any construction going on around here, do you?" He swept a dinner-plate-sized hand around, indicating the motel.

"No," I admitted, and that was puzzling indeed. "But it's been over three weeks since it happened, and I figured maybe you guys had already repaired the place."

Jenkins shook his head. "Takes the boss-lady forever to get any maintenance done around here. Of course, a burned down room would be a priority, so maybe I'm wrong. But I definitely would have remembered if anything like that had happened, and it hasn't." Folding his arms, he peered at me with beady eyes. "You sure this is the right motel?"

"Yes," I growled, fisting my hands at my sides. Goddammit, I'd gotten the details from the file Captain Randall had given me this morning. I'd seen the pictures. Hell, I even knew which room he'd been in. "Take me to room 104."

Jenkins frowned. "Now hang on there," he protested, "I can't just go letting you barge into motel rooms and disturbing our—"

I slapped my badge on the sliver of counter in front of the window. "Take me there now, or I'll arrest your ass for obstruction of justice."

Jenkins stared at me for a long moment. Whatever he saw in my eyes made him decide not to fuck with me, because he hefted himself out of his chair with a curse. He squeezed himself out of the shack, muttering under his breath the entire time, and I thought I heard him say "bitch cop" as he locked the door behind him.

And here I thought he was about to bring me flowers.

The enormous key ring at Jenkins's belt jangled with every lumbering step as he led me across the lot and to the room in question. We stopped in front of one of the many dark green doors, and I inspected the peeling brass numbers as he fumbled with the lock.

104.

Here we go...

The door swung open, and I pressed my lips together as I entered the room ahead of Jenkins. There was not a single hint of fire in the space—not a whiff of smoke or a touch of blackness on the white walls or the wooden bed frame. The pale brown carpet beneath my feet might have been ratty, but it was intact, not even a scorch mark or cigarette burn to be seen.

"See?" Jenkins demanded, folding his arms across his massive chest again. "No fire."

"I do see," I murmured, running my fingers across the bedspread. I frowned when nothing happened—usually I got a good flash when I touched a bed of any kind, and yes, that was a pun. But I saw no naked people rolling in these sheets, or watching TV, or even sleeping.

"What are you doing?" Jenkins demanded as I walked the room, gliding my fingertips across every available surface. "I don't have time to stand here while you waltz around."

I twisted my lips as I skimmed my fingertips across the dresser. "Yes, I'm sure playing Tetris on your phone is very important."

Huffing, Jenkins pulled out his phone, presumably to play on it while I worked. The space was small, but though I touched nearly every available surface, I couldn't get a single vision. Just like in Maddock's nightclub, somebody had wiped every trace of memory from this place.

Sighing, I leaned against the radiator, wondering what my next move was. My fingers brushed against the grate, seeking warmth, and I got a flash of a man standing in the middle of the room.

The drapes were closed, the space tinted yellow by the single light fixture hanging from the ceiling, and the man's trench-coat-covered back faced mine as he muttered some kind of foreign language under his breath.

He pointed toward the bed, and my eyes widened as the mattress burst into flame. The fire grew faster than I thought possible, devouring the mattress as it stretched upward, outward, licking at the flames and the carpet. I was sure it would reach the man next, sure that he would be burned to a crisp...

Except the man was gone.

"Ma'am, I really do need to get back to the front desk now." Jenkins's voice snapped me out of the vision, and I saw him leaning against the doorjamb.

"Yeah, sure." I let out a shaky breath, then pushed myself off the radiator. I wasn't sure what I'd seen just now. I needed some time alone to process it. "I've got what I need."

I let Jenkins usher me out of the room, then returned to my Jeep without complaint. As I sat in the driver's seat, leaning my head against the headrest, one thing became certain to me: whoever had tried to wipe that room clean hadn't wanted me to see the man in the trench coat.

But now that I'd seen him, I was going to figure out who he was and what he'd *really* done with Tom.

eight

By the time my shift was over, I was in a foul mood. My trip to the motel had given me more questions than answers, and Detective Baxter and I had been stuck dealing with whiny perps all afternoon. We'd finished off the day booking a dumb-ass teenager for driving straight into a picket fence after downing a six pack of Bud Light, something that rubbed me the wrong way on *so* many levels.

I mean, DUI is bad enough. I'd seen so many families broken from drunk-driving accidents it made my stomach sick if I thought too much about the needless tragedy. But to add insult to injury, the little shit had gotten drunk on Bud-fucking-Light. Seriously. That was like getting drunk on water, and the fact that he'd gotten behind the wheel when he couldn't even hold beer-flavored water was enough to make me want to drop-kick him all the way into the Boston Harbor.

I need a punching bag, I thought as I left the precinct. But since one wasn't handy, I opted to walk home. The exercise would help burn off some of this pent up energy and frustration and maybe clear my head enough so I could think.

The brisk walk did me some good—the cold wind on my face cleared some of the simmering resentment from my head, and the beautiful sunset lightened my heart a little.

But just as I was crossing the street, a lean, hooded figure on the opposite sidewalk caught my attention. His shoulders were hunched against the cold, hands shoved into the pockets of his hoodie, and because the sun was almost gone, it was hard to see his face. But there was something strange about him, and when he stopped at the corner and turned to face me, I caught a flash of glowing purple eyes with vertical pupils.

We both froze, and time seemed suspended as I tried to figure out what the hell I was looking at. Aside from the vertical pupils, the figure's eyes were remarkably similar to mine. But before I could think any more about it, he darted around the corner.

"Hey, wait!" I dashed after him, curiosity burning in my chest. I knew the thing I was following couldn't be a vampire, because vampire eyes were red, but it definitely wasn't human. Aside from the eyes, it was so fucking fast that I could barely keep it in sight as it led me on a chase through dark back alleys. I twisted around corners at breakneck speed and slipped on too-slick pavement that was still damp from this afternoon's rainstorm.

My breath came fast and hard as I turned another corner, then skidded to a stop as I realized I'd come upon a dead end.

Standing at the edge of the alleyway, I aimed my weapon and peered into the darkness, trying to figure out if he was hiding in the shadows. The moon shone plenty of light from above, though, and I couldn't see any place for him to hide.

A flicker of movement caught my eye, and I turned to my left just in time to see the figure jump out of a shadow that was *way* too small for him to hide in. A pale, clawed hand knocked the gun from my grip before I could squeeze off a shot, and it clattered to the ground.

I ducked a right hook, then made a grab for my gun, but the figure kicked me in the stomach. Breath whooshed out of me as I skidded backwards, falling on my side, and it was only through sheer force of will that I got my legs under me before he could strike me again. I caught his booted foot on my way up and yanked it to me, and a vision of a cold, dark cavern with strange symbols painted on the damp walls assailed me.

Unable to afford the distraction, I pushed it aside, then back-fisted him in the face with all my strength.

There was a loud crack as his head snapped sideways, and the hood slid off. Not that it made much of a difference—my assailant's skin was nearly as pitch black as his hair, and even with the light of the moon I could barely make out his features. But he did bare long, pearly-white fangs at me, and that was the last straw.

"Fuck this," I snarled, pulling my vampire gun from beneath my blazer. It was time to end this thing.

But before I could fire a shot, the creature recovered and knocked the weapon from my hand. I cursed at the thing's inhuman speed—this never would have happened with a human.

Swings came in quick succession, and I had to eat a couple of them to avoid the more dangerous blows. I managed to turn my body into the last one, though, and my momentum threw my assailant off balance. Before he could recover, I kicked him back, lifted my gun, and buried two shots in his chest.

For a moment, I thought I had him. The creature stumbled backward, head bowed as he clutched at the holes in his chest. But instead of turning to ash, he simply stood there for a moment, then lifted his head and gave me a feral grin.

"Uh-oh." If two wooden stake bullets to the heart didn't kill this guy, then I was in *big* trouble.

The creature charged me again, and I dodged, heart-pounding as I tried to figure out how to get to my other gun before he killed me. I doubted that lead bullets would be any more effective than the wooden ones, but maybe if I shot him enough times, I could slow him down.

As the figure turned toward me, I braced myself, but before he could charge me again, a shot rang out.

His body shuddered, and something glistened on his lips that might have been blood. He dropped to his knees, but instead of falling forward or turning to ash, he melted into a puddle of darkness that oozed away, assimilating with the rest of the shadows clinging to the walls.

"Vampire bullets?" Detective Baxter asked.

Shocked, I whirled around to see him standing behind me. But instead of his button-up and slacks, he was dressed in a priest's robes, and the smoking gun in his hand was definitely *not* police issue.

This definitely isn't Detective Baxter.

"Y-yeah," I stammered, still a little shaken. "I'm guessing you're Guy Baxter's brother?"

"Yes." A slight smile curled his lips, and he stepped forward. As moonlight bathed his face, I realized that although he shared similarities to my new partner, his mouth was wider and he had rounder cheeks and a softer jaw. "My name is Father James Baxter. Guy and I are often confused because our voices sound so similar, in addition to the familial resemblance, but most people can tell us apart after talking to us for a minute. How do you know my brother?"

"I'm his new partner." I watched the man tuck his weapon back into his robes. Then glanced over my shoulder toward the spot where my assailant had just melted into the pavement. "What the hell did you use on that thing?"

"Iron. It's much more effective on their kind."

"Their kind?"

His smile broadened, and he held out a hand to me. "Come. Let's go find somewhere warm to talk."

Father James took me to the Gateway Church off Warren Street, which turned out to be only two blocks from where he'd found me. He told me he'd been heading to the convenience store to grab a sandwich when he'd heard strange noises coming from the alleyway behind the building, so he'd come out to investigate.

"Do you usually carry a gun when you're walking to the store, Father James?" I asked as he led me down a hall off the left of the main entrance, away from the nave.

"At night I do," he admitted as we walked past a series of doors that I imagined led to offices and meeting rooms. "Dangerous things walk these streets when the sun goes down, like the shade that attacked you in the alley."

"Shade?" I furrowed my brow as I remembered the way the creature had leapt from a shadow that had been too small to hold him, and then melted into a shadow after Father James had shot him. "I guess that's an appropriate name."

"Indeed." Father James stopped in front of a door with his name on it, then pulled a key ring from his belt. "They are creatures of shadow, so they cannot truly be killed. But if you pierce them with iron, they are forced to rejoin the darkness, and it takes them a long time to regain a more corporeal form."

"It sounds like you know a lot about them," I said as he led me into his office and flipped on the light.

It was a pleasant space, with honey-wood furniture and a large cross that hung from the powder blue accent wall on my left. The wall to my right was covered floor-to-ceiling with book-laden shelves, and the one behind his desk boasted commendations and certificates from the town and various charity organizations. The certificates were framed in gold and neatly organized around a window that looked out onto a small garden.

"When one's job is to shepherd the Lord's flock, it is difficult not to run across His enemies." Father James sat, gesturing for me to do the same. "Thankfully, I've learned that the fae are highly susceptible to iron, so I had a gunsmith specially craft these bullets for me." He pulled a small wooden box from one of his drawers, then pushed it across the table to me. "Take these. You'll need them."

I popped open the box to find twenty bullets neatly nestled into grooves carved into the wood. "Oh no," I said, pushing it back toward him. "I couldn't."

He pressed his hand gently over mine. "I insist. I have plenty more, and I suspect you're going to need them more than I do."

The ring on his third finger brushed against my skin, and I got a flash.

Crunching metal. Blood. Skidding wheels. A scream.

A car accident, I thought as it faded away, looking at him with a new light. One that had almost killed him.

"All right," I said, slowly pulling the box back toward me. "I'll take them. Thank you."

"You're welcome." Father James smiled. "I can't count on being around the corner the next time you run into a fae, so I'll feel better knowing you have those."

Nodding, I tucked the box into one of my inner jacket pockets, then settled back in my chair. The large cross hanging from the wall caught my eye again, and my fingers fluttered to the one hanging from my neck. Being in the church was a comfort, even if I wasn't in the nave itself, because Tom had been very religious. I'd gone to church with him every Sunday, so I couldn't help but feel his presence in this place and wonder if he was watching down on me.

"Did you know a Tom Garrison?" I wondered aloud.

Father James's eyebrows shot up. "Why, yes. He was a special member of my flock," he added, his eyes sparkling with fond memories. "Did you know him?"

"He was my fiancé," I told him around the lump that swelled in my throat.

His eyes widened. "Oh, you're Brooke Chandler!"

I nodded, just now realizing I'd been too shaken up to introduce myself sooner.

"Tom told me a lot of good things about you when he came back to Salem to help the local police with that old case." His expression grew somber. "I was very sorry to hear that he passed in such a terrible manner."

"Me too." I hesitated, wondering if I should mention what I'd found. But hell, he already knew about this hokey shit, didn't he? "I went to the motel where it happened and asked if I could check out the room, but the clerk told me there had never been any fire and he couldn't remember Tom."

Father James sat up straight in his seat, his dark eyebrows pulling together in a troubled frown. "That's not right," he protested. "Tom's death was all over the local news."

"Right?" I slapped the top of his desk, then winced as an elephant-shaped paperweight trembled. "Sorry. But it didn't make any sense, and when I had the clerk open up the room, it was pristine. Like nothing had ever happened." I searched his troubled gaze. "Do you think this could be something…supernatural?"

"It's quite possible," Father James conceded. "A fae could have done it, or perhaps even a vengeful spirit. I've banished my fair share of wraiths from the homes of desperate parishioners during my time here."

"Banished wraiths?" I leaned in, eager to know more. This was the first person with knowledge of the supernatural I'd run into who was actually willing to talk to me, and I was going to soak up every bit of knowledge I could. "How do you do that?"

"Banishing evil spirits takes a level of skill that cannot be taught in a single conversation," Father James said lightly. "However, if you should run across one, a little prayer and faith will go a long way. Simply focus all your willpower and shout *"Capsicum annuum!"* as loudly as you can. You have to really mean it, but if you do it right, you should render the wraith immobile. If you need help after that, give me a call, and I'll come banish it permanently."

"Thanks. That's really good to know." I hesitated. "Does Guy know about this stuff? He never mentioned anything."

Faather James shook his head. "I think it's best we not mention this to my brother. Not everyone can see these things the way you and I do, and I've learned the hard way that you can bring more trouble to your door than is worth it by forcing people to see when they're not ready to."

I nodded, though I wasn't sure I agreed. Was that what Oscar thought? That I hadn't been ready to know the truth? Look where that kind of thinking had landed me.

I glanced at my watch, then rose. "I should get going. Thank you for saving me, and for taking the time to answer my questions." I held out a hand. "Maybe we'll cross paths again."

"I would very much like that." Father James rose, then shook my hand with a smile. "Be careful with your investigation into Tom's death, Brooke. If my hunch is right and the supernatural are involved, things could get very dangerous for you."

I thanked him again, then hoofed it home as fast as I could without breaking into a run. I made sure to stick to well-lit areas, not wanting to run into another shade, or any other type of fae, really. I might have some new iron bullets, but that didn't mean I wanted to confront creatures that I still knew little about.

Once I was safely behind the locked door of my apartment, I whipped out my phone and called Uncle Oscar. I hadn't intended on calling him so soon since I knew how he felt about me coming out here, but after the day I had, I wanted to hear a familiar voice.

"Hey kid," he said, and his deep, gruff voice was like a balm to my frazzled nerves.

"Hey Uncle." I sat down heavily on the couch. "How's it going?"

"That's what I should be asking you. Last we spoke, I thought I might not be hearing from you again for a while. You were pretty upset."

I snorted. "If you'd really been worried about me, you'd have blown up my phone with calls and text messages."

Uncle Oscar let out a gusty sigh. "True. I figured you were probably just simmering down after our last argument."

"You could say that." I let out a sigh of my own.

We'd fought bitterly before I left, had both flung barbs at each other that still stung whenever I thought about them too much. So I hadn't thought about it, had shoved it aside so I could focus on what mattered. Finding Tom.

"So, how is it going?" Uncle Oscar asked. "Made some good use of your vamp gun yet?"

"No, actually," I admitted. "But I did get into a fight with a shade tonight."

The phone went silent for several seconds before Uncle Oscar exploded. "What the hell?" he shouted, and I winced as my ear rang. "What do you mean you got into a fight with a shade? You're not trained to fight shades! You're not supposed to even know what they are!"

"Calm down!" I ordered, hardening my voice. "I survived, okay? A priest came around the corner and shot him with some iron bullets. He gave me some, and now I know what to do next time. In fact, this might have been less of an issue if you'd *prepared* me for such a scenario!" A scathing tone entered my voice.

There was a sharp intake of breath, then a long silence. "Jesus, kid. Just what the hell are you getting into over there?" Oscar finally asked.

I told him everything—Captain Randall's refusal to let me work the case, Detective Baxter's strange inability to remember my fiancé even though everybody knew him, my encounter with Maddock Tremaine at his strange club, the motel room that was mysteriously untouched by the fire that had reportedly killed Tom, and my run-in with the shade and the priest.

"The more time I spend here, the more I'm convinced that Tom got mixed up with the supernatural community here, and it got him killed," I finished.

"Damn right it did." Uncle Oscar growled. "And if you keep this up, it's going to get you killed, too."

"Uncle Oscar—"

"Come home, kid." There was a strange note beneath his voice, and if I didn't know better, I'd say it sounded like a plea. "Get out of that crazy town before you end up the same way Tom did. You're in way over your head, and you know it."

"I'm *not* coming home." I dug my free hand into the couch cushions. "I didn't come all the way out here to turn tail and run at the first sight of supernatural activity— after all, I came here *looking* for it. I've *always* known there were things—supernatural things—besides vampires. It's about time I found out what they are."

"No, it's not!" Uncle Oscar's voice bubbled with frustration. "Not like this! Come home, Brooke. Come back to Chicago, let me give you a little more training. You're not ready to deal with this stuff."

The use of my name, plus the offer to train, gave me pause. But then I let out a bitter laugh and shook my head. "You had your chance to train me, Uncle Oscar, and instead you decided to keep me in the dark. I'm grateful for everything you've done for me, but I'm a grown woman now. I don't need you making my decisions for me."

"You're being incredibly foolish. If you'd just let me give you some more training—"

"And how exactly do I know that you're even going to give me this training when I come back?" I demanded. "How do I know that you're not going to try and lock me up or convince me to abandon my investigation into Tom's death?"

The ringing silence on the other end of the line was all I needed to hear.

"That's what I thought," I said quietly, my heart aching. I'd hoped that Uncle Oscar would deny it, but he was too brutally honest for that. He might have intended to train me, but that didn't mean he wouldn't do everything in his power to prevent me from going back to Salem afterward. "I'm not doing this with you, Uncle Oscar. Not anymore. Goodbye."

I hung up the phone, let a single tear trail down my cheek, then wiped it away.

No more tears. No more guilt. Finding out the truth about what happened to Tom meant I had to let go of everything that was holding me back, and if that included cutting my ties with Uncle Oscar, then that was what I'd do.

nine

I'd barely settled down after my phone call with Uncle Oscar when my front door buzzer sounded. After the day I'd had, I considered ignoring it. But curiosity trumped my desire to be alone—after all, I was new in town. Who on earth would be knocking on my door?

Switching the burner underneath my pot of marinara sauce to low, I stepped away from the stove and peered through the peephole. Shelley was standing on the other side, looking nervously down the hall, and the strain on her face suggested she wasn't here for a social visit.

Sighing, I disengaged the locks and opened the door. "Hey, Shelley. What's up?"

"Brooke." Her voice brimmed with both relief and anxiety—she'd probably been worried I wasn't home. "Sorry, I mean Detective. I should be calling you Detective, right? But I don't remember your last name…"

"It's Chandler." I gently took her by the shoulder and led her into my living room. "But it doesn't matter; you can call me Brooke. Why don't you tell me what happened?"

"I…" Shelley allowed me to steer her to the sofa, and she sat beside me, folding her hands neatly into her lap. "It might be nothing."

"It's not nothing if it's got you worried enough to come to a cop's doorstep."

She let out a sigh and twisted a strand of her long hair around a finger. "It's my eldest son, Jason. He's acting very secretive, refusing to let me in his room, giving me strange glances, clamming up when I ask him questions about his day. And he's been staying out late, very late. I…I think he's mixed up in some kind of gang."

"Huh." I frowned, thinking over the small bits of information she'd given me. "Are you sure it's a gang, and not just a group of friends? I mean, no offense, but what you've described to me sounds like common teenage behavior."

Shelley bit her lip. "That's true…but there's been other things, too. He's been wearing scarves and using makeup to hide injuries. And one time, I walked in the kitchen at one in the morning to find him washing what looked like *blood* off his hands." She shuddered. "He refused to discuss it with me, of course, and just stalked back into his room and slammed the door in my face. I've tried grounding him, but I've got so much to do with working full-time and taking care of Tyler…" Her voice grew thick, and she wiped at a tear sliding down her cheek. "He blames me."

"Blames you? For what?"

She sniffed back more tears. "His father died last year. Killed in an accident." Her eyes flicked away, then back again. "He was abusive, and a drunkard…but he and Jason loved each other. He doesn't say it anymore, but I know he thinks that if I'd tried harder, if I'd just pushed David to get treatment, that everything would have been okay."

"You and I both know that's not true," I said calmly, pushing down the anger rising in my throat. "You were the victim, Shelley. His behavior was not your fault."

"Maybe," Shelley whispered, eyes downcast. She clenched her fists in her lap, and her voice grew stronger. "Maybe, but if I'm honest with myself, I didn't want to help David. Not after all the bruises, all the broken bones, all the tears. I just wanted to leave him. And that's why I can't face the look in Jason's eyes sometimes. Because I know that in a way, he's right. I didn't try to get David help."

"Shelley, look at me." I placed a hand on her trembling thigh and waited until her tear-filled eyes met my steady ones. "How long were you married to David?"

She sniffed. "Fifteen years."

"So I think it'd be safe to say you knew him pretty well then, huh?"

"Better than anyone else." An ugly note entered her voice. "He put on an act for the world, made himself appear to be the doting father and husband, the hard-working man. He saved the real David for when we were behind closed doors."

"Right. So in your estimation, do you think that David would have listened to your suggestion to seek treatment, or go after it himself?"

Shelley was quiet for a moment. "No," she said eventually, shaking her head. "No. He would have beaten me for suggesting it."

"Then put the guilt aside," I said firmly. "I know it's hard, but blaming yourself for something that isn't your fault isn't going to help your son. It sounds like the two of you need to talk out your issues, maybe with a mediator, or that you need to seek help yourselves. I can try to get some recommendations for you, but beyond that, I don't think I'll be much help."

"I'll try that," Shelley said, though she didn't sound very hopeful, "but in the meanwhile, is there any way you could try and find out what he's been up to? Like, maybe follow him around and see if you can catch him doing any gang-related activity?"

I lifted an eyebrow. "You'd probably be better suited hiring a PI for that."

"I would, but I don't have the money." Shelley looked up at me, her dark eyes pleading. "Please, Detective. I need to find out what my son's gotten into before it gets him killed."

Salem was a small town—finding out the names of the local gangs would be simple, and compared to what I'd dealt with in Chicago, would be small time. It probably wouldn't take a whole lot of time to figure out what Jason had tangled himself up in.

"All right." I sighed a little. "I'll look into it."

"Thank you." Shelley flung her arms around me. "Thank you so much." She dug out a picture of him from her pocket, then handed it to me. "If you need anything else, let me know."

I walked her out to her car, which she'd parallel-parked by the curb in front of my building. As I watched her drive off, I mused over what she'd told me...and also what she hadn't.

She'd broken eye contact when telling me about her ex's death, and while she might not have been lying, I had a feeling there was more to the story. And then there was still the matter of that vision I'd had when her ring had touched me. She'd been mixed up with vampires at some point, and that made me wonder if her son was involved with something as run-of-the-mill as a human gang, or with something more sinister.

Bitter wind nipped at my cheeks and bare arms, and I tilted my head toward the stiff breeze. Most people shied away from cold, but I loved it. There was something so invigorating about an icy wind. But I only allowed myself a moment before I headed up the stairs and back into the apartment—after all, I still had dinner cooking.

My stomach rumbled at the scent of hot marinara sauce, and I headed toward the stove to turn it off before it burned. But before I'd made it two steps, an unseen force knocked me back. Hard.

I stumbled, tripping over my own heels, then fell into the side table next to my couch. Pain radiated up my back as the new vase I'd bought crashed to the floor, and I rolled to the side, working to get my feet under me while simultaneously trying to find my attacker. That same unseen force gripped me by the throat, and I choked and sputtered, grasping at fingers that weren't there. Fear escalated to panic as the force *lifted* me off the ground, and I kicked out, feet dangling uselessly above the carpet.

The air around me blurred, and the next thing I knew, I was in my bathroom. The shower curtain was ripped aside, and I slammed into my tub with so much force that my head rattled.

I heard the *thunk* of the stopper being pushed into the drain, and I yelped as cold water jetted out of the faucet on full blast. I thrashed around, trying to get up, but something heavy was pinning me to the tub, and I couldn't move more than a few inches. Soon the water was up to my collarbone, and I began to panic. It was only a matter of time before it rose above my head.

I was going to drown.

ten

"Help!" I shrieked, thrashing against the unseen force pinning me against the rapidly-filling tub. "Someone, please help!"

God, please let these paper-thin apartment walls be good for something!

Tears sprang to my eyes as the icy water brushed my jawbone. Whether it was the violent rush of the tub filling or the next-door neighbor's blaring country music, nobody could hear me scream. Or maybe they didn't care, didn't want to get involved.

I was going to die here.

Not at the hand of a vampire, or a crazed drug addict, or a bloodthirsty gang member...but by drowning in my own goddamn bathtub because some ghost—or otherwise unseen force—had it in for me.

"No!" I growled as anger bubbled up inside me. I wasn't going out like this. I wasn't! There had to be something I could do to get this stupid spirit off me.

"Banishing evil spirits takes a level of skill that cannot be taught in a single conversation." Father James's words came back to me. *"However, if you should run across one, a little prayer and faith will go a long way. Simply focus all your willpower and shout,* "Capsicum annuum!" *as loudly as you can. You have to really mean it, but if you do it right, you should render the wraith immobile."*

A wraith. That had to be it.

"Capsicum annuum!" I screamed, focusing all my effort and energy toward the ghost.

My desperate shout echoed off the tile walls, and for a moment, nothing happened. Then the temperature in the room plunged so sharply I was amazed the water didn't turn to ice. The pressure on my chest dissipated, and a glowing blue figure coalesced in the air above my abdomen.

My scream faded into silence as the two of us stared at each other in shock.

The wraith was…not what I expected. She was a woman in her early twenties, wearing full colonial garb: a floral-printed gown with a petticoat and sleeveless ruffles. A matching hat was perched on her head. She would have looked like she was dressed for an outing with friends, if not for the fact that half of her lovely face had been burned away.

I shuddered at the way her left eye stared at me; the eyelids had been burned off, as well as much of the skin on her cheeks, giving me a glimpse of the bone and sinew beneath. I didn't know why her eyes were bugging out, though—*I* was the one who'd been attacked.

"What the fuck are you?" I demanded.

Those wide eyes blinked now—or at least the right one did. The woman reached up to touch the unmarred side of her face. "I…I'm a ghost?"

"Yeah, no shit." My body was still trembling with fear, but I forced myself to get over it. The ghost wasn't attacking me anymore, and I needed to get out of this damned tub and into dry clothes. Cold was one thing, but I *hated* being wet.

I levered myself out of the tub, which was no easy feat, and dripped icy water on my navy blue bathroom floor mat. The back of my head was throbbing from its impromptu encounter with the tub, my sodden clothes weighed me down, and my silver hair plastered against my scalp and face. Not wanting to track puddles all over the new carpet, I shed my clothing on the bathroom floor and trudged into my bedroom stark-naked to grab something clean and dry to wear.

To my irritation, the ghost-woman followed me, hovering by my bed as I rummaged through my closet. "Do you mind?" I snapped irritably as I shoved my legs into a pair of underwear. "I'm not exactly decent."

"I'm not looking," the ghost said, her eyes averted to the ground.

"Well, what *are* you doing?" I hooked on a bra, then tugged a black sweater over my head. I grimaced as my hair soaked the back of my sweater, and quickly wrapped my silver strands in a bath towel. "Waiting for another opportunity?"

"No," the ghost said sadly. "You've stripped me of my corporeal form. I can't touch you now."

The stench of burning sauce caught my nostrils and derailed my train of thought.

"Fuck!"

Abandoning my questions, I dashed out of the room and went to turn off the stove before my apartment caught fire. The ghost perched herself on the counter and watched as I scavenged what sauce I could and finished cleaning up. I gritted my teeth as she began whistling the tune to Greensleeves off-key and swinging her legs back and forth.

"If you're going to hang around here," I growled, "at least tell me something useful. Who are you, and where did you come from?"

"My name is Celia Johnson." The leg swinging stopped. "I'm from here, Salem. In fact, the house I used to live in stood just a few blocks from here before they tore it down and built a shopping area there. A butcher's shop sits where my house used to be, and I usually haunt that."

"Interesting." I snapped the lid onto a piece of tupperware, then glanced up at her. "What made you decide to leave the butcher's shop?"

"Oh, well, I've stayed at the shop for so long because it's where I died. I was cooking dinner in the backyard, and my stepmother knocked me into the fire pit." An ugly look crossed Celia's face as she reached up to touch her burned skin. "I got vengeance on her, of course, but I guess it wasn't enough because I'm still trapped on this plain. But the man who came to talk to me yesterday said that if I killed you, I could move on." Her face brightened momentarily before she sank back into a sulk. "Except now I can't anymore."

"Whoa, whoa, whoa." I held up a hand, my head spinning as I tried to process what she'd just told me. "Back up a second. You said that a man sent you to kill me? Who?"

Celia opened her mouth to speak, then shrieked as flames sprang up around her body. I jumped back with a cry of my own, grabbing for the fire extinguisher. But even as I swung the heavy red canister around, the flames vanished, and Celia along with them.

Breathing heavily, I set the canister down, then carefully approached the counter. A white rose bouquet rested exactly where Celia's ghostly butt had been perched. There was no yellow card this time, but it didn't take a genius to figure out where they'd come from.

I crushed the fragrant blossoms in my hand, then tossed them into the trash before storming away to grab my jacket. I was done with this. It was time I got my hands on Maddock Tremaine and dealt with him once and for all.

After my near-death experience in the bathtub, I needed to get out of my apartment for a little. Yeah, so the spell Father James gave me had worked, but that didn't mean I wasn't still feeling the aftershocks from my encounter. Sitting around in my apartment wasn't going to get me anywhere, so I took my laptop and made a beeline for the nearest coffee shop so I could do some more digging into Maddock Tremaine.

I was only a block away from the coffee shop when I caught sight of a tall, lanky teenager coming out of a vape shop across the street. He was dressed from head-to-toe in black, his hair dyed to match, and he had a lip piercing, but I still recognized him from the photo Shelley had given me.

Well, well, Jason Williams. Let's see what you're up to that's got your mother so worried.

I hefted my laptop bag a little higher on my shoulder, then crossed the street so I could follow him. I kept a cautious distance, although it wasn't really necessary—with his earbuds jammed into his ears, his shoulders hunched from the cold, and his moody eyes downcast, he was too wrapped up in his own little world to notice me. I pulled a beanie out from my jacket pocket and tucked my damp silver hair beneath it so I wouldn't draw attention to myself, then followed him eastward for a couple more blocks.

Soon we were in downtown Salem, just a few blocks from Essex Street, in the same part of town where Maddock's club was. I frowned, wondering what he was looking for. Was he headed into one of the witch shops? Had he gotten himself mixed up in something occult?

The answer became clear when Jason crossed the street to where a non-descript, but expensive-looking black sedan idled. The windows were tinted, so I couldn't see who or what was inside, but when the back door opened and Jason climbed in, I thought I caught the glitter of a pricey cufflink.

He's definitely not hanging out with a local gang, I thought as I started across the street to stop him.

A large hand curled around my shoulder, fingers digging in harshly, and I was unceremoniously yanked back onto the sidewalk. Heart pounding, I grabbed my gun as my assailant spun me around, then froze as I came face-to-face with a thunderous-looking Maddock Tremaine.

"Get in," he growled, jerking his thumb toward a shiny silver BMW parked on the curb just a few feet away. "We need to talk."

eleven

I probably should have been pissed, or scared, or some combination thereof. After all, I was smack-dab in the middle of a confrontation with a guy who'd tried to have me killed. Twice. Within the last twenty-four hours.

Instead, I burst out laughing.

"I dinnae see what's so funny," Maddock said tightly. A muscle in his jaw twitched as I only laughed harder. "Are ye suffering from hysteria, Detective Chandler? Because if so, ye might want to holster that gun before you shoot yer own leg off."

"I'm not suffering from hysteria." I chuckled, straightening up, and leveled the barrel of my gun at his chest. It only had regular bullets, but I was willing to bet they'd still hurt Maddock, whatever he was. "I just think it's funny that you think I'm stupid enough to get into a vehicle with you after you tried to have me killed. Twice. Now get on your knees and put your hands behind your head. You're under arrest for attempted murder."

Maddock's eyes narrowed. "I haven't tried to kill ye, Detective. If I had, ye'd be dead."

I rolled my eyes. "Save that cliché for someone who hasn't heard it." I clicked off the safety and gave him my best glare. "I will shoot you if I have to."

"All right."

Slowly, Maddock dropped to his knees, putting his hands behind his head. It was a good thing, too, because we were drawing attention from passersby, and this was a busy area. I really didn't want to have to shoot him in front of all these people. Most of them were giving us a wide berth, but there was always a chance Maddock could make a move that would end up getting someone else hurt.

"Smart man," I murmured, keeping my gun trained on him as I approached. I walked behind him, and as I moved to secure his wrists, the most amazing scent hit me. It was heather and woodsmoke and whiskey and rain all at once, and I inhaled deeply. A second later, I realized the scent belonged to Maddock, and my cheeks flamed. I was supposed to be *arresting* him, not sniffing him like a goddamn dog in heat!

"Maddock Tremaine," I began, sheathing my weapon and grabbing hold of his wrist. My voice trembled despite myself, which made me even angrier. "You are under arrest for—"

A wave of dizziness hit me, and the world started spinning. The next thing I knew, Maddock Tremaine was pressing his very big, very *hard* body against mine, driving me against a back alley wall behind a dumpster. My stomach pitched, and I choked, nearly heaving my guts onto the shoulder of his blazer.

"If ye throw up on my suit, I'll make sure to send the bill to yer apartment, Detective Chandler," Maddock growled. "Trust me when I say, the damage to yer wallet would be considerable."

I snorted, and my stomach roiled. "Give me some breathing room, then," I hissed out between clenched teeth. "I don't know what the hell you just did, but it's really not agreeing with my stomach right now."

"Since that was likely yer first time teleporting, I'm hardly surprised." There was a hint of amusement in his Scottish burr now. "The nausea will soon pass."

"Okay, but that doesn't mean I want you on top of me," I snapped.

He *was* right though—the nausea *did* seem to be easing off. Unfortunately, it was replaced by butterflies in my stomach, and my heart began fluttering in response as well. He was far too close, his addictive scent surrounding me, *claiming* me. Heat pooled low in my belly, and I gritted my teeth.

"Don't you?" he murmured, his lips so close I could feel his breath on my skin. One of his big hands drifted down to my waist, settled there for a moment, and then slowly moved up beneath my blazer.

"Get off me!" I stomped on his foot as hard as I could, wishing I was wearing boots or stilettos instead of my flats. Pain radiated up my ankle as I realized he had steel toes in his leather dress shoes.

He smirked.

"Ye ought to be careful," he said, drawing back. "It wouldna do to have ye break yer ankle when ye've only been on the job two days." He twirled both my guns in his hands like he was some Wild West cowboy, then tucked them beneath the rear waistband of his pants.

"Give those back!" I lunged for him, but my hands met empty air as he disappeared right before my eyes.

"Yer wasting time, Detective."

I spun around at the sound of Maddock's voice. He was leaning casually against the alley wall behind me, a few feet away from where he'd pinned me just seconds ago.

"The longer ye draw out this conversation, the longer I'll hold onto yer weapons," he continued. "I've no intention of keeping them, but I'm not going to let ye shoot me."

"You bastard," I hissed, but relented. What was I going to do, run away? I'd wanted a confrontation with Maddock Tremaine, and now I had one. I just wished I'd loaded my new iron bullets into my gun and used them on him to begin with, spectators be damned.

"What the hell do you want?" I demanded. "Why do you keep trying to kill me?"

"I haven't tried to kill ye." Maddock crossed his arms over his chest, the frown returning to his face. "Some cop ye are, by the way. Ye were going to arrest me with no evidence."

"You don't know—"

"Aye, but I do. Because there is no evidence to be had. All I have done is tell ye to stay out of my club. But I never tried ta kill ye. As I said before—"

"Yeah, yeah. If you wanted to kill me, I'd be dead." I waved a hand impatiently. "If that's the case, then what were your goons trying to do to me when you had them drag me to the back alley? Because whatever it was, it didn't work. The wraith you sent to kill me would have been more effective, if I hadn't beaten her back."

"Wraith?" Maddock's eyes narrowed. "What wraith?"

I scoffed. "Don't pretend like you don't know." But if he was lying, he hid it very well. I didn't detect anything beyond surprise in his voice and expression. "The ghost of a colonial woman tried to drown me in my own bathtub less than an hour ago. It really ruined my night, by the way. And then when I was interrogating her, she disappeared, and you left behind a bouquet of white roses, just like you did when you returned my gun."

Maddock scowled. "I had nothing to do with this wraith. Ye've clearly mixed yourself up with someone dangerous, which isn't at all surprising considering how easily ye attract trouble and how reckless ye are in yer actions."

"And what the hell would you know about me and my ability to attract trouble?" I demanded. "You don't know me."

"I know that yer a recent transfer from the Chicago Police Department and that yer looking into the death of yer recently deceased fiancé." He smirked. "It's easy enough for a man of my means to find out most anything I want to know."

"Well, if that's the case, then it should be easy enough for you to tell me what's really going on in this town." I wasn't going to let him intimidate me. "You'mre clearly right in the center of the supernatural community."

"Yes, and I'd prefer that ye stay as far away from it, and me, as possible."

"If you don't tell me, I'll make your life hell. I can have cops breathing down the necks of you and your cronies at every turn. I'm sure that'll put a real cramp in your secretive lifestyle."

Maddock threw his head back and laughed. White, even teeth gleamed in the moonlight, and I cursed myself as the butterflies in my stomach whipped themselves into a frenzy.

"Ye dinnae scare me." He sneered, the humor disappearing from his face as quickly as it came. "And neither does the Salem police department. Yer the one who should be afraid, Detective. This city is too dangerous for a little girl such as yerself. You should pack yer bags and head back to Chicago while ye've still got the chance."

"I'm not a little girl." I seethed, balling my hands into fists. Oh, how I wanted to punch him in that ridiculously handsome face of his! "I've been fighting vampires since I was a teen. Chicago's infested with them. If I can handle that, I can handle whatever else is around here."

Maddock tilted his head, regarding me curiously. "Did yer fiancé know about yer little hobby?"

"Yes," I snapped. "In fact, we worked together, killing vampires while we were on the job."

A pang of grief and loneliness hit my chest—I longed for those days again, when it was just me and Tom, stalking the dark streets of Chicago and kicking vampire ass. At least fifty percent of the homicides we'd dealt with were vampire-related, so it wasn't like we were doing it for fun. But I'd still enjoyed it, not just because we were making a difference, but because I had someone I could share this part of my life with. Someone who'd understood.

Not anymore, though. Everyone around me who knew anything about the supernatural were bound and determined to keep me away from it. And I was sick of being treated with kid gloves.

Maddock sighed, uncrossing his arms and pushing his hands into his pockets. "I can see that I'm not going to dissuade ye from this foolhardy path, and that yer going to cause me trouble regardless of whether or not I give ye information. I suppose it would behoove me to tell ye a few things, so that ye dinnae go blundering around and causing even more problems."

"Gee, thanks." My heartbeat picked up with excitement, but I was careful not to let it show on my face. "I'm all ears, buddy."

"ENVY, the club I manage here, is the premiere supernatural hotspot in this city and the whole of New England as well." Maddock picked some imaginary dirt from his fingernails, as if this conversation was utterly boring. "Its location is technically in Underhill, but it's anchored in this world as well and serves as a sort of go-between."

My eyes popped. "You're saying that your club is a gateway to faerie?"

"That's one way of putting it." Maddock inclined his head. A lock of inky hair fell forward, giving him a rakish look, and I told the butterflies in my stomach to pipe down.

Jesus, did he have some kind of magic mojo that was throwing me off like this?

"As a high-ranking member of the Seelie Court, I have responsibilities to ensure that our domain is well-protected. In addition to that, I also keep an eye out in the area for any newcomers…such as yerself." His eyes narrowed. "And my guards keep tabs on any humans who are trying to get into the supernatural community. For example, that young teenage boy who ye watched get in that car. He's been snooping around for weeks, trying to get a vampire to turn him."

"What?" I straightened up at that. "Are you fucking kidding me? Why didn't you let me go after him? They could be turning him right now!"

Maddock let out a sigh. "They're not doing any such thing."

"And just how do you know that?"

"Because the men he got into the car with weren't vampires," he said patiently. "They were some of my own men. They're going to wipe his memory of the club and take him back to his mother's house. Ye won't find him snooping around here again."

"Oh." Some of the tension coiled in my gut eased. Which was silly, because I had no idea if I could even trust Maddock Tremaine. "You'd better not be lying to me, Tremaine. I promised that boy's mother I would help him."

"Well, now ye can keep yer word," Maddock said silkily, a little smirk playing on his sensual lips. "Better yet, now that I've helped get that off yer plate, ye have some time to help me."

I stiffened. "Help you with what?"

"A number of supernaturals have been going missing in the last few months." Maddock's face hardened. "Someone is taking them, and I need to know why, and where they are. Since yer both a detective *and* a supernatural, I'd like to enlist ye in my search for them."

I pursed my lips. "Are any of them kids?"

"Both children and adults have been taken," Maddock confirmed. "And whoever is doing it is using magic to mask their trail."

"Huh." I pursed my lips. Tom came here to investigate missing kids, and now Maddock was telling me supernaturals were going missing as well? That couldn't be coincidence. But still… "What's in it for me?"

"If ye help me locate my missing kin, I'll help ye uncover the truth about yer fiancé."

I glared suspiciously at him. "How do I know that you'll keep your word?"

"The fae cannot lie," Maddock said simply. "If you doubt that, simply ask yer Uncle Oscar. He knows that to be true."

I pressed my lips together, annoyed that he knew so much more about me than I knew about him. I needed to fix that, to level the playing field between us. He held too many cards.

"Fine," I agreed, because it benefited me all around. "I'll help you."

"Excellent. I'll be in touch." A smile curved his lips briefly, and then his brilliant green eyes hardened. "In the meantime, stay alert, Detective. Yer activities have painted a large target on your back, and I'm sure the wraith attack won't be the last attempt on yer life."

And with that, he vanished.

twelve

Even though I turned in early, I did not sleep easy. My dreams were full of wraiths and vampires and shadowy figures with glowing purple eyes. They stalked me mercilessly, clinging to me like glue no matter how fast I moved.

"Get away from me!" I cried, batting away the bluish figure of a ghostly little girl.

My hand passed through her form as she swooped down, and a chill swept through me, sending a shiver across my skin even though I normally enjoyed the cold.

"But why?" The girl pouted, her voice echoing strangely in the darkness. "We're family."

I glared at her. "I may not remember my parents much, but I'm pretty sure that you're not from my family tree."

"We may not share blood," someone hissed from my left. I whipped my head around to see a vampire smiling at me, his white fangs gleaming despite the lack of light. "But we do share a heritage of sorts, Brooke Chandler," he continued. "You're one of us."

"No!" I pulled out my vampire gun and shot him in the chest. Blood bloomed on his chest as the wooden stake bullets ripped through his flesh, but instead of disintegrating into ash, he simply fell to his knees and laughed, and laughed, and laughed...

"Detective! Wake up!"

A demanding male voice dragged me kicking and screaming from the dream. Strong, firm hands curled around my shoulders, shaking me, and I lashed out with my fists.

"Mac Soith!" Maddock cursed as my fist connected with his perfect jawline. He grabbed my wrists in both hands and pressed me into the mattress. "Stop struggling, will ye? I'm not trying to attack!"

I blinked up at him, staring into leaf-green eyes that crackled with annoyance.

"W-what are you doing here?" I sputtered.

I should have been angrier, but that delicious heather-whiskey scent of his was sinking into me, muddling up my thoughts, and the hard, muscular body pressing me into the mattress wasn't helping things, either.

"I came here because I wanted to speak to ye regarding the investigation ye agreed to help me with," Maddock growled. "But ye were screamin' too loudly to hear me bangin' on the door."

"Oh." Heat flooded my cheeks, and it took everything I had not to look away in embarrassment. "Well, now that you're in here, can you get off me? I'd like to be able to breathe now."

Something hot flickered in Maddock's eyes, and his gaze dipped downward. "Is that why ye sleep with naught but a sheet over you?" He raised an eyebrow. "Because ye 'need to breathe'?"

My entire face flamed. "That's none of your business!" I tried to shove at him with my hands, which he still held firmly in his grip. I slept in the nude because I tended to overheat easily—if it were warmer weather I would have foregone the sheet as well, which had me thanking my lucky stars for the cool autumn weather as of late.

"Get off me before I arrest your ass for breaking and entering!"

Maddock chuckled as he released me. "There was no breaking," he informed me. "Teleporting into yer apartment is an easy enough matter, just as it was when ye tried to arrest me last night."

"Get out of my room," I snarled, clutching the sheet to my chest as I sat up. "I'll meet you in the living room in five minutes."

"If ye don't, I'll assume something went wrong and come back in to check on you." He smirked and then vanished.

Cursing, I whipped the sheet off my body, then glanced at the clock by my bedside. Six-thirty. Who the fuck came to visit anyone at six-thirty in the damn morning? The sun hadn't even cracked the horizon, I noticed as I peered through the curtains of the window beside my bed.

Then again, I guess it was good he came so early. I had to be at the precinct by eight-thirty, and I wasn't going to give Captain Randall another reason to bust my ass by being late.

I eyed the bathroom longingly, wanting a shower, but the last thing I needed was for Maddock to spirit himself back in here while I was drying off because I'd used up my allotted five minutes. So I settled for my fluffy blue bathrobe with glittering snowflakes, and the matching slippers, then tied my hair into a messy bun before heading into the living room.

Maddock had already made himself comfortable on the couch, sipping coffee from a to-go cup and reading something on his gigantic phone screen as if he were sitting at some café instead of in a cop's living room. His black hair was pulled back into a low tail today, and he wore a woolen coat just a few shades darker than cobalt over his business suit.

"I see you've made yourself right at home," I sneered, sitting in the recliner across from him. I wanted to sit on the couch, dammit, but I'd already decided it was best to keep as much distance between us as possible. I wasn't the type of woman to go weak at the knees for a pretty face, but Maddock was a fae, and whatever mojo he had was messing with my ability to think clearly whenever he got too close.

"I dinnae see why I cannae be comfortable if I have to relegate myself to sitting here in this dingy apartment of yers."

"I'm sorry," I said sweetly, crossing my legs and placing my hands on my knee. "I should have rented a castle instead, so that you could feel more at home."

Maddock lifted a second to-go cup sitting on the coffee table and handed it to me. "Drink this. With any luck, coffee will take some of the pissiness from yer tone."

I eyed the cup suspiciously. "Aren't you not supposed to accept any food or drink from the fae?"

Maddock rolled his eyes. "That's only if yer *in* Underhill, Detective. And even then, only if ye dinnae want to be trapped there."

"Hmph." I took the cup from him—after all, the fae couldn't lie, right?

Maddock eyed me strangely as I took my first sip. "You really dinnae know anything about the supernatural world, do ye?"

"Not nearly enough." I scowled at him over the rim of my coffee cup; he was really spoiling my morning coffee. "And if I'm going to work with you, you're going to need to start filling me in."

"Indeed." Maddock's eyes narrowed as he looked around the space. "There's magical energy in here. I sensed it strongly in yer bedroom."

"Yeah, no shit." I rolled my eyes. "There was a wraith here last night, remember? She tried to drown me in the bathtub?"

"Hmm." A thoughtful look clouded in Maddock's gaze as he set his coffee cup back on the table. "Do you happen to have any chamomile, sage, and honey on hand?"

"Yes." I eyed him warily. "Why?"

"Bring them to me, and I'll show you."

I thought about refusing, but I was curious as to what he wanted with some herbs and sweetener. I had a feeling he wasn't planning on using the stuff to flavor his coffee. So I went and fetched the items from my kitchen cupboard, then brought them to him along with a little bowl.

"So, what now?" I asked as he mixed the ingredients together. "And don't tell me you need candles or some shit."

"Dinnae be so daft. I'm not a witch, Detective." Maddock finished mixing up his little concoction, then rose.

Slowly, he wandered around the apartment, following some kind of strange trail that only he could see. After a few minutes, he stopped at the wall behind my dining table.

"Here," he murmured, dipping his hands into the honey mixture. Then he proceeded to use the mixture to draw a series of complicated symbols on the wall.

"Hey!" I snapped, swatting at his hand. "What are you finger-painting on my walls for?"

Ignoring me, he closed his eyes and muttered something in a strange, musical language that sent a weird hum through my body. In the next second, the symbols he'd drawn melted away, and I gasped as a black 'O' with three jagged, vertical slashes appeared instead.

"What the hell is that?" I demanded, leaning in to sniff at the stripes. They were a dark, rusty red color, and I recoiled at the coppery tang that hit my nostrils. "Is that *blood?*"

"Aye," Maddock said grimly.

"What the fuck!" Rattled, I paced the short distance between the wall and my kitchen counter. "What kind of sicko would come here and do this?" I paced back. "And whose blood is that?"

"It belongs to whoever drew the mark," Maddock said. "As far as what the mark is, I've been doing some research into that. It seems to belong to an ancient sect of witches that call themselves the Onyx Order. They lived near Salem for a long time, but vanished a good two-hundred years ago. Nobody had seen or heard from them since then, so they were thought to have been annihilated or disbanded." He glared at the symbol. "But it would appear they are back."

"Hang on." I held up a hand. "You're saying you've seen this symbol before?"

"It's appeared in the home of every supernatural who's gone missing," Maddock said. "I thought it was simply a calling card they were leaving, to taunt the friends and loved ones of the victims. But since ye haven't been taken, I'm thinking now that it's a mark. A sort of beacon, to highlight their next target. I believe they're coming for ye, Detective."

I hissed, then shoved my hands into my pockets and stopped pacing so I could glare at the offending mark. "Is there any way to scrub that thing from my walls? Get rid of this so-called *beacon*?"

Maddock shrugged. "I'm sure I could figure it out, but I doubt it would stop them. For whatever reason, they've got ye in their sights now, and they intend to have ye."

I threw up my hands. "Why? Because I'm poking into Tom's death? They don't want me uncovering the truth, so they're going to get rid of me instead?"

"Perhaps," Maddock allowed. "But you've plenty of power in that little body of yers, and I'd wager that's attractive to them, too."

I narrowed my eyes. Aside from my psychometry-like talent, which wasn't apparent enough for him to know about, I didn't have any power to speak of. "I don't know what you're talking about."

Maddock smirked as he wagged his finger at me. "Aye, but ye do."

I groaned. "Come on, Tremaine. You've got to tell me *something* about what's going on here. Before yesterday, I didn't even know the fae were real. My scope was limited to vampires, and now you're telling me there's witches, too? What else should I expect? Gnomes? Djinn?"

"Ye met a gnome the other night, when ye were snooping around in my club," Maddock said. He tilted his head, then added, "Billy. The little man in the back alley who unsuccessfully tried to mind-wipe you."

"Gee, why am I not surprised?" I thought back for a minute. "What are your mountain men? Giants?"

"Trolls."

"Jesus." I pulled my silver hair from my messy bun and reset it, more out of a need to do something—*anything*—other than just stand here, listening to this. "Just how many different types of supernaturals are there?"

"Many, but dinnae concern yerself with trying to learn every single type. What's important are the sub-species."

"Sub-species?" Jeez, he said that like it should mean something to me. But instead, it just made me feel more overwhelmed. "Care to elaborate?"

Maddock made a sound in the back of his throat, then pulled out one of my dining chairs and straddled it. He looked up at me through those sinfully black lashes of his, and even though his eyes were glittering with ire, my stomach still fluttered in response. *Damn him.* Why did he have to be so annoyingly sexy?

"Since it seems I have to give ye a history lesson, I may as well make myself somewhat comfortable," he said, misinterpreting my annoyance. "My kind, the fae, were the first magical beings to exist on Earth, and all supernatural creatures are, in a way, our children…such as yerself."

I chose my next words carefully, speaking slowly and pausing occasionally to assess if he did, in fact, really already know about my gift. "So…" I said, "the fact that I can see things others can't means I have fae ancestry?"

"Ye could say that." Maddock wrinkled his nose, as if he found the very idea distasteful. "Because fae magic is so potent, it tends to take on a mind of its own. Nymphs and dryads, for example, are creatures that sprang into being simply because the fae lived in their habitats for too long. Some of our creations occur by accident, others on purpose, but all of them are our responsibility. In particular, the Seelie Court has given me the responsibility of making sure the balance is maintained between the supernaturals living in this sector of the world. And the witches are throwing off that balance."

"Hmm." I looked down at my hands. They seemed normal enough, aside from the fact that I could use them to see into the past. Was there fae blood running through these veins? "So witches are a product of the fae as well?"

Maddock nodded, his features twisting in displeasure again. "Their ancestors were humans that learned to harness residual fae magic and use it for their own. Entirely forbidden, of course, but by the time they came into their own, there was little we could do about it, and the Seelie Court ruled that they should be recognized as a proper sub-species." Bitterness entered his tone. "That was one of our poorer choices."

"Why?" I studied him curiously, wondering why he appeared to harbor such animosity toward witches. "What's so horrible about witches versus any other supernatural?"

"They're conniving, manipulative, and take things that don't belong to them." Maddock hissed, then shoved to his feet. "Such as the fae that have been going missing recently."

"Well, I can't argue with that," I muttered, eyeing him warily. He was glaring at me, as if this were somehow my fault. "But how do you know it's the witches doing this? A symbol on a wall isn't what I call concrete evidence."

Maddock crossed his arms and glared down at me, making my

heart jump into my throat. "So yer defending them now? Somehow I'm not surprised."

His sarcastic tone was so accusatory that his behavior suddenly made sense. All the animosity, the condemning glares...

"You think *I'm* a witch, don't you?" I jabbed a finger at him. "That's why you don't like me, and why you always look at me like I'm a piece of shit stuck to your shoe."

"I dinnae know what ye are," Maddock growled, clamping his hand around my forearm. "Aside from a heaping of trouble. But right now, I need ye, which is why I'm tolerating yer presence in this city. Now let's get going already. I've something to show ye."

"No!" Energy sizzled in the air around us, and I tried to pull away, instinctively knowing what was coming.

But it was too late. We were already gone.

thirteen

"I swear to God, if you *ever* do that again without warning me first, I will shoot you in the crotch."

Bracing myself against the yellow-papered wall of a parlor room I'd never seen before, I took in deep breaths as I fought against the desire to retch. It was a good thing I hadn't eaten anything today, or I would have thrown up all over the thick, red rug that covered the glossy wooden floor of this fancy-looking apartment.

"I'll try to keep that in mind," Maddock said lightly. He didn't flinch, as most men would have at my threat. In fact, something that looked suspiciously like laughter entered his eyes as his gaze roamed over me, and my cheeks flamed as I realized I was still wearing my bathrobe.

"I fucking hate you," I growled, tugging the bathrobe tighter around my body—the belt had loosened during our impromptu travel through time and space. I was never going to appear in front of him again without being fully dressed.

"Dinnae worry. I'll have ye back to yer apartment soon." His gaze moved away from me, trailing across the room, and in the next instant, his expression hardened, green fire snapping in his eyes. "*Bloody hell.* This was a waste of time."

"Why?" I narrowed my eyes as I followed his gaze, trying to see whatever he saw. Red and gold drapes that matched the carpeting and expensive-looking art on the walls—normal enough. But the humongous couches and chairs—it would probably take me less effort to mount a horse than it would to climb into the stuffed armchair sitting by the fireplace—and the ridiculously high ceiling gave me pause.

"What are we even doing here?" I asked. "And whose house is this?"

"We're in the residence of one of my staff, Garin Barclay. He's a giant," Maddock added in answer to my unspoken question. "He's been missing for about a week."

"A giant?" I paled a little as I studied the furniture again, mentally gauging just how large their owner had to be. Maddock measured an easy six foot three, and I was willing to bet with all that muscle he'd pressed up against me earlier that he weighed at least two-twenty. And yet, two and a half of him could probably fill out that arm-chair, with room to spare. "How the hell does a guy like this walk around in public?"

"Glamour," Maddock answered, a bite of impatience in his voice. "Both higher and lesser fae learn the skill early on, as our true forms are often...*unpalatable* to the human eye."

I eyed Maddock warily. "Does that include you?" It would be a relief to know that underneath the sexy skin he wore, Maddock actually looked more like a troll.

A smirk curved his lips for just a moment. "Ye wouldn't be able to keep yer hands off me if ye saw my true form."

"Oh, as-if." I pushed aside the barrage of images my mind spewed as it tried to figure out what Maddock's true form looked like. "Let's get back on track. Why did you say it was a waste of time to come here?"

"Because witches have wiped the place clean." Maddock growled, his eyes narrowing again. "You won't be able to use your talent to discover anything."

I stiffened. "What talent?"

Maddock rolled his eyes. "Please, Detective. Dinnae be so naïve to think that ye could hide such a thing from me."

"Don't give me that shit." I propped my fists on my hips and turned to face him. "I don't believe that you somehow dug up information like that about me. I haven't told anybody about my talent, not even Tom. I bet you're bluffing, and you don't even know what it is."

"Ye can see into the past by touching objects," Maddock said dryly. When I gaped at him, he added, "One of my guards reported seeing ye walking around the club and running yer hands across various surfaces. It didn't take me long to reach that conclusion."

"Hmph." I still didn't quite believe that he'd managed to make the leap that quickly, but he *was* right, so what could I do? "So you're saying that you don't think I can find anything here because the place has been wiped clean?"

"Aye."

"I don't know about that," I murmured, moving forward to

run my fingers across a mahogany tabletop. "I stopped by the motel room where Tom was murdered and that place seemed to have been wiped clean, too. But whoever did it was sloppy, because they missed a spot, and I got a vision."

"Did ye?" Maddock stood a little straighter, eyeing me curiously. "What did you see?"

I told him about the mysterious figure in the trench coat who'd set fire to the place, and he frowned.

"And yet ye say the room was untouched by fire, and the clerk said there was no such incident?" he asked.

"That's right." I skimmed my fingers over the back of one of the ginormous couches. "Hard to believe, eh?"

"Very," Maddock said firmly. "It would take an extraordinary level of skill to burn a motel room to ashes and then reconstruct it. It also sounds like a colossal waste of time and energy. I would have simply placed an illusion to make it appear as if the place had burned, and then once the investigation was over, simply lifted the spell so it would return to normal."

I frowned. "But wouldn't that also require altering the memories of the staff? And any long-term resident?"

"Aye, but such things are possible." Maddock regarded me silently for a moment. "Strange, though, that someone would go through such trouble. If they wanted to make it appear as though yer fiancé had died in a fire, why try to cover it up afterward?"

I shrugged. "Maybe in case someone came along and tried to reopen the investigation?"

Maddock arched an eyebrow. "Ye mean someone like yerself?"

I paused. "Are you suggesting that somebody knew I would be coming?"

Maddock snorted. "If I were the one who'd killed yer fiancé, I'd be counting on it. Yer a detective, and you were in love. Why wouldn't ye come out here to look into things?"

I turned that over in my mind as I finished searching the apartment. Unlike my search of the motel room, I didn't get lucky—whoever had covered their tracks here had done a good job. Frustrated with my lack of productivity, I kicked at one of the chairs. It moved, fractionally, and something winked from the darkness beneath it.

"Hmm."

I dropped to my hands and knees, then fished a pearl earring out from beneath the chair. As I held it up to the light filtering in through the curtains, it glowed, and a vision hit me.

"Well shit." A brunette wearing black skinny jeans and an equally black button up shirt sneered up from above me. A similarly dressed blonde stood next to her, gripping a bloody silver knife in her hand. "What the hell do we do now? We weren't supposed to kill anyone. Just take him alive."

The blonde's cruel features screwed up in distaste. "We'll have to hide her somewhere. Not that it'll be easy lugging this fat bitch around." She kicked at something I couldn't see in front of her, something I suspected was a dead body. "Where can we bury her, that the cops won't dig her up?"

"The old mill up in Wenham," the brunette said. "It's well-shielded, and nobody'll think to look in there." She glanced over her shoulder. "But first, we have to get him back to the coven before he wakes up. It was hard enough taking him out the first time."

The vision faded. A sinking feeling started in the pit of my stomach as I stared at the pearl earring, processing what I'd just seen.

"I'm guessing ye saw something?" Maddock's deep voice drew my gaze toward him, and he nodded toward the pearl earring in my fingers. "Your aura changed when you picked that up."

I frowned. "You can see my aura?"

Maddock shrugged. "Aura, life force, whatever ye'd like to call it. It makes it easy for me to tell when someone is using magic, which ye clearly were just now."

I shifted uncomfortably on my knees, not sure how I felt about that. I didn't really consider my talent to be magic, but what else could I call it? It also had me wondering what else he could tell about me from my aura...such as my unwelcome attraction to him.

"Yeah," I said, scowling now. "Apparently your giant had a lady friend. The two women who came here to capture him killed her. I saw them discussing how to dispose of her body. They mentioned a mill in Wenham."

Maddock blinked. "I dinnae know of any mill up in Wenham."

I smiled, then pulled my phone from my pocket. "That's what Google Maps is for."

Maddock brought me back to my apartment so I could change, but once I was showered and clothed, I refused to let him teleport me again. Since my Jeep was still at the precinct, he reluctantly agreed to have someone bring his Mercedes around, and we drove to the mill in comfort and style.

On the way there, I called Baxter and told him that I was checking on a lead in connection with one of our cold cases and would be running a little late. He had questions, of course, and I was forced to give him vague answers—after all, I couldn't very well tell him I was investigating the murder of a Giant's lover.

Our little field trip took us north, onto the highway for a few miles, and then into Wenham itself, which was a small town with colonial style homes tucked away into neighborhoods with narrow, winding roads shielded by oak and maple trees. There were plenty of dirt and paved roads that branched off the main road, leading up to houses or fields where animals grazed, and my GPS led us up one of those dirt roads.

"Bloody hell," Maddock growled as a stone shot out from beneath one of his tires and pinged against the underbelly of his car. He scowled, clenching his jaw. "I should have called for the Land Rover instead."

I snorted. "Spoken like an entitled rich guy."

He swung his glare toward me, but I ignored him and pretended to examine my nails instead. So what if he was annoyed? Maddock seemed to be perpetually irritated about my existence, so I might as well make the most of it. Besides, most of the time he annoyed the shit out of me too.

"There it is." I pointed to a crumbling stone structure, about twenty feet tall and half-covered with moss and ivy, jutting out of the field to our left. A rickety-looking waterwheel hung off the side, suspended over a dry creek-bed that had once turned it and powered the structure. Maddock parked on the side of the road, and we picked our way along the small path leading up to the door.

"There's a faint glamour covering this place," Maddock murmured as he held up a hand, signaling for me to stop. "A simple one that shields it from anyone who wouldn't already know it was there."

"Which explains why we can see it." I tapped my foot impatiently. "Is there anything else I should be aware of? Like traps?"

Maddock studied the building, then shook his head. "All seems clear." He gestured to the large, wooden double doors. "Ye can go on in."

I lifted an eyebrow, a little smirk playing on my lips. "Not going to open the door for the lady?"

Maddock eyed the large metal rings on each door that served as handles with distaste. "Those are made of iron."

"Oh." Understanding, I curled my hand around the cold metal and gave it a tug. The door opened with a loud, rusty creak, and I wrinkled my nose at the smell of moldy hay, freshly-turned earth, and...blood.

"The body's definitely here somewhere," I insisted as I stepped inside the mill.

My eyes widened as I took in the main room. The same symbol I'd seen in my living room was painted across the millstone in the center, and different symbols were painted on the walls in what had to be more blood.

"Wait." Maddock made a grab for my arm as I moved toward the millstone, but I was already there, my hand on it, and—

The little boy screamed and writhed, his naked skin chafing against the millstone as he tried to break free. Ram's horns curled back from his temple, and though his small face should have been smooth and unlined, it was shriveled and wizened like an old man's.

Rope crisscrossed over his torso, holding him to the stone, and his vertical pupils rolled with fear as he stared up at the naked woman looking down at him. Other naked people frolicked around them in a circle, men and women dancing and chanting in a strange language that sent a crackle up my spine.

"Please don't," the boy sobbed, and then suddenly I was the boy, tied to the millstone as golden tears leaked from the corners of my eyes. "Please don't kill me. I can be useful, I swear." My voice was weak and feeble, as if I were at the tail-end of my strength.

"Your time has come." The woman stepped forward, her voice distant, a faraway look in her cool grey eyes. "You will serve the Onyx Order in death, as you have done in life."

She lifted the blade—a black-handled dagger with a five-pointed star carved just above the hilt. The chanting rose, gradually coming to a fever pitch, and as the edge of the blade flashed in the moonlight, the woman brought the blade down, straight toward my heaving torso.

I screamed.

"Brooke!" Maddock's powerful fingers dug painfully into my shoulders as he shook me. "Brooke, wake up! It's not real."

"What?" I blinked up at him, shielding my eyes with my right hand. It was too bright in here, with the sunlight streaming in through the windows—it had been night, the only light coming from flickering torches and the moon just a few seconds ago in my vision. "Oh, right. Sorry, I just…I was having a vision."

"I noticed." Lines of disapproval bracketed Maddock's mouth. "I told ye to wait, but ye went charging in and touching things anyway. Symbols like these tend to hold power long after they've been used."

"Well, that explains why that happened," I muttered, batting Maddock's hands away and rising to my feet.

"*What* happened?" Maddock demanded, rising with me.

I told him about the vision I'd witnessed. "I've never had that happen before," I admitted, a little shaky. "Usually when I get a flash, I'm just an observer. I've never suddenly *become* one of the victims before."

"Perhaps this will teach ye to be more careful next time before rushing to touch things in an old ritual site," Maddock said dryly. His piercing green eyes searched my face. "Are ye sure yer all right?"

"I'm fine. Why?"

"Because," he said softly, lifting a finger to touch my cheek. "Yer cryin'."

It was only when his warm finger slid up the curve of my cheek that I realized there was cold wetness there—tear tracks. Mortification made my cheeks bloom with heat, not just because of the tears on my face but because of the way his eyes softened with something that looked suspiciously like sympathy.

"It's just an after-effect from the vision." I swatted his hand away, then briskly wiped the tears away from my cheeks. "The boy I became was about to be stabbed by a crazy naked woman with a wicked-looking knife, so it's not really surprising that he was crying." I paused, remembering the ram's horns curling from his scalp and the strange wrinkles on his skin. "I'm guessing he was fae?"

"That would be the logical assumption." Maddock pressed his lips together. "Fecking witches, thinking they have the right to take our young and steal their power."

"Young?" I echoed. "So you're thinking he was a boy even though he had all those wrinkles?"

Maddock's eyes flashed dangerously as he glared at me. "The reason he had those 'wrinkles,' Detective, is because those witches

116

drained him of his life-force. True witches depend upon fae magic for their powers, and when they can get their greedy little hands on one of our people, it's like Christmas morning because they can chain us down and use us as a never-ending supply source. They drain us over and over again, until something finally breaks and we can no longer serve as their magical battery. Once that happens, they squeeze our last drops of magic out of us in one of their depraved rituals, then seek out another fae to draw from instead."

Every ounce of blood drained from my face, leaving me feeling cold inside.

"Is that what I saw?" I whispered.

"Undoubtedly." Maddock cast a scathing glance at the bloody symbols painted on the walls, faded but still undeniably there. "These symbols are consistent with such a ritual. A barbarism of fae magic." He spat on the millstone, and I tensed, half-expecting it to sizzle.

"Right." I let out a long breath, then squared my shoulders. "Let's get back on track. Do you have any super-special fae ability that can tell me where the body is that we're looking for?"

Maddock lifted his head, nostrils flaring as he sniffed the air. "This way."

I followed him out of the front room and down a narrow hall. Wooden floorboards creaked beneath my feet, and the smell of earth and blood grew stronger. We turned into a large room with a pile of large, moldy sacks to our left, and off in the corner, I could see the hard-packed earth had been dug up and patted back down again.

"Shit," I muttered, toeing the spot with my booted foot. "I could really use a shovel right now."

Huffing, Maddock lifted a hand and spoke a strange word that made my eardrums throb. "Ye dinnae need a shovel," he told me. "Ye have me."

The earth beneath my feet shifted, and I jumped out of the way as dirt spewed out of the ground, almost as if it was being vomited by the bowels of the earth. My stomach lurched as the decomposing body of a large woman popped out of the soil, her flaxen curls and flower-printed dress bedraggled and stained with blood and dirt.

"There she is," Maddock said without preamble.

"Great." I propped my hands on my hips, not sure whether to glare at Maddock or the dead body. "Now how the hell am I supposed to explain this to the precinct?"

fourteen

It took a good thirty minutes for the local and state police to arrive on scene, and another half hour after that for the medical examiner to get here, as there was only one and he was based out of Boston. During that time, Maddock and I discussed how best to proceed. After all, if a coven of witches was involved, was it really a good idea to involve local law enforcement?

I believed in the law, of course, but guns were of limited use against magic, and Maddock was of the stringent opinion that humans should have as little involvement with the supernatural world as possible. We argued back and forth for a few minutes, trying to work out a compromise that would serve us both.

In the end, we decided to let the local police department take the body in and make the appropriate notifications to the woman's family, and that Maddock would pull whatever strings he had to in order to keep the authorities in the dark regarding the supernatural nature of this case. In the meantime, he took his car and left the scene—having him around would raise too many questions.

It didn't feel totally right, lying to Captain Randall about this case, but since he was lying to me, I figured that made us even. I was going to dig up whatever secrets he was hiding, but first I had to figure out what was going on with these disappearances and now murders. After all, I was the only cop around here who could.

"Jesus, Baxter," I snapped into my cell phone as I watched the crime scene tech carefully go through the mill, looking for any evidence that I might have missed. "It's been close to an hour. Aren't you coming?"

"I can't." Baxter growled. "I caught a murder of my own this morning. Domestic violence gone south, and it's not pretty. I'm going to be tied up with this all day."

"Dammit." I jutted out my lower lip. "I was really hoping I could at least get a ride from you." The medical examiner had already left, and I wasn't exactly looking forward to cramming myself into the van full of crime-scene equipment, though I'd do whatever I had to.

"Oh, well if that's what you need, I can always ask my brother to grab you." Baxter paused. "He told me you stopped by the church the other day."

"Oh, Father James?" I relaxed a little. "Yeah, that'll work. Your brother's a nice guy." And he might be able to answer some questions about what the hell had gone on at this mill, too.

"All right, I'll give him a call."

I helped the crime scene technician finish up in the mill, careful to keep my gloves on at all times so I didn't touch anything directly with my hands. Breaking down and crying mid-vision in front of the crime scene technician would be exactly the type of nail Captain Randall would love to pound into my coffin.

Unfortunately, without my special ability, there wasn't much to see. The technician took blood samples from the symbols, but despite the disarray of the old mill and the presence of a dead body, there wasn't much else to find.

"You sure you don't need a ride home?" the tech asked as he loaded his equipment back into the dusty white Ford van he'd driven here. He was a skinny guy in his early thirties, but the smattering of freckles on his nose and his baby face made him look a *lot* younger. "I'd hate to leave you out here stranded."

"I'm good, thanks." My grumbling stomach belied the words, but I ignored it. I could afford to wait an extra few minutes for Father James to get here. He was already on his way, so it would be rude of me to leave him waiting.

By the time Father James arrived, the sun was hovering directly overhead, and my stomach was crying out for lunch. I jumped to my feet eagerly as a black Camry pulled up in front of the mill and was at the door before he had a chance to roll down his window.

"Thanks for coming to get me, Father," I said as I slid into the passenger's seat and shut the door behind me.

"You're quite welcome." But the words weren't sincere, and the tone in his voice was enough to drag my attention away from the seatbelt I was fastening. I expected him to be looking at me, but instead his attention was fixed on the old, crumbling structure of the mill. "I'm curious to know what you were doing all the way out here without a car."

"Huh?" I was momentarily thrown when he turned his

narrowed gaze at me. Why was Father James so suspicious? "I took a cab out here," I said, repeating the same lie I'd told my peers. "My car's in the shop."

"I see." He studied me for a moment, then shifted the car into reverse so that he could turn and head back up the dirt road. "You shouldn't have come up this way alone, Brooke. It isn't safe."

"I'm a cop, Father James, and I was chasing down a lead. Staying safe isn't really part of my job description."

"And did your lead pan out?" he asked, voice tight.

"Yeah. I found a dead body." My voice hardened in response to his judgmental attitude. "Just what is your problem, anyway?"

Father James swung his head around to face me even as he kept his foot pressed down on the gas, careening us up the pebble-strewn road. "My *problem* is that you're sticking your nose into places where evil abounds. I warned you about the dangers of this place, tried to give you protection, but there's only so much I can do. If you keep wandering off the beaten path, you're going to end up like Tom."

"What do you know about Tom?" I demanded, but he was already turning away. I itched to grab his arm, to pull his gaze back to mine, but he was heading onto the highway now, and the last thing I needed was to distract him while he was piloting a moving vehicle.

"I know that he was just like you," Father James replied. "Determined to find answers, determined to find truth. And as much as I believe in the Lord, and that shining His light into the darkness is the only way to banish evil, I also believe that around here, it's the quickest way to get yourself killed."

I tried to get more information out of Father James, but he was remarkably tight-lipped, and the drive back to the precinct was shorter than I'd have liked. I spent the rest of the day handling the paperwork regarding the victim I'd found this morning and also helping Baxter wrap up the case he'd caught.

The prettily-dressed woman I'd found buried in the old, rundown mill was born Marjorie Graham and was a thirty-two-year-old resident of Salem. She owned a bakery a few blocks from the apartment where she'd been killed. I wondered if the Giant she'd become lovers with had romanced her from over the glass counter of her bakery shop or if the two of them had run into each other on the street and hit it off. Had she known he was fae?

She had to have known, I thought, drumming my fingers against my desk as I paused in the middle of writing my report. There was no way she'd spent any length of time in his apartment, and not to mention his bed, without knowing.

And now she was dead, and her family would never know the truth of what had happened to her. Even if I hunted down the women dressed in black who had done this to her, Marjorie's family would still never know the entire truth, because Maddock wouldn't allow it.

I curled my fingers around my mouse, digging angrily into the hard, white plastic. God dammit, but why did Maddock get to decide? Who was he to pull strings and press buttons, to have autopsy and police reports doctored so that no hint of the supernatural would come up in any investigations? Who was he to leave so many cases dangling, so many families without closure?

And just what good is closure when you're lying on the inside of a closed casket?

I sighed. That was true enough. What was the point in telling someone that the boogie man was real if you couldn't also arm them with the knowledge they needed to defend themselves against him?

If I went up to Captain Randall—or any of the cops here, for that matter—and even *hinted* at what I'd seen, they'd have my badge and lock me up with the crazies. And then how was I going to help anyone?

No, much as I wished I could tell people the truth, it wasn't the right choice. Aside from the fact that they'd think I was crazy, I also didn't know enough to teach them what to do about all of this crap anyway. I still had too much to learn myself.

As the day went on, I half-expected Captain Randall to call me on the carpet for being late and pursuing a murder without Baxter, or at least grill me for the holes that any cop worth his salt would find in my vague report. But as the end of the day drew closer, I began to see that Maddock had kept his end of the bargain.

Nobody would be looking into this. Nobody but us. Which meant that if I wanted to find out what was going on, I needed to get out of here.

As soon as my shift ended, I was out the door and in my Jeep. It felt good to have the steering wheel under my hands again—walking around Salem had been interesting, but now that I knew strange creatures haunted the shadows, I felt safer driving home.

As I pulled into the lot in front of my apartment building, which was part of a complex of several buildings located just off

Bridge Street, my attention snapped to a huge black guy dressed in a tailored suit. He was leaning against the trunk of a shiny black Mercedes, and as I slid into my spot, he inclined his head, his brilliant amber eyes glinting with recognition.

A shiver slid down my spine as I killed the engine, and I gripped the steering wheel tighter. Maybe it was his strangely-colored eyes that gave him away, or maybe it was some kind of built-in supernatural intuition, but I just *knew* he was fae.

"Good evening, Detective Chandler." The man inclined his head to greet me as I got out of my Jeep, his deep, rich voice washing over me like a wave of molasses.

"Good evening." I paused in front of him, folding my arms across my chest. The action hitched my blazer up a little, drawing attention to the gun and badge at my hip. "Since you seem to be waiting for me, mind telling me what I can do to help you?"

"Staying inside would be the easiest," the man said. "Lord Tremaine sent me here to secure the perimeter and make sure nothing comes to attack you tonight."

I arched an eyebrow. "Tremaine sent me a bodyguard?"

"I guess you could call it that." The guy shrugged, drawing attention to his massive shoulders. Jesus, was being built like a behemoth a job requirement for working with Maddock Tremaine? "I've had the doors and windows of your apartment warded, so nothing should be able to get in unless you let it in."

"Oh." My first instinct was to be angry that somebody had been sniffing around my place and setting up magic spells. But after nearly being drowned in my bathtub, I considered that some magical protection voodoo might be nice. "Well, thanks, I guess. But if there are wards protecting my apartment, I don't think you need to be out here. I can take care of myself, and fae are being targeted right now."

The man laughed, exposing white teeth with incisors that were just a little too long. "Your concern is touching, but there's no reason to worry. This is my job, and besides, I'm an iron fae." He thumped his chest. "Nothing can cut me."

"An iron fae?" My brow furrowed as I tried to figure that one out. "What, does that mean your skin is made of iron? How does that even work if the fae are allergic to iron?"

"My kind are an anomaly amongst the fair folk," my new guard said. "A scientist would say we are a genetic mutation—nature's attempt to help the fae adapt in this world full of steel and glass and iron bars that the humans are building." His upper lip curled. "There is a reason we prefer smaller towns and cities."

Huh. Was that why I'd never run into a fae, then? Because Chicago was a big city? "I'm guessing that means vampires and other supernaturals born of fae magic aren't susceptible to iron?"

"Yes, which is why they are able to thrive by comparison." The sneer deepened, and I raised my eyebrows at the clear prejudice in my guard's amber eyes. "Vampires, shifters, witches, and the myriad other supernaturals out there make their homes in the iron-clad cities where we cannot dwell, and so they are able to carve out their own territories. If we shared the same lands, you can bet that we would be on top, and that all the other races would bow to our will."

"Er, so are you saying that the other supernaturals around here *do* bow to fae will?"

"Not as much as they should, these days." The guard scowled. "Lord Tremaine will yank them into line, though. He always does."

"I'll keep that in mind," I said, starting to head toward the entrance to my apartment. "I better head in. Have a good evening."

The guard returned my farewell, and I went inside, mulling over what I'd just learned as I trudged up the stairs.

Maddock had told me he was here to oversee the supernatural community in this area, but were his intentions simply to protect the residents, or to subjugate them to fae rule? If the bodyguard's views were any indication, the fae considered themselves far superior to their magical by-blows and felt all supernaturals should defer to them. I bet that created all kinds of animosity toward the fae.

And maybe, just maybe, even the kind of animosity that would lead an old coven of witches to start kidnapping fae citizens.

I wanted to delve into research the moment I set foot in my apartment, but my body demanded food and relaxation first. So I whipped out a TV dinner from the freezer, then drew myself a hot, luxurious bath.

As I sank into the water, a shiver of apprehension trickled down my spine. I'd nearly *died* the last time I was in here. But I pressed my lips together and pushed the feeling away. I was not going to let the experience keep me from enjoying my bath. I'd discovered long ago that the best way to get over a traumatic experience was to face triggers head-on rather than letting them squish me into a little ball of fear. That might not work for everyone, but it worked for me, and I wasn't about to stop now.

Sighing, I rested my head on the lip of the tub and touched the cross that rested on my soap-covered chest. I felt as if I was getting dragged out to sea by getting mixed up with Maddock in his quest to find these missing fae, and I needed to ground myself, to remind myself why I was really here. To find out what happened to Tom.

But as my fingers brushed the metal, a vision hit me, one of the most disorienting I'd ever had.

Yellowed, linoleum-tiled halls. Nuns dressed in long, black habits. Children of various ages wearing bedraggled uniforms. A picture of a group of kids outside a church-like building hung on one of the walls, with a large sign out front that read "New Advent Home for Children."

A room with rickety wooden desks and a dusty chalkboard. A struggle. The room spun as fists flew, metal flashed.

Blood. So much blood.

The world tilted, and then I was on my side, liquid seeping onto the scratched tile beneath me. And that was when the screams came.

Gasping, I shot straight up in the tub, water sloshing over the sides. My heart galloped so hard I thought it might burst through my chest. God, but what had I just seen? I knew from conversations with Tom that the New Advent Home for Children was the orphanage where he'd grown up. But what was up with all that violence, all that blood? Had someone been killed?

From the vantage point that I'd witnessed the battle, the wearer of the cross hadn't been a child, but an adult. Was this a recent vision? Had Tom been at the orphanage? Was *that* where he'd *actually* been killed?

They'd sent me his cross, saying that was all they could find left of him. Had he died wearing it in a fire, or in a battle inside of an orphanage? The whole thing had never sat right with me. The cross would have been ruined by the fire, and the flames would have left behind *some* remains.

Bodies don't just disappear, and the excuse that Tom's body must have been moved was sloppy—if they thought that, why hadn't they searched for it? All these questions were a part of why I was here now. Tom's case needed to be investigated *properly*.

I scrubbed myself clean as quickly as I could, then left the bath and hurried into a pair of shorts and a tank top. Curling up on the couch with a can of coke, I opened up my laptop and ran a search on the New Advent Home for Children. Google told me it was located in Boston, about an hour's drive from here.

Had the missing kids Tom was talking about actually been from Boston? That would explain why Captain Randall didn't seem to know about them…but then why hadn't he mentioned that Tom was digging around in Boston? And why hadn't Tom told me the truth about where he was going? The two of them were covering something up…and only one of them was alive to tell me the truth.

Angry now, I shrugged on a hoodie over my tank top, then went outside to talk to my new bodyguard. I wanted to get a hold of Maddock and see what he knew about this. Cover-ups seemed to be his specialty, after all, and he *had* offered to help me find out what happened to Tom. I was going to get his help, and then I was going to Boston.

I trotted down the steps and out the front door of the apartment building, then approached the black Mercedes. It was dark out, so it wasn't until I was standing next to the driver's side door that I noticed the shadowy outline of the guard sprawled in his seat.

Alarm bells rang in my head, and I instinctively placed a hand on my weapon. I didn't know the guy, but he'd struck me as a professional. No way was he going to just fall asleep in his car when he was supposed to be protecting me.

Sucking in a deep breath, I braced myself for the worst, then yanked open the car door. The thick, salty stench of blood instantly clogged my nostrils, and my eyes widened in horror at the sight of the guard slumped against a tan leather seat. His supposedly unbreakable skin was sliced open in a hundred places, blood seeping from all the wounds. Lifeless eyes stared up at the car's roof, the amber irises I'd found so interesting devoid of spark.

And just as I reached out to check his pulse, to determine if he really was dead, his body disintegrated in front of my eyes.

fifteen

I pulled up outside Maddock's club with screeching brakes, then slammed out of my Jeep. The line of people waiting to get in snaked through the parking lot and around the block, just like last time, but I bypassed them and stormed up to the Mountain Man guarding the front door.

Said man moved his bulk to block the door and fixed his cold blue eyes on me. "You can't go in."

I pushed back my blazer, revealing my badge, and rested my hand on the butt of my weapon. "Like hell I'm not. Let me through. I'm here to see Maddock Tremaine on official police business."

"Lord Tremaine would be more than happy to meet you at your precinct at a time of his choosing if you need to discuss official business with him." The bouncer's face was stony. "But you're on the no-entry list, Detective, and that isn't going to change."

"If you don't let me in *right now*, I'm going to rain every kind of legal hell I possibly can down on this club, and I will *never* help your boss again."

The guard smirked. "I doubt Lord Tremaine is concerned about that, considering that you don't actually have any jurisdiction in Salem."

Damn. So he'd found out about that. Aware that all eyes were on me, I leaned in close enough that my nose nearly brushed the bouncer's chest and glared up at him. "The guard that *Lord Tremaine* assigned to keep watch over my house is *dead*."

Mountain Man's nostrils flared. "Caid? Dead? That's impossible."

"He was sliced up like sashimi and shoved into his car, but I can't prove that since he disintegrated shortly after I found him." I scowled at the bouncer. "Are you going to let me in, or not?"

"One moment." The bouncer pulled a radio from his belt, then moved a few paces away and spoke into it quietly. A muffled voice crackled back. This went on for about a minute before he finally turned back to me.

"Lord Tremaine will see you now." The guard opened the door, and loud bass music spilled out into the night along with dark laughter and the scents of booze, expensive cologne, and sex. "Someone will escort you."

I stepped into the dim interior to find another Mountain Man waiting for me. This one's head was shaved bald, and he had a long, wicked scar slashing vertically across the left half of his face. Consequently, the left eye was milky white and unseeing, but that didn't lessen the potency of his frigid stare as he looked me up and down.

"Right this way, *Detective*." He angled his big body so that I could pass by. "Down to the end and then up the stairs."

Right. Just like last time. Except that this time, there was a behemoth herding me up the stairs, his body so close to mine that I could feel the menace rolling off him, sending warning signals skipping up my back.

I didn't even think about stopping to stare at the other patrons or skimming my fingers along surfaces to see if someone had gotten sloppy and I might find anything here. There was a time and a place for everything, and I knew that within these walls, the fact that I represented the law didn't matter. I needed to hold myself in check, at least until I was in front of Maddock.

I thought we would be going to the same room where I'd first overheard Maddock and Vox conversing, but Mountain Man guided me farther down the hall, to a room on the left. He knocked on a large door with wild beasts carved into the dark wood, angling his body in such a way that I couldn't easily grab the doorknob and push my way in.

"Enter," Maddock's deep, richly-accented voice snapped, and Mountain Man pushed the door open.

"Sir, she's here—"

"Yes, I am, and you don't need to talk for me." I brushed past him and into the room—a study, I realized. Dark, heavy wood, sumptuous red carpeting, and shelves lined with books both old and new. A large oil painting of a woman draped in red silk dominated the wall across from his desk, and his dark, exotic scent filled the space, marking it unequivocally as his.

Maddock's green eyes pierced me like a lance—his eyes glittered like gems, his face granite, and I knew right then that he was furious.

"Leave us," he snapped at the guard.

The guard bowed, then backed out of the room as if Maddock was the goddamn Queen of England. I would have rolled my eyes if the situation wasn't so serious.

"Sit," Maddock said softly, indicating the buttery brown leather chairs arranged in front of his desk. "And tell me exactly what happened."

"Fuck you." I folded my arms and stayed right where I was. "You don't get to sit there and tell me to make myself comfortable, as if ten seconds ago I wasn't being told I was blacklisted from this club. What the hell, Tremaine? I thought we were working together."

"We are," he said coldly, "but our partnership does not require granting ye access to my club. The only reason I let ye in now is because you told the bouncer Caid is dead. Is that true?"

"He was sliced up and left to rot in that expensive Mercedes you gave him." I felt a twinge of sympathy for the dead fae, but I brushed it aside—I needed to hold onto my anger. "I came here to let you know, thinking maybe you'd have some answers and we could hash out a plan together. But apparently I'm not even allowed to see you."

My strides took me across the room, and the next thing I knew my hands were splayed across his desk, palms pressing into papers neatly organized into small stacks. Maddock's eyes widened as I leaned in, baring my teeth at him, and I took satisfaction at his surprise—I bet he thought I didn't have the guts.

"So what is it, Maddock Tremaine? Did you think this was going to be a one-way street, where you can teleport into my living room, leave guards outside my apartment, and otherwise call on me wherever you like, but I'm not allowed to do the same with you? Do you think that you can sneer at me like I'm less than the dirt stuck between the crevices in your shoes, and yet look at me like...like..."

"Like what, Detective?" he asked, his eyebrow arching.

My face burned with unfinished thought. He knew damn well what.

"Like you are now," I said, and I hated the breathless note that entered my voice. He had a way of looking at me not just like he was undressing me with his eyes, but as if I was *already* bare.

Maddock leaned back in his chair and peered up at me, one corner of his mouth tipping up almost into a smile. "Ye mean like I want to pin ye to the wall and fuck ye until ye can't breathe anymore?"

I swallowed, trying to block out that image.

"Well, Detective, I am not sure who wants that more...me, or ye? But I do believe ye had something more important to whine about. The matter of my guard, Caid? If ye could, please get back to that bit."

We could play this game all he liked, but I wasn't about to let him win. I refused to let him get to me. So I leaned in even closer, until I could feel his breath on my cheeks, until his deliciously masculine scent was dangerously close to overwhelming me.

"If you think you're getting away with either one of those things, you've got your head so far up your ass, I'm surprised you can see anything."

"Oh, I can see just fine," Maddock said. His Scottish burr was whisper-soft, and his eyes had shifted from brilliantly cold to blisteringly hot. "And what I see is a little girl standing in front of me, pretending to be a woman. A little girl who thinks she can intimidate me by entering my personal space and using foul language. You may be bold, Detective, but yer bloody foolish as well."

"Just because I'm not a thousands-of-years-old fart like you doesn't mean I'm a little girl." I meant to snap the words, but they came out just as softly as his. "I'm a woman, and you should damn well start treating me like one instead of like a child who can't take care of herself."

"Fine." Maddock's hands banded around my upper arms, and I gasped as he yanked me forward. "Then yer about to find out what happens when a *woman* drapes herself across my desk."

I landed in his lap with a flurry of papers and a loud thud as something heavy— probably a paperweight—fell to the floor. And then his lips were on mine, his hands in my hair, his hard body molded against my own. Rough stubble scraped my cheeks as he kissed me, *devoured* me. His teeth nipping at my lips, his tongue exploring my mouth so completely that I couldn't help but melt into him. My body was molten, a sizzling live wire, and I sank my fingernails into his shoulders. Hunger was a living animal inside me, clawing to get free, and my desperate desire only seemed to excite him more.

Our hips shifted in the commotion, and then his arousal ground against me, hard and hot even through the layers of clothing that separated us. We both gasped at the sensation, and the shock of the sexual charge was enough to snap me out of the funk, enough to let me rear back and slap him across the face.

Hard.

"Fuck." The word exploded from him as his head snapped to

the side, but it didn't seem to be in response to the blow. It was in response to the violent lust that had surged between us, a lust that was so strong it had obliterated all common sense. And here I was, panting with need, while Tom was barely cold in his grave.

"No." Cold horror and disgust rose in my throat, and I scrambled off his lap and pressed myself against the wall, as far from Maddock as I could manage. "*No.*"

Maddock turned slowly to face me again. His eyes glittered, harder than diamonds now. "Are you satisfied?" he growled. "Do you now see why I can't have you in my club? Why I insist on keeping distance between us?"

"Yes." I let out a slow breath, ordering my heart rate to return to normal.

I didn't know what the hell this attraction was between Maddock and me, but I didn't like it one bit. We barely knew each other. There was probably some kind of supernatural explanation for it, but if there was I didn't want to know. All I knew for sure was that there could be nothing between us.

Ours was a partnership of convenience, and once we'd both attained our goals, we'd be moving on our separate paths. Maddock Tremaine was a cold, manipulative bastard who was out for himself, and I wanted nothing to do with him.

But for now, I needed him.

"We have to find a better solution," I said once I was confident I could speak normally again. "I need to be able to contact you if something comes up."

Maddock pulled a business card out of his inner jacket pocket and tossed it onto the desk, a faintly annoyed expression on his face. "I thought a detective of yer caliber could do something as simple as produce a phone number, but since ye can't...*here*."

I snatched up the card, stuffed it in my pocket, and plopped down in the chair. "Save me the speech and tell me what kind of spell or weapon can cut up a fae who supposedly had unbreakable skin."

"There are ways of enchanting weapons to make them powerful enough to do such a thing." Maddock's expression turned grim. "The spells are costly, usually requiring some kind of sacrifice, and the enchantment is not permanent. But if that's what occurred, it means the Onyx Order has at least one iron fae-killing weapon. We can only hope the enchantment on the weapon is temporary." He pressed his lips together. "I am not willing to sacrifice more of my men, and yet I must keep ye safe until we have solved this mystery. Ye are very close to becoming more trouble than yer worth, Detective."

"Yeah, well you passed that point a long time ago," I snapped. "Besides, didn't you say that you warded my apartment? Isn't that supposed to keep enemies away?"

"Yes, but it won't stop them from attacking ye when ye step outside."

"Why don't you let me worry about that." I patted the side of my blazer, where my second gun was nestled snugly. "I've got vampire and fae ammo at my disposal, and plenty of old-fashioned bullets, too. I'm hardly a damsel in distress."

Maddock snorted. "Ye've never been that."

I nearly asked him what he meant by that, but I didn't want the conversation to get de-railed again. "Just before I went outside, I had a vision concerning Tom," I quickly caught him up to speed on the details. "I want to go to the Boston orphanage and see what I can dig out of them."

"Then go."

I rolled my eyes. "I want you to come with me."

"Why?"

Was he determined to be infuriating? "Because you agreed to help me find out what happened to Tom, and it's time you started keeping up your end of this arrangement. Besides, I think you and I both know the two are connected. It can't be a coincidence that the same coven of witches who've been kidnapping your fae have been gunning for me the second I set foot in this town, and that all evidence of what happened to Tom has been erased."

Maddock stared at me for a long moment, almost as if waiting for me to say something more. Or maybe he was just trying to frazzle me with that thousand-yard stare. I gritted my teeth; I wasn't going to let him mind-fuck me. I needed to be in control, for once.

"Just come with me tomorrow. We'll pretend to be a childless couple looking to adopt. You can distract the nuns while I snoop around."

His eyebrows shot up. "But Detective, I do believe that would be illegal. This isn't official police duty. The Salem police department might kick ye back to Chicago."

"Is that a threat?" I asked, narrowing my eyes at him. "That's some seriously passive aggressive behavior."

"I assure you, when I'm aggressive, there's nothing passive about it." He leaned forward now, entwining his fingers in front of him on his desk. "I just wanted to make sure we are on the same page, since ye seem to like flashing that badge around so much and using it to make threats against my club."

"Don't—"

"Please. I'm past done arguing with ye, Detective. I'll pick ye up from yer apartment at four o'clock, and we'll go visit this orphanage. Don't be late. Now get out of here." He turned to his computer, angling his chair away from me.

And just like that, I was dismissed.

sixteen

I worked at the precinct until three o'clock, then hurried home so I could change out of my cop clothes and into something a little more appropriate for my excursion with Maddock this afternoon. I told Baxter and Captain Randall I was following up a lead in Boston, and while Baxter had wanted to come, the Captain had been surprisingly accommodating about letting me go on my own. He hadn't even asked many questions.

Maybe I'd misread him, and he wasn't such a dick after all.

I had an early dinner, then switched out my slacks and button-up shirt for a white, knee-length dress with a square neckline and faux pearls that gleamed softly at my ears and throat. Low heels replaced my boots, and I swapped my blazer with a red woolen pea coat and a black leather concealed carry purse.

I couldn't fit both my guns in, so I opted for the 1911—after all, wooden stake and iron bullets were effective on humans, too.

And I was being the furthest thing from a cop as I could think of today—my instincts told me Maddock wouldn't be dressing down to make us look like the friendly neighborhood couple, so I was going to have to pretend to be a socialite instead.

Fun.

Finished dressing, I rummaged through my closet and pulled out a short black wig styled into an A-line bob. I'd used it before, both on the job and off, when I wanted to maintain a low-profile. My silver hair was eye-catching and memorable, neither of which I wanted to be today. So I tucked it under the wig, then pulled out my make-up kit and made sure my eyebrows matched. My lavender-blue eyes were still going to draw attention—there was no getting around that without colored-contacts, which I'd never gotten the hang of putting in—but I ditched the eyeliner and mascara and went bold on the lipstick to try and draw attention away from them.

I was just finishing up with my makeup when phone buzzed. Maddock's name flickered onto the screen along with a text message: Come outside.

My heart skipped a beat, and I ruthlessly squashed the butterflies that threatened to rise in my stomach at the reminder of the scorching-hot kiss I'd shared with him last night.

You have to move past that, I told myself sternly. That kiss hadn't been an invitation for more, but a warning of what would happen if we let ourselves get too close to each other. I needed to heed that warning. There would be no more kissing, or unnecessary touching, of Maddock Tremaine while we worked together. And the sooner this partnership was over, the better.

Yeah, good luck with keeping your hands to yourself today, a snide voice snickered in my head as I locked my apartment door behind me. *You guys are supposed to be a couple this afternoon.*

I sighed as I headed down the stairs. Why did life have to be so unfair?

Maddock was waiting at the curb inside a silver Aston Martin, of all things. Determined not to be impressed by the sleek, sexy coupe, I pulled open the door and slid smoothly into the black leather passenger's seat as if sitting my butt down in a three-hundred-thousand-dollar car was an everyday occurrence.

"You're a real show-off, you know that?" I said as I buckled my seatbelt.

"I fail to see what the point of having endless amounts of wealth is if I cannae 'show off' every once in a while, as you put it." Maddock's eyes narrowed as he took in my appearance. "Ye look better than I expected."

I bit the inside of my cheek on that one. Nothing bugged me more than people assuming I had to be some certain way just because I was a cop. There was more to me than my job.

"I'm a woman, Tremaine," I said mildly, refusing to rise to the bait. "I know how to dress up."

"Indeed," he murmured, his eyes lingering on my painted lips for a moment too long. Heat flashed through me as the sensation of his mouth against mine suddenly came back to me. He'd tasted dark and spicy and utterly delicious, and hunger clenched low in my belly. It was like a craving, an addiction, and I needed to shake it fast.

Maddock's nostrils flared, like a beast that had scented prey, and I braced myself, ready to fend him off if he decided to grab me again. But he jerked his gaze away from me, almost violently, then shifted into gear and shot into traffic.

Was it just me, or was the pull between us getting worse?

"So." I let out the word with a slow breath, trying to relax. I needed to ease the tension between us so I could focus. "Has anyone else turned up missing or dead that I don't know about?"

"No." Maddock's hands flexed, almost imperceptibly, on the steering wheel. "From what I've observed, they only take one at a time, and since ye've been marked, that means the others have a reprieve until yer taken."

"Huh." I pursed my lips as I ingested that piece of information. "So I'm guessing the best way to ensure no one else is missing is to keep me safe?"

"Correct. That's one of the reasons I assigned Caid to watch ye yesterday. Except I lost him instead." A muscle in his jaw twitched.

Guilt twanged in my chest. "I'm guessing Caid wasn't just a bodyguard to you."

"While I do have many employees, most of the ones who work closely with me are fae that I've known for too many of your lifetimes to count." Maddock's voice held no emotion, but his body language said everything. Caid had meant something to him. "Forming bonds is unavoidable when ye've been around someone for such a long time."

"I see that," I said softly. I wondered what that would be like, to have a friendship with someone that lasted hundreds, maybe even thousands of years. "How old are the fae, anyway? How long do they live?"

"Millennia, and indefinitely. We do not age, nor do we die of 'natural causes' as yer people do. And when we do die, we are eventually reincarnated, though it can take quite a bit of time."

"Jesus." I tilted my head back against the seat rest. "How many times have you been reincarnated?"

"That's none of yer business."

I huffed. "Well, what's the average? I mean, since iron can kill you guys, I imagine you don't all go through life without being reincarnated at least a couple of times."

"Ye underestimate us if you think we can be killed so easily, even with iron." Maddock's tone was frigid. "And ye take me for a fool if ye think I will just give up the secrets of our race to anyone who asks."

"Fine." I crossed my arms and glared out the window. "I'll stop asking. But you should get me a list of all the fae who've gone missing. I can't very well do my job as a Detective if you keep side-lining me. There might be patterns and clues you're missing, things that could get us closer to finding the victims."

A pause. Then, "Very well. I'll see what I can do."

The tension in the car lightened, and I let out a little sigh. Maddock and I would never get along, not completely, but if we could keep our eyes on the prize, then maybe we could stop tearing into each other.

Relaxing in my super-comfy seat, I pulled out my phone to review the information I'd gathered regarding the orphanage, and relayed it to Maddock so we'd both be prepared when we got there.

"So it's a Catholic orphanage?" Maddock asked, his voice dripping with derision.

"Yes." I slanted a look at him. "What, you don't like Catholics?"

"They've persecuted pagan religions throughout history, including many of the humans who worshipped my kind. So no, I'm not a fan."

"Oookay." I wasn't touching that subject with a ten-foot pole. Talking about religion and politics was the fastest way to send a conversation south. Especially when the person you were conversing with didn't like you much in the first place. "Well, anyway, the New Advent Church of Salem was founded in 1833, and they opened the orphanage about ten years later. I did a run on them this morning at the precinct, and they've got a surprisingly clean record."

"Why 'surprisingly'?"

"Because any orphanage that has starving and poorly-dressed children, and where adults beat each other bloody in classrooms, can't be a great place." My voice hardened as the memories from the vision flitted through my mind again. "There's a huge problem with the search I ran, though."

"And what is that?"

"The orphanage moved to a larger, newer building about five years ago." I let out a frustrated breath. "And the old one was demolished. The vision I saw happened in the old building."

Maddock swung his head around to glare at me. "If what yer saying is true, then why the fuck are we going there? Your fiancé couldn't possibly have died at the orphanage if the vision you had happened over five years ago!"

"Because something fucked up is going on in that orphanage, and I want to know what, and why!" I snapped. "And just because that incident happened five years ago, doesn't mean it's not relevant! If Tom went there five years ago, as a grown man, and ended up in a fist-fight, then I want to know why. I want to know what brought him back to the orphanage then that got him into trouble, and if that same trouble got him killed this time around."

"Fine." Maddock turned back to the road. "But we'd better find something. I don't appreciate having my time wasted, Detective."

We pulled into the parking lot of the New Advent Home for Children—a large, Romanesque building with gorgeous turrets and a large cross jutting up from the central building. It was two stories high, with huge windows framed with ornate molding. Definitely more than a couple steps up from the building they used to own. The records listed that they'd received an anonymous donation which had allowed them to purchase the larger building, but I hadn't had time to do more digging and find out who had given them the funds.

Maybe I would, after this. Because if my vision was any indication, they definitely didn't deserve the upgrade.

"Wipe that disgruntled look off your face," Maddock murmured as he killed the engine. "We're supposed to be the happy, excited couple."

"Right." I took a deep breath, then flipped down the visor and used the mirror to check my reflection one more time. "Okay, so you're going to use your fae mojo to distract the nuns while I snoop around, right? Because otherwise they're going to think it's weird that you're touring the place without me."

"That is the plan." Maddock reached over and snapped the visor back into place. "Stop worrying about yer appearance, Detective. It's more than fine."

The butterflies in my stomach momentarily broke free at the unintentional compliment. "All right."

We got out of the car, and I looped my arm through Maddock's, allowing him to pull my body against his.

He was very polished today, in a black woolen overcoat and a suit that drew the eye to his powerful shoulders and impressively large form. That large form felt very solid against mine, and absurdly, the sensation of being pressed against his side made me feel safe. That must have been some kind of primitive reaction from me, because there was nothing safe about him.

"Are you ready, darling?" he asked, turning to face me, and the smile on his face and the warmth in his eyes took me aback. Jesus, but was this the same man who'd been bitching at me about wasting his time not ten minutes ago?

It was then I realized there were two children at the top of the steps, clean and dressed in uniforms, watching us. We were on display right now, and this was show time.

He's just acting, I told myself. *Now get your head in the game.*

"Of course." I smiled sweetly at him, snuggled in a little closer. "I can't wait to meet our future daughter."

I felt a little bad as I watched the faces of the two boys fall— they must have heard my comment. But I pushed the feeling aside as Maddock and I headed up the steps; we weren't actually here to adopt any of the children, after all. It was kinder to not get their hopes up.

"Good afternoon, and welcome to the New Advent Home for Children." A nun seated behind a honey-walnut reception desk greeted us as we stepped into a long hall with vaulted ceilings. The number of lines in her round face told me she was in her sixties, and she had kind grey eyes and a nice smile. "How can I help you today?"

"Good afternoon." Maddock smiled, and it was as if the clouds had parted to reveal the sun in all of its glory. The woman's face lit up, and she sat up a little straighter in her chair. "I'm Max Graves, and this is my wife, Brandy. We have an appointment with Sister Walsh."

"Oh! Yes, I see you're here on the appointment list." The nun tittered a little, and damn if she wasn't blushing. It would have been adorable if the object of her affection wasn't a millennia-old fae. "Why don't you have a seat, and I'll let her know you're here."

It didn't take very long for Sister Walsh to come to us. Her heels clicked down the hall, and we turned to see a middle-aged woman with sharp blue eyes approaching.

"Good afternoon, Mr. and Mrs. Graves. I'm Sister Catherine Walsh." She smiled briskly, shook our hands with a firm grip. "Why don't you come this way to my office."

We followed her down the hall, past rows of classroom doors where I could see children studying or working on various activities. They were all nicely groomed, anywhere from six years old to sixteen, and the classrooms seemed to be clean and neat. But the younger faces were subdued, the older ones hard, and there was none of the mischief or carefree attitude that I normally associated with children.

We were led into the sister's office—a grand space with religious paintings hanging from the walls, shelves lined with gold-leaf, leather-bound books, and ornately carved mango-wood furniture. The visitors' chairs she guided us to were the color of brown sugar and butter-soft, and the computer system she had at her desk was state of the art.

Yeah, this definitely wasn't a struggling orphanage. In fact, it was more like a private school.

"So, tell me about yourselves," the nun said as she settled into her own chair. "Why are you looking to adopt?"

Maddock and I launched into our rehearsed script, explaining that we'd been married for three years and worked at the universities in Cambridge—he was a professor at MIT and I worked in one of the administrative departments at Harvard. We'd been trying to conceive for nearly two years now, but with no success, and the fertility specialist had said my egg count was unusually low and there was little hope for me conceiving naturally. We were just a wealthy, responsible, loving couple who dearly wanted a child to call our own.

As if.

While the nun droned on about options, I allowed my gaze to surreptitiously wander around the room. Various certificates of achievement and photographs on the wall told me that she'd been around for a long time. Long enough to have known Tom, perhaps?

My heart skipped a beat as I caught sight of a group photo of several nuns with the orphans all gathered outside the original building—it was nearly twenty years old, and one of the gangly youths looked a lot like Tom. A younger version of Sister Walsh stood to the left of the children. She was here at the same time he was, which meant the two of them knew each other.

Damn! If I were here as a cop, I could just come out and ask her about it. But my instincts told me that she wouldn't tell me anything useful. No, going undercover like this was the best way.

I snatched my phone out of my pocket and texted Maddock from under the edge of the desk. The nun was mid long diatribe about how the children here were being raised with strong Catholic roots to give them excellent moral fiber, and she was so wrapped up in her monologue that she didn't even notice.

WORK YOUR MAGIC ON HER. GET HER TO LEAVE THE ROOM. I WANT TO SEARCH THE OFFICE.

"Excuse me, Sister Walsh." Maddock's sexy Scottish burr brought the nun's speech to a startled halt. "Would ye mind showing me to the restroom?"

"Oh, certainly, it's down the hall and to your—"

"Your institution is so magnificent that a person could get lost without your assistance." Maddock rose, then extended a hand toward the nun. "Please, sister, I would greatly appreciate it if ye could show me the way."

The nun initially looked like she was going to balk—she was a stern-looking woman who I imagined wasn't easily seduced—but she went starry-eyed, softening up just like the receptionist had.

She nodded. "Of course, Mr. Graves. Follow me."

I let out a little sigh of relief as Maddock led the nun away. As soon as their footfalls receded down the hall, I was out of my chair and searching the room. I didn't find anything suspicious at first— just the usual odds and ends one found in an office space and lots of folders filled with forms and paperwork.

But in the back of one of the drawers, I found a small wooden box with a gold clasp. I opened it carefully, and surprise jolted me as I found a note resting on top of a gold and blue object that looked suspiciously like a badge.

No. Not *like* a badge. It *was* a badge.

When I lifted the note, a Salem PD badge peeked up at me. My first instinct was to pick it up first, but I ignored it in favor of the piece of paper, which seemed more important. Unfolding it, my fingers trembled a little as I recognized Tom's bold handwriting.

Dear Sister Walsh,

I just wanted to thank you and Father James again. Without your guidance and training, I never would have made it this far, and definitely wouldn't have this opportunity here in Chicago right now to help make a difference and further the cause. Since I won't be using this badge anymore, please take it as a show of my appreciation, and think of me.

Until we meet again,
Thomas

My heart swelled with pride, and tears pricked at the corners of my eyes as I stroked my fingers over the sweet words. They hadn't been for me, but I felt the affection in them anyway, and it only made me miss Tom even more, which I hadn't thought was possible.

I put the note aside and lifted the badge from the box, tempted to take it even though I knew I shouldn't. As my fingers curled around the cold metal, another vision hit me.

Tom was standing in our bedroom, the Chicago skyline backlight glittering in the darkness outside our window as he paced on the side of the room opposite the bed. A bed that I was lying in, my body turned toward the wall, my silver hair a wild mess that gleamed in the moonlight that filtered in through the window.

He held a phone to his ear, nodding silently at whatever the speaker on the other end was saying, a grave expression on his face. His replies were whispered, and I strained my ears, trying to catch what he was saying.

"I don't think so."

"…haven't seen anything yet."

"Maybe we're wrong. I've tried everything."

"No, she doesn't know. Yes, I've been careful. Yes, I'm sure."

Frustration blanketed Tom's face, and he tossed the phone onto the nightstand. Raking a hand through his sandy hair, he turned to look at my sleeping form.

"What are you, Brooke Chandler?" he whispered into the darkness. "Just what the hell are you?"

seventeen

The badge slipped from my fingers, clattering onto the desk. As the vision broke, I stared down at it in confusion, eyebrows pulling together as I tried to figure out what I'd just seen.

Who the hell had Tom been talking to on the phone? The way he'd been talking, and what he'd said after he'd gotten off the phone, made me think he'd been talking about *me*.

But that couldn't be right. Could it?

Needing some air, I quickly put everything back where I found it, then left the room. I needed more information. The thing about visions was that they could easily be taken out of context and slanted to mean a variety of things. The vision I'd seen of the orphanage when I'd touched Tom's cross was proof of that; I thought I'd watched his murder, but it turned out to be an event that happened years ago. An event that I still had no clarity on.

I moved briskly down the hall and out the back door, then

headed into the gardens. I couldn't go snooping into the other rooms—that was frowned upon in places like this, where the privacy of the children was paramount. But I could wait out in the gardens for a little bit, catch my breath, and regroup before I went back inside. If any of the nuns found me outside, it would be easy enough to tell them I just wanted some fresh air.

The garden behind the building was a small but elegant arbor full of rose bushes and vines crawling up lattices and small, neatly organized rows of herbs that the kitchen probably used. I sat on a stone bench, then looked up to see Maddock and the nun in one of the rooms upstairs, having a conversation of some kind that involved the nun "talking with her hands" a lot. Was he getting any useful information out of her? Ugh. Why couldn't I have his ability? If I could spell people into being open, honest, and transparent, it would be easy enough to interrogate them and get all the information I needed.

I rose, intending to go back into the building, but an inexplicable urge tugged me farther into the garden, to the edge of the property. We were at the outskirts of the city, and beyond the garden fence was a thickly wooded area.

I walked through the trees, not sure where I was going, letting my feet guide me along the leaf-strewn path. The sun was dipping closer to the horizon, tinging the sky with red and gold and purple, and it lit up the trees around me, making it appear as if the turning fall leaves were catching fire.

The quiet tinkle of a small stream caught my attention; before long, it came into view. A large maple tree stood just on the other side, and a chill shot down my spine as I noticed the Onyx Order symbol carved into the trunk, the shape larger than my face.

Maddock's warning not to touch it echoed in my head, but the pull was too strong, and my feet took me across the stream and to the tree before I could will myself to resist.

With a pull like this, I was certain I was being led by magic. If I tried, I was sure I could resist it, but I was a detective because I was willing to do whatever it took to find answers. I couldn't just walk away from this.

Slowly, I lifted my hand, then ran my fingers across the rough bark, dipping them into the wickedly carved grooves some unseen hand had left.

Suddenly, I was no longer in the woods, or at least not the woods as I knew them. Instead, I was inside a house—a huge, lodge-style cabin.

It was the strangest house I'd ever been in.

Live birds flitted from potted trees that grew upside down from the ceiling, and the air was thick and sultry, as if I was in a tropical forest. The furniture was exquisitely carved into the shapes of animals, with gem-like eyes that glowed so brightly they seemed real. A fireplace roared in a lapis lazuli hearth. Gold covered every inch of the floor I stood on, except for an impossibly blue, bubbling creek that ran *through* the space, disappearing down a hall and off to who knew where.

A hand touched my arm, and I turned to see who it was. Shock rippled through me at the sight of Maddock wearing a deep green frock coat with a tan contrast, replete with matching vest, breeches, and frothy lace jabot. The garb of a wealthy colonial man.

Looking down, I realized I was dressed in a long, ice-blue velvet dress with side panels and bell-sleeves, a brocade insert highlighting my otherwise well-covered cleavage.

"W-what?" I gasped, pulling away, but Maddock drew closer, whispering some numbers in my ear.

And then the vision vanished.

Gasping, I clutched at the tree, using it to steady myself as I tried to return my world to its axis. That wasn't a vision. It was some kind of message...something that never happened to me before. But who was it from? And what had it meant? Had someone from the Onyx Order left it here for me? But how could they possibly know I would have come?

I ground my teeth together, realizing the answer to my question the moment I'd thought it. *Magic.* Of course. They didn't just leave me a message; they'd led me to it. But if they wanted to kidnap me, why not wait for me here?

Coordinates, I thought, running the numbers Maddock had given me in my head. Those numbers had been coordinates—I was certain of it. I plugged them into the Maps app on my phone and found that they were a short distance from here, just half a mile. I could make it there in no time, before it got dark out.

Glancing over my shoulder, I wondered if I should rush back and get Maddock, but knowing him, he would have suggested I go home and to let him handle it. I shook my head. No way. It was probably safer for me than for him at his point, considering every time the Onyx Order came around his kind, they ended up dead. On the other hand, they could have snatched me at any time and hadn't. That had to mean something, and I wasn't going to find out unless I followed the trail.

Besides, this was my *job.* I wasn't some damsel in distress heading into a trap, even if that's what the Onyx Order might think. I was armed and dangerous, and I was tired of running from these unseen forces. It was time these witches learned who they were dealing with.

I made my way to the forest, following the directions my phone provided me. It was tough going, as there wasn't any discernible path through the woods in the direction I was trying to go. Branches from bushes scratched my legs, and dirt and tree sap smudged my coat. I definitely didn't know how I would explain that to the nuns when I got back to the orphanage, but I decided not to worry about that right now.

Seriously though, next time I did something like this, I would be sure not to wear white again.

It didn't take long for the terrain to become a steep slope—something these white pumps were definitely not made for navigating. I fell and scraped my palms on rocks so many times that I considered ditching the shoes, but I didn't want to add bloody feet to my list of ailments, so I continued on. Eventually the landscape leveled out again, and the trees thinned, revealing a huge lodge-style cabin with a river running through it.

No fucking way.

I braced myself against a tree, then jumped as I realized the bark beneath my arm belonged to a palm tree. In fact, all the trees up here were of a tropical variety, and the air was thick and sultry, just like in the Not-A-Vision I'd experienced.

The call of a parakeet drew my attention upward, and my eyes widened as I stared up at a cloudless blue sky peeking through the trees that was very much *not* the red and gold sunset streaked sky I'd been looking at earlier.

What the hell was this place? Was I even still in Boston? It seemed impossible that something like this could exist here. And yet, here I was.

Hesitantly, I took one step forward, then another. The ground here was softer, not quite boggy but definitely not the cold, hard-packed earth I'd been stumbling across earlier. And there were tiny grass shoots peeking out here and there.

I made my way across a small bridge that led over the stream and to the front entrance of the house, then tugged carefully on the golden door handle that had been cast into the shape of a curved branch.

I shouldn't have been surprised to step into the exact same room as the one I'd seen in my vision. Half of me expected it, of course, but the other half was still stunned to find the tropical birds flitting around the trees hanging from the ceiling—how the fuck did they stay there?—and the golden floor with the river running through it.

I looked down at myself, checking to make sure that I wasn't dressed in Colonial garb, but fortunately I was still in my now-stained and scratched up outfit.

"Well, hello there."

I jumped at the sound of a female voice—my *own* voice—greeting me. Twisting in the direction of the voice, I watched as a red armchair situated near the fireplace slowly turned, revealing an exact copy of myself, wearing the *exact* clothes I'd had on in the not-vision.

Her eyes were wide with the same shock and surprise I felt, but she recovered much more quickly than I did.

"Fancy seeing you here," the Not-Me smiled, and I reached for my gun.

eighteen

Just as I was drawing my weapon, the front door flew open behind me. Maddock barreled in, a combination of fear and stark rage on his face. He flung out a glowing hand, and I jumped out of the way, irrationally thinking he was about to attack me. But instead he blasted the Not-Me who was still sitting in front of the fire.

Not-Me sprang out of the way with an alien hiss, clearing the blast with room to spare. The chair disintegrated, leaving not so much as a speck of ash behind, and Not-Me threw out a blast of her own, albeit weaker, at Maddock.

Maddock deflected it with his bare hand, but it gave Not-Me the opportunity to jump him, transforming as she went into a black-skinned humanoid with a long, forked tongue and cloven hooves.

Maddock twisted away from the Definitely-Not-Me's wickedly

sharp claws and raised his hand, probably to blast it again. But I had already drawn my gun from my purse, and I squeezed off a shot, aiming for the thing's head. The gun kicked in my hand, and the creature let out a shriek as the wooden stake ripped through the side of its neck, leaving a nasty-looking hole.

Damn, I thought as I watched the hole close up. *I should have loaded up with iron beforehand.*

Thankfully, the shot was enough to scare the thing away. It dodged another blast from Maddock, then flung itself through the front door and disappeared.

"Bloody unseelie scum," Maddock growled, stalking toward the door.

For a moment, I thought he was going to chase it, but he simply slammed the door shut, then knelt down and pressed his hands to the base of the wall. He muttered a series of strange words that sent weird sensations through my body, and a series of runes flared to life, racing along the bottom of the wall and around the entire room. Some kind of protection spell, maybe?

"Umm, hello?" I waved my arms in the air, trying to get his attention. "You wanna tell me what the fuck that was all about?"

"In a minute."

I gnashed my teeth, but Maddock ignored me, walking a perimeter around the room and then leaving it, presumably to check the rest of the house. I would have followed him, but he flung out a hand and told me to stay where I was. And whether it was because enough strange shit had happened to me or because I was just too damn tired, I listened.

Sighing, I flung myself down on one of the couches, staring at the birds twittering above me. They weren't any kind I'd ever seen before—their feathers glittered like jewels in a variety of colors, and they had glowing eyes I was pretty sure no species on Earth did.

I turned onto my side so I could study the room, and as my nose brushed against one of the pillows, I caught a strong whiff of Maddock's smoky-sweet scent. My body stilled as I considered the implications of that. If this pillow smelled like Maddock, that meant he spent a lot of time here.

Footsteps thudded in the hall, and I lifted my head to see Maddock stalking into the room, looking right pissed. His dark eyebrows were drawn together in a thunderous scowl, and he leveled a glare at me that could have reduced a mountain to dust.

Thankfully, I was made of stronger stuff.

"What the hell are you looking at me like that for?" I demanded, rising to my feet. "I didn't do anything wrong."

"Really?" Maddock sneered, not slowing down one bit. I reached for my weapon, but he'd already backed me into the wall. His big body radiated such intense fury that I actually started to sweat.

"Ye dinnae think that running off into the woods by yerself, instead of coming to me to get my help with whatever it was that caught yer attention, is wrong?"

"So you could help me, or so you could stop me?" The words exploded from my mouth with child-like belligerence, and my cheeks burned with embarrassment. But I plowed on. "I thought about going back for you, but I wanted answers—something you seem hard-pressed to give me. And before you go acting like I shouldn't have done that, I'll remind you that my shot slowed that thing down. I didn't need you. Now, tell me what's going on, so maybe next time I can trust you enough to ask for your help. What is this house? What was that *thing*? How did you know to find me here?"

Maddock's scowl deepened, but there was a flicker of emotion in his eyes that told me my point had been made and would not be refuted.

"The creature ye encountered is called a phoukas," Maddock spat. "It's a type of unseelie that can mimic the forms of certain creatures, usually humans and a select number of beasts. As for the house…this is my home."

"Your *home*?" Stunned, I looked around again. The place was stunningly beautiful—completely at odds with the brutally suave fae club owner I thought I was coming to know. "Why do you live here instead of in Salem?"

"I spend many of my nights at the club these days, but this place has been my home for a long time, and I'm rather…fond of it." Maddock's jaw clenched. "Somebody managed to disable the wards without it alerting me, and they used magic to lead ye right to it."

"If it helps, I knew I was being led on. That's not exactly the kind of thing that stops me—I usually just find a way to work the situation to my advantage, which I would have done on my own. I'm guessing the 'somebody' responsible here wasn't the phoukas?" I asked pointedly. "I mean, that thing doesn't look like it's incredibly intelligent."

"It's not, and it could never have done this," Maddock growled. "Likely, it was whoever carved that symbol into the tree down by the stream. I just dinnae understand how they knew ye were going to be here." He let out a disgusted sigh, then eased back, giving me some breathing room. "This isn't the first time the unseelie have sent someone after me, but it's usually not something so insignificant as a phoukas. They must be changing their tactics. But *why*?"

"Maybe start with why was it disguised to look like me," I demanded. "How did it even *know* about me? Are the unseelie watching me now, too? What did you drag me into, Maddock?"

"I doubt ye would be on their radar," Maddock said dryly. "The phoukas simply pulled a memory from the house in order to choose its guise. It was likely trying to throw me off."

"A...a memory? Of me? Here?" I spluttered. "But I've never been here before!"

"Ye have, unfortunately, been here before." Maddock's eyes tightened, and he looked away. "A very, very long time ago."

"What, you mean like when I was a baby?" I asked, half-sarcastic, but my heart thumped a little. Was it possible that Maddock actually did know me as a child? Had he known my parents? What could he tell me about them?

"No." A disgusted expression crossed Maddock's face as he closed the distance between us again. His long fingers clenched around my jaw as he tilted my face up to his.

"What the fuck!" I punched him in the gut, and it was like sucker punching a brick wall. One-hundred percent ineffective, and I came perilously close to breaking my knuckles.

"I didna want to do this again, but it's the easiest way to show ye," Maddock growled, and then he crushed his mouth against mine.

At first, my senses were overwhelmed by him—his heather and woodsmoke scent; the spicy-sweet taste of his mouth; the weight of his big body pressing mine into the wall—but all that was abruptly replaced by a vision...or rather, a memory.

"Yes. More." *Shocked, I watched myself beg, lying naked on satin sheets, through the eyes of someone above me. Someone inside me.*

My tousled silver hair was spread across the pillow, my cheeks were flushed, and my hands were gripping the shaking headboard so hard my knuckles were turning white.

"Harder!" *I moaned, letting go of the headboard and reaching down between my legs. The man above me groaned, a low, animalistic sound, and a thrill shot through me as I realized I was hearing Maddock's voice.*

How was that possible? There's no way I would have forgotten something like this.

But the memory was part of me. And even though I was viewing myself from Maddock's eyes, I could feel every sensation rippling through me-then's body, could witness each moment in a way I could never deny as truth.

Maddock's fingers curled around my rib cage, his fingertips digging into my skin. It was passionate, not aggressive, but he didn't know his own strength. Still, his bruising grip was a nearly imperceptible feeling beneath his powerful thrusts.

The arousal building inside me was unlike anything I'd experienced before, almost like magic. Hell, it probably was magic. Some kind of preternatural fuck magic—a mind-warping, skin-buzzing, simmering spell that had me on the verge of explosion but somehow held me there, begging this man for more.

Certain I was about to shatter completely from the pleasure, a panic fluttered through my chest at the thought of him stopping. The me-then bit into his shoulder, apparently believing that would get a reaction.

It did.

Maddock pulled my hair, his urgency rising to meet my frenzied need for completion. Something came over me as the magical sensation sparked over every nerve cell in my body, shifting my moan into something more primal as I came, screaming his name. Moments later, the Maddock from the vision groaned again, burying his face in the crook of my shoulder as he found his release.

The memory shifted then, moving so that I could see both of us lying in a hand-carved wooden bed that was fit for a king. It was strange, watching my hands stroke his broad back, brushing droplets of sweat away as every muscle in his body relaxed. As Maddock's eyes closed, a strange mix of tenderness and sadness filled my eyes, and then they hardened with what looked like determination.

My hands continued stroking Maddock's back, but they took on a faint blue glow. The more they stroked, the brighter the glow grew, until my entire body was engulfed in the strange energy.

I gasped as I began to see a pattern—the energy was wafting up from Maddock's body...and into *mine.*

"No!" Maddock's eyes flew open as he growled the word. His big body shuddered, and he braced himself using his knuckles, trying to rise. But whatever I was doing to him left him too weak, and he collapsed on top of me again, helpless against whatever voodoo I was performing on him.

When I was done, his tanned skin had taken on an ashy tint, and I was resplendent with power. Smiling, I pushed him off me as if he weighed nothing, then sauntered over to a chair on the other side of the room, where a blue velvet dress and some lacy undergarments were draped.

The same blue dress I'd seen myself wearing in the other vision.

"Bitch…" *Maddock croaked, his body still trembling. The fury radiating off him was palpable, but he couldn't do more than shift his head to glare at me. "I'll kill ye the next time I see yer bloody face."*

"Don't be so angry, darling." *I pulled the dress over my head. It was really strange to hear myself speaking with a Colonial accent. "We both know you were using me, and now it's my turn to use you. I need your power for something important, and besides, it isn't as if you won't regenerate it. A week of bed rest and some chicken soup, and you'll be just fine."*

I winked as I tied a bonnet over my silver curls and slipped my feet into elegant slippers. A coat came on next, and then I headed for the door.

"I wilna…forget this…" *Maddock gasped, still struggling to move from the bed.*

I turned back to face him, profound sadness weighing down my features. "I know. But at least I can take comfort in the fact that if I succeed, you and I will both live on to remember this. Even if you do hate me for the rest of your eternity."

The vision broke, and Maddock shoved away from me, his chest heaving. He glared at me, but the anger in his eyes was tempered with confusion.

He snarled. "How did ye do that?"

"W…what?" I was still gasping for breath, still reeling from what I'd seen. "How did I do *what?*"

A muscle beneath Maddock's left eye twitched. "You tampered with the memory. You *changed* it."

"How the fuck could I have done that?" I cried. "How would I even know what to change, since I've never seen it before?"

"I dinnae know!" Maddock snapped, raking a hand through

his dark hair. He cut his gaze away from me, looking like he wanted to break something. "But that last bit...yer parting shot... I dinnae remember that. I've never remembered that. *It didn't happen.*"

"As far as I've always known, *none* of this has ever happened!" Fed up, I stalked toward him, curled my fist into his collar and yanked his head down to face me. I was done letting him push me around; let's see how *he* liked it for a change. "Are you telling me that we used to be lovers several hundred years ago? Because that can't possibly be true. I was born twenty-three years ago, Tremaine. I didn't live in colonial times. That vision you showed me—it's a woman who looks remarkably like me, but it's *not* me. It's got to be a phoukas or something."

My voice wobbled a little, and I pressed my lips together. I was *not* going to panic over this.

"The woman in that vision *is* ye." Maddock's hand clamped around my wrist, yanking it away from his collar. "Ye went by Veronica Moussall at that time, and ye were a mystery, not a phoukas. Believe me, I would know. Ye were a member of the Sisterhood of the Forgotten—one of the five ruling witch clans in the area of that time—and yet ye were something more, different somehow. I thought that perhaps if I could seduce ye, I could unravel yer secrets. I thought ye might be the key to helping me regain my power."

"Regain your power?" I frowned, looking him up and down. "You look plenty powerful to me." No, I hadn't *seen* Maddock use much of his magic, but the confidence and energy rolled off him in abundant waves. He'd said that he was put in charge of this entire sector by the Seelie Court, which had to mean he was powerful. The idea that he was somehow diminished, that he'd once been even stronger, even more dangerous, chilled my spine.

"Aye, but my strength is not what it once was." Maddock dropped my hand, a muscle in his jaw clenching. I'd never seen him so agitated. "As I mentioned before, my kind cannae be truly killed—we reincarnate after we are vanquished. But it takes a very long time, and we lose some of our magic every time it happens. I have lived for millennia, and have been reincarnated more times than I can count." His narrowed gaze turned back to me. "The fae have long searched for an answer to this affliction, but we've yet to find it."

I let out a soft laugh. "I see. So you tried to seduce me, thinking you could use me to get your power back, and instead I took yours." I shook my head in wonder. "Sounds like you're a sore loser, Tremaine."

Maddock's eyes flashed at that. "Excuse me?"

"You tried to use me, and instead I used you." I folded my arms across my chest and stared up at him. "And because you're a chauvinistic male, you're still butt-hurt about it after...what? A hundred years? Two hundred?"

"Over three hundred years," he growled.

I paused as something occurred to me. "If I'm reincarnated, does that make me fae?" I looked down at my hands—my ordinary, oh-so human hands. Was I really part of a race of such extraordinary beings?

"What ye are, as I said, is a *mystery*." Maddock's expression was stony as he regarded me. "Fae don't reincarnate as quickly as you have. It's unprecedented. Besides, the way that you stole my power...that's something only a witch can do."

"Right…" I said, recalling what he'd said back at the mill. "It's how they fuel their magic. I get that. But it's not something I would do."

Maddock pressed his lips together, agitation darkening his gaze. "It's certainly something you did, though."

I shuddered, remembering the boy with the ram's horns I'd seen in my vision at the mill, and how emaciated he'd looked. Cold horror filled me at the thought of more fae like him chained up in a dark cavern somewhere, reduced to little more as a battery for a group of power-hungry supernaturals. "What they're doing to your people is horrible."

"It is." Maddock glared at me again. "Much more horrible than what you did to me."

I huffed. "According to that memory you showed me, I seemed to have had a good reason for taking your magic. In fact, it sounded a lot like a life and death thing to me."

"Indeed." Maddock didn't sound impressed. "You seem to have a knack of attracting those sorts of things. I meant to show you a second memory…the one of the last time we met, before we broke apart."

"Oh?" A nervous tremor rippled through me. "And what memory was that?"

"I was at the Seelie Court, returned after a long spell away, and I found out they were holding ye there. They wouldn't tell me why, but I gathered that ye'd destroyed something of ours, something powerful enough to merit an execution. They refused to let me speak to you despite my status, but I went to the execution, and ye spotted me as you were led up to the platform." Maddock's eyes glimmered as he spoke, and if I didn't know better, I could have sworn I saw sadness in them. "Ye looked me in the eye as they lowered you onto the chopping block and told me ye would see me again. Ye also told me that when that day came, things would get even darker."

"That's just crazy," I said, rolling my eyes now. "You're making me sound like some kind of prophet or something."

Sure, I had a strange talent, but the idea that I was some kind of powerful, witch-like creature with the ability to reincarnate was bat-shit crazy no matter how you looked at it.

"Do you want me to show you?" Maddock taunted. "Because I assure you, the memory is real." He reached for me again.

"No!" I sidestepped him. "Umm, no, thanks. I don't really have any desire to watch myself get beheaded."

"You were slain with a spear through the chest."

"Fantastic." I glared at him, easing my hip onto an armchair. "Anything else you'd care to share?"

"No. But I will say this." Maddock's face turned stony again. "Ye had better be ready for what's coming, because if yer premonition was accurate, our lives are about to become more hellish than ever. And I've lived a long time, Detective. Long enough to know that if something has the capability to scare me, it might just have the capability to end the world."

nineteen

Maddock's words echoed in my head during the drive home, clawing at the edges of my mind and pulling me perilously close to a panic attack. Reincarnation? End of the world prophecies? What the hell kind of world had I walked into? And why had nobody prepared me for this?

Anger and fear roiling inside me, I slammed my apartment door behind me, then made a beeline for my bedroom. I stripped off my dirty outfit, then flung myself onto the mattress facedown and closed my eyes.

And then I breathed.

Inhale, two, three. Hold, two, three. Exhale, two, three.

I repeated the words over and over inside my head as I followed the breathing exercise Oscar had taught me when I was little. It helped me focus, helped still my thoughts and emotions, and was a great tool in times of stress.

After several minutes, my heart rate finally slowed, and enough tension bled from my body that I was able to unclench my hands and roll over onto my back. Letting out a sigh, I finally allowed my mind to think again, and the first thought that popped into my mind, naturally, was Oscar.

Oscar should have prepared me for this. My parents had given me into his care. Was it really their idea that I not be taught to use my magic, or was it his? I wanted to think that my parents would have wanted me to be well-armed and able to defend myself from all this. But what if they didn't? What if they thought that by keeping me in the dark, they could stop whatever was coming to pass?

And how did they even know anything *was coming to pass?*

Turning over, I pounded my fist into my pillow, half to fluff it up and half in anger. The truth was, I had no idea why my parents had sent me away. They could have been bandits, living a life of crime, and having a kid on the run was too tough. Or maybe I'd been in actual danger.

Either way, I was tired of speculating. I wanted to know the truth. I wanted to know why my parents had sent me away, and more importantly, who they really were. Had I gotten my magic from them? Since Oscar knew supernaturals existed, that likely meant my parents did, too. Were they witches, or something else?

My mind made up, I picked up my phone and speed-dialed Oscar. The phone rang, and I stared up at the popcorn ceiling as I waited, trying to detect patterns the way one tried to find shapes in the clouds. But like my life at the moment, much as I tried to find meaning, all I saw was chaos.

"Hey, kid." Oscar's rough voice drew me back to the present.

"Glad you called. What's up?"

I opened my mouth, wanting to launch straight into my interrogation. But instead, I said, "Everything. And it really, really sucks."

I told him about the events that had transpired—about the missing fae, the assassination attempts, the strange markings on the walls, the dead body I'd found, and what I'd learned about Tom at the orphanage. The only thing I *didn't* mention was the memory Maddock had showed me. Even though Oscar was the closest thing I had to family, I couldn't bring myself to tell him about something so crazy.

Not that I had to. What I told him was enough to make him fly off the handle as it was.

"Dammit, Brooke, you need to come home!" I heard a thud, and I pictured him slamming his hand down on the counter. He was probably standing in the kitchen, drinking a glass of scotch and staring out the glass doors leading to the backyard like he usually did late at night. "Please, come back to Chicago. You can stay with me for as long as you need. I don't care about you paying rent. You just need to stop digging."

"No!" Rage burned hot in my chest as I clenched the phone. "I'm not going to run home with my tail between my legs and more questions than I left with! You've been hiding things from me, and I want answers! You *owe* me answers."

"I don't *owe* you anything!" Oscar snarled. "I took you in and raised you when you had no one."

"Yes, and why is that?" I spat, trembling now. "Why is it that I had no one? Why didn't my parents take care of me? Why did they abandon me?" Tears spilled from the corners of my eyes, and my heart ached fiercely as I ripped open the wound that, most days, I refused to look at. The wound carried by every orphan and abandoned child who thought they were unloved.

"Brooke—" Oscar sucked in a breath. Then he sighed. "Your parents didn't abandon you."

"Oh, yeah? Well, what would you call leaving me on your doorstep and running off into the night?"

"Protecting you," Oscar shouted. "That's what I would call it. Your parents wanted to shield you, to make sure that you didn't fall into the wrong hands, that you stayed off the radar. And you've just ensured their efforts were all for nothing!"

"The wrong hands?" I echoed. "What the hell does that even mean?"

"I—" Oscar stopped talking. "I can't tell you that, Brooke. I'm sorry. I made a promise to your parents."

"Yeah, I get it. A promise to lie." My voice was heavy with bitterness. "What else have you lied to me about? Are my parents even still alive?"

"Brooke..." He sighed. I could almost hear him swallow on the other end of the line. His next words came out strained. "I'm sorry, kid. They were murdered shortly after you came to me. And since then I have done everything to honor their request to keep you safe."

A memory slammed into my chest then—not a vision, but a recollection.

"Hello?" Oscar answered the phone, gruff as usual.

He was standing in the kitchen, his torso visible behind the counter, while I sat on the couch in the living room and read a book. The phone was in the kitchen instead of his study, because for some reason he liked to take his calls there, sitting on one of the barstools or standing in front of the stove and cooking a pot of his famous chili.

I flicked up my gaze for just a moment before returning to my book—I was neck-deep in the Order of the Phoenix and too riveted to care much about anything else.

"What? Are you sure?" The tightness in Oscar's voice pulled me out of my book, and I glanced up to see that he'd gone completely still. His hand was gripping the counter so tightly, his rawboned knuckles had turned white.

"Yes, yes, I understand." His shoulders slumped, and his dark eyes flickered toward me. A strange feeling went through me as I noticed an emotion I'd never seen before in those eyes—sympathy. "Yes, I'll make sure. Thank you for taking care of this. I'll do my part."

He hung up the phone, and I put my book down. "Uncle Oscar?" I asked, coming over to him. I'd never seen him so distraught, and even though I didn't know him well yet, I knew that it wasn't normal for him. He was normally unflappable. "Is everything okay?"

Uncle Oscar said nothing, his back to me as he stared out the window. Then he turned slowly and laid a hand on my head, staring down into my eyes.

"Yeah, kid. Yeah, everything's okay. It's just been a long day." He smiled, then ruffled my hair. "Why don't you go finish your book. I'll let you know when the chili is ready. Everything's going to be just fine."

"Hello? Brooke?"

Oscar's voice pulled me from the memory, and I stared up at the ceiling, unseeing, for a long moment.

"That evening, when you got that phone call. It was a few months after I came to live with you, and I was sitting on the couch, reading. That's when you learned my parents were dead."

"Yes." Oscar sounded incredibly weary. "Please, Brooke. You had just finished settling in. Telling you would have hurt you unnecessarily. You have to understand that everything I've done was for your protection."

"Well stop!" I jumped to my feet, anger forcing me to pace. "Stop protecting me! I'm a grown woman now, and that's not your choice to make anymore! This is *my* life, and you should have told me."

"And if I had, kid? Then what? Would you have run away, tried to find them? Or been consumed with a burning vengeance until you were old enough to strike out on your own and find their killers? The same way you're trying to find your fiancé's killer now? And have you even figured out what you're going to do when you *do* find the person responsible? If this person has been killing and kidnapping so many powerful creatures, what's going to stop them from killing you next?"

"It doesn't matter now. They've already got their sights set on me." My voice was brittle now. "I've got no choice but to see this through, and if you're not going to help me, then maybe I made a mistake calling you."

I hung up the phone, then tossed it onto the bed so hard that it bounced off the mattress, smacked into the wall, and flipped onto the floor. Thank God for cases, although if it had broken, I'm not even sure I would have cared.

I was positively fuming about the fact there was someone out there who might have the answers—somebody who should be on my side—and he wouldn't tell me what was going on. Oscar might have been protecting me when I was a kid, but his insistence on keeping me in the dark was going to get me killed.

A knock on the door pulled me away from the maelstrom of thoughts in my head, and I frowned. Who the hell was calling on me at eight o'clock at night? Annoyed, I pulled on a robe and stalked to the door, then peered through the peephole.

My annoyance vanished when I saw Shelley standing in the hall. Her face was blotchy, her mascara clumped together from tears, and her toddler mounted on her hip like he was a security blanket.

The stark fear in her eyes tugged at my heart strings, vanquishing my problems as I put them aside for hers.

I yanked the door open, and she jumped. "Hey, what's going on?"

"I… Can I come on in?" She pressed trembling lips together, and the toddler wailed, clearly distraught by his mother's grief.

"Of course." I quickly ushered them in, not wanting any neighbors to come out and complain about a crying baby in the hall. "Here, let's sit down, and we can—"

"No." Shelley's voice was somehow both hard and full of desperation. She planted her feet in front of the kitchen, refusing to let me lead her to the couch. "There's no time. We have to go now."

"Why? What's happening?"

"My son's missing. I've called him a hundred times, I've looked for him everywhere, and I don't know what to do." Voice breaking, she shifted the toddler to her other hip and gripped my hand so tightly she ground the bones together. "Please, Detective Chandler. Find my son. I don't care what you have to do, but *find him*."

twenty

"I'm sorry the place is such a mess," Shelley babbled as she fussed with the lock on the front door of her apartment. It was peeling paint, and the brass doorknob looked like it had been at least two hundred years since it had last been polished. But since she was living in the Point, which was considered the bad section of town, that wasn't really surprising. "I've just been so busy, and with Jason going missing—"

"You don't need to apologize, Shelley." I placed a hand on her shoulder, gentle but firm. She looked back at me, her eyes red-rimmed and stark with fear. "I'm not here as a guest. I'm here as a detective. Now breathe, focus, and let's get that door open so I can look through Jason's things and see if there's anything I can use to find him."

"Okay." Shelley took a deep breath, blinked the tears away. "Okay."

On the way over, she'd talked me out of calling backup. She was worried what might happen if he was caught doing something wrong when they went looking for him, so I relented. Finding him and making sure he was safe was the important thing.

Shifting the toddler on her hip, Shelley tried again with the keys. The door swung open, revealing a cramped, but overall tidy living space. The underlying structure was pretty drab—shitty carpet and pale grey walls—but she'd tried to liven it up with colorful knick-knacks she'd placed on various surfaces and shelves.

To my right, a pile of laundry sat unfolded on a threadbare couch and baby toys were scattered all over the floor in front of the TV. To the left, a few undone dishes sat in the kitchen sink. But despite the mess, and the clear poverty, I got the sense that the space was generally well-taken care of, and Shelley wasn't a slob.

"Jason's room is back here," she said, starting toward the hall leading away from the front area. But the toddler began to fuss again, flailing desperately in her arms.

"Shhh, shhh. It's all right," she tried to reassure him, but he just grew more distressed. Nearly in tears again, Shelley turned back to face me. "Tyler's tired, and I need to feed him. Would you mind going ahead without me? I'll be in soon."

"It's okay. Just tell me which room."

Shelley pointed me to the second room on the left-hand side. The directions weren't really necessary—the Mudvayne poster plastered all over the black-painted door was a dead giveaway.

I let myself in, inhaled the scent of pot and stale Doritos, and allowed my eyes to wander. Underneath the heavy metal posters and the black, well, everything, I was looking at the bedroom of a typical teenage boy. Unmade bed, clothes on the floor, a cluttered dresser, and piles of textbooks on the desk and floor. A quick look at those told me that despite his issues, Jason was a dedicated student.

As I approached the bed, a spark tingled up my spine, and I stopped. I was beginning to recognize the feeling, as it had happened a couple of times now. It was a sense of awareness, a sense that something magical had occurred in the area.

Inspired, I went back into the living area. Shelley was on the couch, nursing Tyler, so I let her be and went straight into the kitchen.

"What are you looking for?" She tried to crane her neck around, but clearly the task was difficult when holding a nursing toddler.

"I just need some supplies. I didn't bring my field kit. It's fine, I'll let you know if I need help."

Working quickly, I whisked chamomile, honey, and sage together in a bowl, then grabbed a glazing brush and headed back to the bedroom with my concoction. Kneeling on the bed, I dipped the brush into the bowl and painted the savory-sweet mixture onto the walls. I then muttered the same words I'd heard Maddock use.

It took me three tries to get the syllables right, but when I did, a haze briefly shimmered in the air before revealing the same black O with the three jagged, vertical slashes that had been in my apartment and the giant's.

"W-what is that?"

I nearly dropped the bowl at the sound of Shelley's voice. Twisting around, I saw her standing in the doorway, her eyes round as saucers. She must have finished feeding the baby and gotten him to bed, because he wasn't attached to her hip this time.

"It's a gang symbol," I lied, hastily climbing off the bed and putting the bowl on top of a stack of textbooks piled onto a side table. "I've seen it at a couple of crime scenes recently. They're usually drawn in some kind of weird invisible paint."

"And the ingredients in my kitchen were enough to uncover this invisible paint?" Shelley sounded a little skeptical.

"Yeah." I resisted the urge to run my fingers through my hair. I felt really uncomfortable lying to Shelley about this, but what could I do? "Look, the other crime scenes I'm talking about were all regarding missing persons. I think it's safe to say that this gang, whoever they are, has taken Jason as well."

"But why?" Shelley cried. "Why have they taken my son? What have I done to deserve this?"

Now was the time to take a gamble. "Could your connection with a certain vampire have anything to do with it?"

Shelley stiffened, and the walls behind her eyes slammed down instantly. "What are you talking about?"

"I think you know exactly what I'm talking about."

"No. No." Shelley backed out of the door. "There's no way you could possibly know about that." Her eyes were wide with fear again, but this time the fear was directed at me instead of the unknown enemy who had taken her child.

"Shelley." I gentled my voice as I approached her, as one might approach a skittish animal. "I'm not here to judge you or hurt you in any way. I'm here to find your son, and in order to do that, I need you to be truthful to me. I need you to tell me why you got involved with the vampires, and why your son is so fascinated with them that he's trying to turn himself into one."

"Oh God." Shelley's lip trembled, and tears spilled over her cheeks. "This is my fault. If I hadn't made that deal…if I'd just put up with Daniel for a little longer, none of this would be happening."

"Okay, okay. Slow down." My heart twisted at the sight of her crumpled to the ground, wracked with grief and guilt, but I didn't have time to let her wallow there. Closing the distance, I put one of my arms around her shoulders and grasped her hand, urging her to her feet. "Let's go sit down, and you can tell me what's going on. We'll get through this. Together."

I guided her to the couch and moved the laundry out of the way so she and I could sit down. Rather than looking at me, she reached for a baby monitor sitting on a black side table, then stared at the image of Tyler sound asleep in his crib.

A look of inexplicable tenderness crossed her face, and I felt a pang as I wondered if my own mother had ever looked down at me like that. Had she loved me like that, the way Shelley loved her own children? To distraction? To indescribable grief?

Stop it. This isn't about you.

"This can't be happening," Shelley whispered, her hand coming to cover her mouth as she stared at the baby monitor. She made a sound a little like a hiccup, then traced her forefinger around the edge of the monitor's screen. "Everything I did…I did it for my boys. My actions have only ever been motivated by the desire to keep my children safe."

"Of course," I said gently, squashing the urgency that wanted to seep into my voice. I needed Shelley to be calm, or she would panic and perhaps forget details. A focused witness was a good witness. "I'm not here to judge. Just here to find your son."

"I'm guessing, by your lack of shock and the casual way you speak about vampires, that you are acquainted with the supernatural world?"

"Chicago is infested with vampires, so yeah. I know a thing or two."

Shelley smiled a little. "I imagine you do." Her face turned sober again. "I grew up in New Orleans, which is full of voodoo practitioners and witches, among other things. My best friend's mother was a voodoo priestess, so I knew more than the average person, even though I've no ability of my own."

"Okay." I nodded encouragingly. "So, because of your voodoo friend, you somehow got mixed up with vampires?"

"Not exactly." Shelley took a breath, digging her fingernails into the couch cushions. "My husband, Daniel, was abusive. Not in the beginning of our relationship, of course—he was very sweet and attentive. But after we got married…well, it was just mental at first, but a year after Jason was born, it started getting physical. He would get me drunk before he hit me, so that he could always claim to the police that I just fell and hit my head or that I was just making things up." Her voice shook now. "I stuck it out for my son…but when I got pregnant with my second child, one bad night made me fear for my unborn child's life. I realized I didn't want my kids to have a violent, manipulative drunk for a role model, or for him to one day turn on them the way he did on me."

"And so you tried to leave."

"And so I tried to leave." Shelley nodded slowly. "But it wasn't easy. Daniel caught me trying to escape and threatened to kill me. He told me that the only way I was leaving him was in a body bag." More tears came, but these were slow, silent, the kind that quietly bled from your soul rather than gushing like a waterfall. "I knew that the only way I was going to get rid of him, was by…you know…getting rid of him."

I slammed down on the shock that exploded in my chest. "Are you saying that you put a hit out on your ex-husband?"

"What would you have done in my position?" she snapped, her voice vibrating with anger and grief. Her eyes flashed as she jerked away from me. "My husband had already established a pattern of insanity on my part with the cops by getting them to think I was a crazy drunk, and I knew they'd be more likely to lock me up in the psychiatric ward than prosecute my husband if I came to them and told them that he'd threatened my life. The only way to keep myself safe—to keep my children safe—was to get rid of him."

"All right." I let out a breath. "All right." How could I possibly argue with her logic? I believed in the law, but I certainly sidestepped it every time I staked a vampire. Shelley's husband might not have been a supernatural, but there was no denying that he *was* a monster, and she'd done what, in her mind, she felt she had to.

"So how did you kill him?"

Shelley flinched at the word 'kill.' "I hired a vampire to do it," she whispered.

Jesus. "Why a vampire? Why not a normal hit man?"

Shelley let out a dry, humorless laugh. "Is there really a difference? They're both monsters. And just as vampires run the underground in your home city, so they do in mine. They have their hands in all sorts of criminal enterprises, including assassination. So I hired one of them, then I packed up my life, my children, and moved to Salem."

I was silent for a moment as I processed this. By law, I was technically supposed to report it, but thankfully, her story would sound ridiculous enough to most that there would be little point. There likely wasn't any evidence to follow anyway, and it was a waste of my time and police time when there were bigger things to worry about.

"I'm guessing Tyler wasn't born yet?" I finally asked.

"I was only a few months along." Shelley smiled down at the monitor again, which was still nestled in her lap. "It's hard, being a single mother, but at least he's free of his father's influence."

"And how does Jason feel about the fact his father's gone?"

Shelley's eyes filled with tears again. "He hates me for it," she whispered. "He found out a year after it had been done, and he's never forgiven me. Daniel was never physically abusive to Jason, but he manipulated him, convinced him just like the police officers that I was crazy, unbalanced."

"I'm sorry." I placed a hand on her shoulder, gave her a sympathetic squeeze. I couldn't imagine how horrible it must have been for her, to have her husband turn her child against her. It seemed like, even in death, the bastard was still hurting her.

"Anyway, I think that Jason believes his father is still alive," Shelley continued. "That, instead of killing him, the vampire I'd hired simply turned Daniel and added him to his coterie." Shelley shook her head. "The assassin showed me the body himself—he'd killed him with a clean slash to the throat, not by draining his blood. But I think...oh, I think that Jason believes that if he can convince a vampire to turn him, that he can rejoin his father, and be free of me." She broke down into sobs now, burying her face in her hands. "My son wants to turn himself into an evil monster. And it's my fault."

"No," I said fiercely, and this time I wrapped my arms around her in a tight hug and held her close. "No, Shelley. Don't do this to yourself. This isn't your fault."

"B-but if I hadn't killed his father——"

"Then he would have turned your son into a different kind of monster." Shelley flinched, but I pressed on ruthlessly. "This isn't what you want to hear, but it's the truth. Your husband was turning Jason into a carbon copy of himself, and the best thing you could have done was get him away from that kind of influence. The fact that Jason is still following in his father's footsteps is *Daniel's* fault, not yours."

Shelley said nothing for a long moment, simply turning her face into her hands and breathing. Eventually, she raised her head, turning to stare at me with those red-rimmed eyes.

"It doesn't matter whose fault it is," she whispered. "He's going to die anyway, isn't he? They're going to turn him, and there's nothing I can do."

I shook my head. "I don't think the vampires took him."

Shelley's eyes widened. "You don't?" Hope flared in her eyes. "But you said a gang——"

"Yes, but not vampires. Witches."

"Witches?" Confusion scrunched Shelley's features. "What do witches want with my son?"

I let out a breath. "I'm not really sure," I admitted. "They've been kidnapping supernaturals left and right the last couple of weeks, but this is the first human they've taken. The good news is, no one who's been kidnapped has turned up dead, so there's a good chance we can recover your son."

I left out the part about the woman who'd been killed because she hadn't been kidnapped first, and Shelley deserved a little bit of hope. Besides, there was no point in adding to her worries.

Shelley let out a half-laugh. "Is it strange that I'm relieved? I shouldn't be, because witches can be just as ruthless as vampires, and I have no idea what they're doing to him, but—" She stopped, shook her head. "I'm just so glad it's not vampires."

I smiled a little. "It's not strange, and I'm glad to bring you some comfort." I stood, adjusting my jacket and making sure my weapons were where they should be. "Take care of Tyler, Shelley, and get some sleep. I'm going to do some more digging, see if I can find out exactly where the witches are keeping Jason. And then I'll bring him back to you."

"Are you sure?" Shelley shot to her feet, anxious again. "Is there anything I can do? There must be something—"

"Shelley." I laid a hand on her shoulder. "I know you want to help, but the best thing you can do is stay here and make sure your other son stays safe. I'll update you as soon as I know more."

"Thank you." She threw her arms around me. "Thank you so much for agreeing to help. For promising to bring him back. You don't know how much that means to me."

"You're welcome. I'll keep you posted."

I made a beeline for my car, then opened up the Maps app and plugged in an address. I needed to find out more about the Onyx Order from someone who was an expert in witches.

And I knew just the place to start.

twenty one

Ten minutes later, I was standing on the sidewalk across from Crow Haven Corner, the oldest witch shop in Salem. Or so the tourism guide had told me when I'd been researching the city.

I stared dubiously at the three story barn-house building, which had been painted black and had purple signs with yellow moons and bats hanging over the windows and entrance.

It didn't look like anything more than another tourist trap, but I *had* felt a tingle of magic when I'd passed by this place a few days ago, so it was possible somebody inside knew something.

If not, I supposed I could go to another witch shop. There were at least three others that I'd passed on the way here, and maybe even more that I didn't know about. Probably most of these people weren't 'true witches', as Maddock had called them, but there was probably at least one.

So I headed up the steps and inside. Directly in front of me was a dark purple staircase that headed directly upstairs, but to my right was an open doorway that looked like it led into the shop, so I veered in that direction instead.

"Welcome to Crow Haven Corner, Salem's oldest witch shop," the woman behind the counter said with a small smile. She was in her late twenties and looked normal-enough with her glasses, white blouse, and black jeans. The only thing different about her was her dyed bluish-silver hair. "May I be of any help?"

I glanced around the shop. Strange, colorful balls dangled from the ceiling, incense hung thick and sweet in the air, and the tables and shelves were laden with candles, herbs, dolls, and all kinds of supernatural-looking trinkets that probably did absolutely nothing. Was I really on the right track here?

Stop being so skeptical. You're not going get anything done like this.

"I'm Detective Brooke Chandler." I stuck out my hand with a smile. "I'm doing a little bit of research in connection with a case I'm working on, and I was hoping for a few minutes of your time."

"Sure." The woman's eyes widened a little, and she leaned forward, bracing her forearms on the glass display case. Beneath it lay a variety of sparkly jewelry and decorations. "What can I do for you?

"I was just wondering if you knew anything about this symbol." I pulled a notebook from my inside pocket, then flipped it open to the drawing of the Onyx Order symbol I'd hastily sketched. "I've been running into it a lot in my investigation, and evidence suggests it has to do with witches."

The woman's eyebrows shot up.

"Or at least a group of teens that think they're witches," I added hastily.

"That's so weird," the woman said, her throaty voice growing hushed as she studied the symbol. "I don't think any of the local covens use this symbol. I could ask our owner if she's seen it before, though. She's way more knowledgeable about the different covens around here than I am." Her dark grey eyes flicked up to me, round with concern. "What kind of investigations are you running? I don't know all the covens around here, but the ones I do know would never do anything dangerous or try to hurt our community. We only hex people who are trying to harm others and disturb the natural order of things. Our main rule is to do no harm, and we abide by that very strongly."

"Unfortunately, I can't give out any particulars at this time." I nudged the book at her again. "Are you sure you've never seen this symbol before? It doesn't have to be in connection with a coven. It could have been in a book somewhere."

The woman studied it again, then shook her head. "I really should ask the owner," she said. "If you want, I can take a picture of this and show it to her. Maybe she'll have better answers."

"That would be great." I let her use her phone to take a picture of my sketch, then dug out a card and handed it to her. "Please have her call me if she knows anything."

"I will. I'm sorry I couldn't be of more help, but please feel free to look around the shop while you're here. If you have any questions about the items, I'd be more than happy to help."

"Thanks."

I moved off, leaving room for an eager customer to come up and ask questions about an item she was holding that looked suspiciously like a wand. Sticking my hands in my pockets, I wandered around the shop and considered my next move.

I could try the public library, I mused. Maybe it was still open, and I could ask if they had any old books on Salem's witchcraft history that I could hunt through for mention of the Onyx Order. Failing that, there was Google, but I wasn't sure how much I would find.

Pulling out my phone, I plugged in the term "Onyx Order." The first ten search results were all about Castlevania. Ugh. I tried "Onyx Order Witches" and got pages regarding the use of crystals and other gemstones in pagan rituals.

Yeah. This wasn't going to be easy.

I pulled out the notepad again and stared at the symbol. I might try doing a Google image search or something when I got home, to see if I could find anything in connection with it. With any luck, it wouldn't be a heavy metal band or a role playing group.

"I've seen that symbol before," a quavering voice said.

I glanced up to see an old woman with a cane standing next to me. She wore a black dress with a high collar, and her flyaway grey hair gave her a bit of a wild, unkempt look, like she'd run away from her nursing home and hadn't been picked up yet.

"Have you?" Reluctantly, I shifted the pad in my hand so she could get a closer look. The vacant look in her pale, almost colorless eyes made me think that she was a little off, but I couldn't turn down a possible lead.

"Oh, yes." The woman nodded, smiling blithely. "The Onyx Order. A nasty witch coven with a grudge against vampires."

I froze. "What?"

She chuckled a little. "You thought I was just a batty old woman, didn't you?"

"Well...umm..." I squirmed a little, then fought to get the

conversation back on track. Maybe her cloudy eyes were deceiving, and she'd been spying over my shoulder when I'd run my Google searches. But maybe not. "How do you know about any of this?"

"That's not important," she chided, wagging a gnarled finger at me. "What's important is finding them, isn't it?"

"Well…yeah," I agreed. "But it would be nice to know what your connection is to all of this."

"I'm simply a concerned citizen who wants to ensure the safety of the town I live in." Her eyes sharpened. "Back when the Onyx Order was alive and well in Salem, they held their coven meetings in a mansion located ten miles north of here in what is now Hamilton. I believe the property is off Dearborn Road. If they've resurfaced again, that is where they'll go."

"How do you know the mansion still exists?"

The woman shrugged. "Maybe it does, maybe it doesn't. But it's somewhere to start, isn't it?"

"Yeah, I suppose…" I wasn't sure if this was some kind of trap, or if the woman was really trying to be helpful, but I'd encountered both working for the police force, and one thing I knew for sure was you didn't turn down a lead unless you had a better one to follow. "Thanks for the tip."

The woman's smile widened, a crafty gleam in her eyes. "I accept your thanks, and will be in touch soon to collect on my favor. Good luck, Detective Chandler."

"Wait, what—" I began, but she'd already turned away, disappearing behind a bronze, paisley patterned curtain before I could finish asking her what favor she was talking about. She hadn't mentioned that her information came at a price!

I rushed after her, but when I jerked aside the curtain, there was only a small, glossy round table and two chairs sitting there. A small corner of the shop used for medium readings, I realized, and there was no entrance or exit aside from the curtain I'd just yanked open.

She'd disappeared.

twenty two

Disappearing woman or not, I wasn't about to waste the only lead I had. I jumped into my Jeep, then opened up the Maps app and pinpointed the location as best I could.

The satellite feature on my phone was a godsend—without it, I would have never been able to figure out where the property was, because the area the old woman had mentioned was all woodland—probably mostly used for hunting and trail hiking. But in the center of the forest, there was a large clearing, at least two acres, and though I didn't see any buildings there, it was the only spot that made sense.

I set a course for the area I'd marked, then shared the location with Maddock as a text message.

MEET ME AT THIS ADDRESS. I'VE FOUND SOMETHING, I added quickly, then turned the car on.

I received a text back: WHAT HAVE YOU FOUND?

JUST HURRY UP, I typed back, gritting my teeth. I didn't want to tell him I didn't know yet. I'M ALREADY ON MY WAY.

It took me around half an hour to get to the place, mostly because I took several wrong turns on the way there. But eventually I turned onto the correct road, and it led me to a small parking lot that was unsurprisingly empty considering the time of night. If not for my headlights, I wouldn't be able to see a damn thing, and it was a good thing I had them, because Maddock was standing right in front of the spot I was about to park in.

"Dammit!" I slammed on the brakes and glared at him. There were no other cars here, so he must have teleported. I rolled down my window. "Couldn't you have given me a little warning?"

His glare was even stonier than mine. "Why? I didn't get any warning from you before you sprang this on me. Didn't it occur to you that I might have had plans for the evening?"

I sighed. "It isn't like I did this on purpose. Can you just get in here so I can explain what's going on?"

I pressed a button, and the passenger door unlocked with a click that was far too audible in the cold, empty night.

Maddock said nothing as he approached the vehicle. He looked like a dark specter, dressed in a black overcoat, black slacks, and shiny black shoes. His inky black hair flowed over his broad shoulders, unbound, and his green eyes gleamed like a cat's might when hunting prey from the shadows. A little shiver went down my spine as he opened the door, but I forced down the feeling—Maddock wasn't my enemy. At least, not right now.

"Talk," he snapped once the door was closed and my window was rolled up once more. I pressed another button and locked all the doors, and he raised an eyebrow. "That serious?"

"I wouldn't have dragged you out here in the middle of the night if it wasn't." Grabbing the wheel, I finished parking the car, then shifted the car into park and turned in my seat to face him. "Shelley came to my apartment just minutes after you dropped me off. She says her son is missing."

Something flickered in Maddock's eyes, but the emotion passed too quickly for me to analyze it. "How do ye know he isn't just partying with his other goth friends?"

"Because I went to Shelley's house and searched his room. It's been marked."

Maddock's eyes widened. "How did ye discover that?"

"I used the same spell you did to uncover the mark," I said, a little smugly. I didn't need Maddock Tremaine for everything, now did I?

"No, not that." He looked like he wanted to roll his eyes. "I meant how did ye know where to apply the spell? Trial and error?"

"No." I paused, thinking back. "I just got a feeling as I approached the bed. I guess you could call it some kind of spidey-sense. I've had it a couple times now, and always whenever there was something magical nearby, so I made an educated guess and did the spell."

"Hmm. A second-sight for magic…" Maddock flicked his gaze away, staring out into the pitch darkness. "Yer powers are getting stronger," he muttered, almost to himself.

"What was that?"

"How did yer discovery of the mark lead ye here?" Maddock's voice was hard now. "Did ye touch the mark and get another vision? Because I assumed ye'd have learned from the last time —"

"I didn't touch the mark," I snapped. "I'm not stupid, okay? I found out about this spot another way."

"How?"

I gave Maddock a summary of my visit to the witch shop. When I told him I went there to see if any of the staff recognized the symbol or knew anything about it, he snorted derisively, but his expression grew thoughtful when I told him what I had discovered.

Without outright lying, I was careful to frame the story vaguely enough that he'd assume I got the information from the docent. I wasn't sure why, but I had a feeling telling Maddock about the old woman wasn't a good idea.

"So ye think that the Onyx Order has a residence somewhere in these woods?" Maddock asked. "And ye decided to rush here to check it out now, without any reinforcements?"

"I brought you, didn't I?"

"Aye, but if I'd known what we were getting into, I would have brought a few of my men." Maddock glared at me. "I'm not sure whether to be annoyed or flattered that ye'd think I'm capable of taking down an entire coven of witches by myself."

My cheeks flushed, mostly because I knew he was right. It would have been better if he'd brought his reinforcements. The thing was, I wasn't used to having people I could count on in situations like this. Whenever I'd had to deal with anything vampire-related, the only person I'd been able to call on was Tom. Right this very second, in a professional sense, Maddock was my Tom. And it hadn't occurred to me that he might want to bring anyone else along.

"Well, we're already here," I said evenly. "We can't just turn around now. Why don't we just go there and see if we can at least do some reconnaissance? Find out what we're dealing with. And then we can go back for reinforcements."

Maddock grunted. "I highly doubt this will work out the way yer suggesting. But I am curious to see if the directions ye were given lead to anything at all. The covens were always very meticulous about hiding their locations. I've never known where the Onyx Order kept their residence."

"What, you couldn't just use your fae magic to find out?"

He slanted his gaze at me. "We may be god-like, but few of us are all-powerful or all-knowing."

I snorted as I unfastened my seatbelt. "If that was supposed to be a humble-brag, I'm not sure you succeeded."

We got out of the car, and I checked to make sure my weapons were in place before locking up the Jeep.

"Ye should be wearing something more substantial than that." Maddock growled as he eyed my blazer. "It's bloody freezing out here."

I shrugged as I buttoned up. "The cold doesn't bother me." I lifted my face to the stiff breeze whistling through the night, enjoying the way it tugged at my silver curls. "I kind of like it, actually."

"I can see that." Maddock regarded me for a moment, curiosity gleaming in his eyes. I wondered why he found my affinity for the cold so fascinating. "Are ye going to stand there posing all night, or are we ready to go?"

"I was waiting for *you*," I grumbled, my cheeks heating again. I pulled my phone from my pocket, checked the directions again, then pointed north. "We've gotta head a couple miles that way."

We walked silently, the only sound coming from our frosted

breaths and our boots whispering along the dirt path. I'd learned long ago to tread softly no matter what sort of footwear I sported, and apparently Maddock possessed the same skill.

He's thousands of years old. He probably possesses lots of skills.

I glanced sideways at him as we walked. His face was mostly cast in shadow from the canopy of trees, but dappled moonlight spilled through the branches, highlighting his sharp cheekbones and the brilliant green of his eyes.

A part of me wished that I could question him more, to pry more knowledge out of him about this strange world that I was never more than a sideline member of. But even if I thought he'd answer, now was not the time to talk. The glare from my phone's screen was already alerting enough attention as it was, and if not for the fact that I needed it both to see where I was going and to guide us to our destination, I would have hidden it away.

The occasional rustle sounded through the brush every so often, making the hairs stand up on my neck. But it was always some sort of nocturnal animal—a raccoon foraging for its breakfast, a hedgehog scurrying through the undergrowth, a bat chasing a moth through the trees. Once, we even saw a bear picking what was left of the blackberries off a bush not five yards away. But even though it turned our way and stared for a moment, it largely ignored us and went back to its nighttime snack. I had a feeling Maddock was responsible for that—I felt a strange tingle that suggested he was using magic, maybe to keep some of the bigger animals from attacking us.

I could imagine doing this with Tom, walking hand-in-hand through the darkness, surrounded by silence and peace and nature. Of course, since Tom didn't have Maddock's mojo, we probably would have gotten eaten, or at least almost eaten. But still, it was a nice thought.

Except for the fact that he's gone, and you'll never get the chance to do anything like this with him again.

My throat swelled with tears, and I pushed back the familiar swell of grief. Now wasn't the time for that. And besides, there was a good chance that finding the Onyx Order would also lead to finding out what happened to Tom. He'd been looking for missing children, and the Onyx Order was kidnapping people. Surely there was a connection there. Occam's razor and all that jazz.

After about three miles, we came across what we were looking for. The path didn't change, but to our left, the trees gave way to a wide clearing. The opening was about five feet wide, large enough for me to get a good look, and though plenty of moonlight illuminated the clearing from above, I could see nothing but grass. But I felt that tingle again—the one that told me magic was near.

"It's here," I murmured, taking a step forward. A glint of silver caught my eye, and I looked down to see a lone earring half-buried in the dirt.

"Detective…" Maddock warned, but I was already crouching down, my fingers digging it out.

Boot prints in the ground suggested somebody had stepped on it, and recently, too. There were definitely people here.

A dark, windowless room with a single, bare lightbulb hanging from the ceiling. Beneath the lightbulb, a steel table. Chained to the table, a naked, black-skinned creature with a forked tail and cloven hooves. He was thrashing and screaming, his body lit with an unholy red glow as a pale woman in a black dress pressed both hands to her palms. Her ice blue eyes glowed unnaturally in the darkness as she siphoned his power. Anger and terror swirled in the air, emanating from the chained fae, but he eventually sagged under the weight of defeat—he was powerless to stop this woman.

The scene shifted to another dark room, this one with more lightbulbs, but still dim. Cages lined the walls, filled with various humanoid fae. Glittering, scaly skin and glowing eyes caught what light there was, but it was hard to see more.

A flash of fang caught my eye, and I blinked in shock at the sight of a vampire curled in the corner of his cage, looking more than half-dead. An extraordinarily large cage sat in the corner, and as my vision shifted its way, enormous hands gripped the cages and shook the bars. The bars turned poker-red, the hands started smoking, and a roar of fury split the air.

Another scene change. This one outside. Four men and a woman walked along a forest path. Reddish gold light filtered in through the trees, sunset lighting their way enough that flashlights weren't necessary. Jason was being carried on a stretcher between them, bound hand and foot. His black hair was matted with blood on the side of his head, and his pierced lip was swollen and bloody.

The path widened, revealing the same clearing Maddock and I had just discovered. This time, I could clearly see the colonial mansion that lay beyond, but before I had a chance to get a good look, Jason's eyes popped open.

Instantly, he began thrashing against his bonds, surprising the men enough that they dropped the stretcher. Somehow, he managed to roll free and get to his feet. The wild look in his eyes made my stomach drop with sympathy and fear.

"Stop!" a voice ordered from out of sight. The earring's view neared Jason, and I realized the voice was the one wearing the earring.

Jason twisted, his bound hands swinging out, and he knocked her a good one toward the earring—or rather, the person wearing it. The view tilted, then there was a blur that ended with the earring's view of a woman overhead—the blonde from earlier.

My brow furrowed. How had the silver earring recorded her in its memory earlier, if she'd been wearing it? Unless—

Oh. The realization hit me hard. The first visions must have been someone else. Had they been spying and wound up dead, and if so, what kind of sicko wears the earring of one of their victims?

Before I could process another possible scenario, the earring showed me the rest of the vision. The blonde staggered backward, and the other men grabbed Jason and started beating him back into submission...

The vision broke, and I stared at the little silver earring in my hand, my gut roiling with emotion. I wanted to crush it in my fingers, and then I wanted to find its owner and grind her into the ground with my boot until she was reduced to ash.

"What did you see, foolish woman?" Maddock whispered softly.

"A phoukas," I murmured, slowly rising. "She was chained to a table, and a blonde woman was siphoning her power. I also saw fae and other supernaturals in cages. And I saw Jason, right here, struggling against his captors. He's here, Tremaine. I know he is."

"Then we'd best retrieve him."

twenty three

I didn't tell Maddock that the last person who'd spied on this house and its happening had likely wound up dead. Or that apparently these people liked to keep belongings from the people they killed. I figured painting the witches out to be violent creepers might not surprise him, but wouldn't inspire him to move forward, either, and I couldn't waste time waiting for his backup—not with Jason's life potentially on the line.

"There's supposed to be a house here." I turned back to the empty clearing and glared at it, as if I could will the structure to appear. "A colonial mansion of some kind. I saw it in the vision with Jason. It's got to be here."

"It *is* here," Maddock said. "I can see it right now."

I scowled at him. "How the hell can you see it but I can't?"

He smiled smugly. "A fae of my age and power can see through most illusions without relying on the use of incantations or other devices."

I rolled my eyes. "That's great, O' Powerful One. Think you could help bestow some of that great power unto little ole me?"

To my surprise, Maddock's lips twitched. "I thought ye'd never ask."

He grabbed my hand, and I gasped as a surge of energy shot through my arm. Fire blazed through my nerve endings, but even though it was hot, it didn't hurt. It felt...good. Like I was glowing from the inside out, incandescent with power.

No, not 'like' I was glowing from the inside out. I literally was. The white light radiating from my body reflected in Maddock's eyes, and I caught my breath as I noticed the look in them. His eyes were warmer than I'd ever seen, filled with not just desire but...admiration? As if I were somehow awe-inspiring?

"Brilliant," he said softly as the glow faded, and I was glad for the darkness right then, because my cheeks were probably redder than burning coals—they were certainly about as hot. "Ye don't seem to be able to access yer power at will for some reason, so I've given you some of mine to tide ye over for now."

"Oh." My insides squirmed with guilt, and before I could think better of it, I reached out and touched his arm. "You don't have to do that. You should take it back."

After seeing how tortured that phoukas had been, as well as how violated Maddock himself had been when I'd stolen his power in a past life, it didn't feel right to take his magic.

"And then what?" Maddock arched an eyebrow. "If ye run in there with a gun as yer only weapon, ye will force me to spend all my time acting as a shield for ye. We'll be more effective if ye use some of my power. Think of it as splitting ammunition between two people instead of only one having a gun."

"Good point." I took a breath and let it go. The glow had faded, but the power still thrummed in my veins, and it felt damn good. It would have been hard to give it back, and I understood the witches a little better. I didn't agree with what they were doing. But if I was raised my whole life to believe that a fae's power was for the taking, and I knew what a rush it was every time I did so, I would damn well be siphoning it off them every chance I got.

Such a thought made me wonder if that's the kind of person I'd been in my past life. Had I taken power from the fae whenever I'd felt like it? Or had I only done it in moments of great need, as the memory Maddock had shared with me seemed to suggest?

God, it was still so weird to think I even had a past life. A whole other timeline I couldn't remember at all.

Either way, I didn't feel good about what I'd done, and I vowed silently to myself that I wouldn't be that person this time around. I wouldn't go out of my way to steal power from the fae.

But man, I hoped whatever power Maddock thought was hidden inside me would hurry up and manifest. I hated relying on others. In the human world, that'd never been an issue for me, but the supernatural world was a whole other thing.

"Okay, so what now?" I asked, staring hard at the clearing. It remained stubbornly empty. "I've got your power, but I still can't see anything."

Maddock chuckled. "I only gave ye a fraction of my power, Detective. Yer going to need much more than that, and practice, before ye can see through illusions the way I do. Until then, you'll need an incantation."

"Well, hurry up and tell me already!"

He told me the words, and I repeated them. Like the other spell

I'd mimicked from him, the words were thick and strange on my tongue, and it took me a few tries to get it right. But once I did, the air in front of me shimmered like a heat wave, then cleared to reveal the mansion I'd seen in the vision.

The two-story structure was dark and foreboding, with steeply pitched tile roofs, a solid stone exterior, and casement windows with the drapes drawn tight.

"Jesus, this looks like something straight out of Colonial times," I murmured, staring at the mansion in awe.

I mean, yeah, I knew it was supposed to be there, but knowing that in my mind and watching it appear before my eyes were two different things. I really needed to get used to this magic stuff.

"It *is* something straight out of Colonial times." There was a touch of amusement in Maddock's voice, and I glanced sideways at him. Was the cantankerous bastard actually warming up to me? "Now are ye going to stand there and gape at it like a tourist, or are we going in?"

"And here I was thinking you were actually being nice," I muttered.

Maddock's expression turned stony. "Don't make the mistake of letting yer guard down around me, or any other fae, Detective. Humans are little more than chattel to my kind, a fact ye would do well to remember."

I stiffened. "I'm not human, remember?"

His cold eyes blazed. "Even more reason for ye to be on yer guard. We tend to annihilate anything that could potentially be a threat."

An icy shiver slid through me, and I turned away. So much for getting along. Maddock seemed determined to remind me that we were immortal enemies, or at least that we were supposed to be. Whether I was human or supernatural, it was apparent that I was still the enemy unless he needed me for something.

I scowled inwardly. Maybe that's why Previous Lifetime Me didn't care so much about using *him*. We approached the clearing, treading softly along the path that clove its way through the tall grass and up to the front entrance of the house. The sense we were being watched through the sightless windows crawled up my spine, and the feeling grew more intense the closer we got. But there was no stopping now. We were here.

By unspoken agreement, Maddock took the back of the house while I took the front. There was nobody around, not so much as a mouse scurrying through the grass. It was impossibly quiet, like the calm before the storm that was sure to break as soon as we entered the house.

Maddock circled back around to the front and gave me the all clear signal. I drew my weapon, checked that it was loaded, then approached the front door. The porch creaked beneath our boots, and the wind picked up speed, whipping my hair in a frenzy around my face.

And then the door burst open.

A woman with long, fiery red hair rushed out. She was dressed head-to-toe in black, and her outstretched hand glowed with yellow-red energy that she flung in my direction. I squeezed off a shot, and she staggered back through the open doorway, a bloody red hole in her forehead. The energy died in her fingertips as she collapsed into the darkness of the house, and I blinked, surprised that I'd actually killed her. I thought she'd use her magic to deflect the shot or something, but apparently not.

I guessed bullets worked on witches, too.

"Fuck," Maddock hissed. He grabbed my free hand and pulled me through the door, leaping over the body of the dead witch as he did so. Inside was a large foyer, and past that a main hall with couches and chairs and tables from another time.

Curved stairways led to a balcony on the second floor, and more women rushed down the stairs, their faces illuminated by wall sconces that held flickering candles. Their hands glowed with energy, and I raised my gun, hoping I could take down a few more before they launched their magical missiles at us.

"Stay back!" Maddock growled, shoving me out of the way.

He raised his own hand and spoke quickly. A large blue shield shimmered into existence, surrounding us in a protective cocoon. Just in time, too, as several of the witches loosed the glowing balls of energy they'd been building in their hands. Purple, green, orange and more splashed against the shield as they converged on us.

"Shoot them!" Maddock yelled. "Take them out while I cover you!"

I did as I was told, aiming for the closest witch. I took her out with a shot to the heart, and she crumpled, revealing angry brethren just behind her. Planting my feet wide, I squeezed out shot after shot, taking down as many as I could while Maddock simultaneously deflected their blasts and returned fire with his other hand. I needed to focus on the fight, so I tried not to think about how awe-inspiring he was. But it was difficult. After all, it must take an extraordinary amount of energy to simultaneously defend and attack.

"You think you're so powerful," one of the witches spat as she pushed herself to the forefront. Anger burned hot in my chest as I realized it was the blonde I'd seen in my visions. "But you are only one, while we are many." A wicked smile curved her perfect red lips as she eyed Maddock up and down. "You will fall, fae, just like the many who have come before you."

She joined hands with her sisters, and they began chanting. Maddock tried to blast them, but other witches closed ranks, deflecting Maddock's blows and returning them with more blasts. One of the blonde's blasts, however, sliced right through Maddock's shield with such resounding force that the explosion of energy catapulted us to opposite sides of the room.

My shoulder crashed into a wall, shooting pain all the way down into my hands so suddenly that I nearly dropped my gun. Through the chaos and the crowd of witches, I couldn't see Maddock from where I'd impacted the wall.

I lifted my gun despite the pain in my shoulder and shot two more. But as I tried to shoot a third, my gun clicked empty. Frantically, I grabbed for my second magazine, fumbling in my efforts to reload as fast as possible. I fired enough shots to take down some of the witches between Maddock and I, then bolted to his side. He started trying to get the shield up, but that was the same moment a blindingly bright glow surrounded the chanting witches, and it just didn't take.

Maddock looked at me and shook his head, and he didn't have to say it. I knew. That shield wasn't going back up until Maddock's energy regenerated. The witches advanced now in hordes, and I aimed my reloaded gun right at them.

"Oh, no you don't!" I shouted, as I shot one of them in the throat. I aimed again, but somebody sideswiped me and I staggered, thrown by the unexpected blow. My gun clattered to the floor.

"Enough with the bullets." A witch with black hair and burgundy lips sneered. Her eyes glowed red in the darkness as she lifted a blazing hand toward me. "Let's see if you've got what it really takes to be one of us."

"To *be* one of you?" I shouted as I ducked her blast. I tried to make a grab for my gun, but another witch kicked it across the room, advancing on me as well. "Why the fuck would I want to do that?"

"Because you *want* to belong, and the only place you belong is among us."

More witches approached, closing ranks around me, but strangely enough, only the blonde raised her hand again. The rest stood at the ready, clearly able to attack if needed, but not making any moves. Not that I was complaining—but why hadn't they killed me already?

As I glanced over at Maddock, who was fighting off his own pack of wolves—or rather, witches—the blonde scoffed.

"Why do you worry about him?" she snapped. "He is not on your side, Brooke Chandler. He is fae—he is our enemy. You belong with us."

I turned slowly to face her. "I don't know who I belong with, but it's most definitely not with you."

Her expression turned ugly, and she blasted me, shouting the words to some kind of enchantment. I threw myself to the side, but the blast grazed me, and my left arm went numb. The witches I stumbled into shoved me back into the center of the strange little mosh pit we'd formed, and somehow I knew that the spell the blonde tried to hit me with was intended to paralyze me.

Cold anger filled me, and a rush of power the likes of which I'd never experienced spread throughout my body. Acting purely on instinct, I threw my hands out to either side of me, and a string of strange syllables burst from my lips.

Icy-blue energy rippled out from my palms in a shockwave, blasting the ring of witches off their feet. Their bodies clattered to the floor as if they were made of stone, and a bluish tint settled over their features, almost as if they'd been *frozen.*

A wave of tiredness swept through me, so sudden and fierce that my knees nearly buckled. But a gasp drew my attention, and I turned my head to see that all the witches who were fighting Maddock were standing stock-still, staring at me open-mouthed. Bodies littered the ground surrounding Maddock, who was staring at me with a similar expression of shock, but he recovered before they did, and blasted them with a wave of green energy that sent them all skidding back.

"Go!" he shouted, engaging them again.

I didn't need to be told twice. We hadn't come here to fight; we'd come here to find missing persons. We needed to do that and get out of here. Battles could be fought another day.

Unfortunately, the witches didn't feel the same.

twenty four

Heart pounding, I sprinted up the stairs, trying to put as much distance between myself and the witches as possible. I raced along the mezzanine corridor, ducking and swerving to avoid the occasional blast from below, but Maddock kept them occupied.

Even so, I needed to get out of the open before one of them actually hit me, so I threw myself through the first available doorway. This one led down a long, dark corridor with dusty old portraits and paisley blue carpeting. Red wax candles flickered in their holders as I raced past, throwing open door after door as I tried to figure out where the hell I was.

The first two doors led into empty bedrooms, but as I came to door number three, my second-sight tingled. Somehow, I knew there was a single witch beyond the door, and that she was waiting to blast me. So instead of throwing the door open, I drew my gun and fired three shots at different angles. A cry rang out, and I kicked open the door, gun at the ready in case my shots hadn't struck anything good.

But the witch was sprawled on the floor, blood gushing across the carpet beneath her. My shot had struck her barely an inch above the heart. Still alive, she struggled up onto her right elbow. Magic crackled weakly in her left hand, but she was losing blood too fast, and her magic was already winking out by the time I placed my boot on her wound and pressed down.

The witch let out an ear-splitting shriek, collapsing beneath the weight of my leg and the excruciating pain I was causing her. Unrepentant, I leaned in and pinned her with my stone-cold glare. "Tell me where you're holding the prisoners."

"N-never" the witch shrieked.

She bucked her hips, but stopped when I applied more pressure. My noisy interrogation was likely going to attract all kinds of attention from other witches in the hall, so I removed my boot and straddled her instead, poising my knee directly above her wound so I could apply more pressure as needed.

"If you scream again," I told her calmly, "I'm going to apply more pressure. And if that doesn't work, I'm going to start shooting. But not in the head, or the heart. I'll blow your fingers off, one by one, and then your toes, until you bleed to death."

I wasn't actually going to do any of those things—it would be a serious waste of bullets—but I wanted her to see me as an even bigger monster than her own kind. "And after that," I continued, "I'll hunt down your loved ones and do the same to them. Unless you tell me what I need to know."

"F-first floor," the witch stammered, her eyes glazed now. Her voice was growing weaker, and I knew she didn't have much time left. "Toward the back...is where you'll find them."

"Are they guarded?" I demanded. "How do I get in?"

"S-secur-ity c-c-c—" She gasped, and then her eyes rolled back in her head. Her body went limp as she expended her last breath. And then she was gone.

Cursing, I searched her body until I found what she must have been talking about. In the back pocket of her jeans was a security card, and as I touched it, I got a flash of the woman swiping it, then punching in a code.

6612.

Damn, was it really going to be this easy?

Footsteps echoed down the hall, and I launched myself to my feet, spinning around to face my attackers. So much for easy. A witch barreled in, magic already blasting from her palm. I twisted out of the way and rolled, then came to my feet and aimed my gun straight at her forehead. She dodged the shot, but the witch that rushed in behind her wasn't so lucky. She took it right in the eye.

Ouch.

"You bitch!" the first witch cried, flinging another blast at me. I didn't move out of the way fast enough, and the ball of energy hit me in the right arm, rendering it completely numb. Panic rose up in my chest as my firearm clattered to the floor.

The witch smiled smugly. "Not so tough without your bullets, are you?" she purred. "I don't know what you did to the others in the main hall, but you won't be getting away with it again."

She extended glowing hands, clearly intending to paralyze the rest of me.

"Fuck you." I swung to the left, my dead arm acting as a counter-weight, then side-kicked her in the stomach. She flew into the wall, head cracking against the plaster. Her eyes rolled shut as she slumped to the floor. In the movies, she would have gotten back up again, but in real life, when the back of your head is slammed up against a wall, it tends to knock you for a loop. Even if you are magical.

Not wanting to wait around for more of them to show up, I snatched my gun from the ground and made a break for it. There would be more like her, though, and I wasn't as good of a shot with my left hand, but I'd make do.

I dashed to the end of the hall, took three turns, evaded another magical blast, blew another witch's head off, then stumbled down a flight of steps. My foot missed the last step, and I narrowly avoided face-planting in the hall. But my left foot landed a little too hard, and pain shot through my ankle, sending me hobbling against the wall like an old lady.

Only two bullets left, and then I was going to have to pull out the vampire gun. Hopefully, my right arm would start to work again soon, because it had taken me three shots to kill the last witch with my left hand. I didn't have that kind of ammo, and the witches seemed to be endless around here. Just how big was this damned coven, anyway?

Thankfully, the number of witches seemed to be thinning out, because I encountered no one as I limped along a narrow corridor. The walls were dark and bare here, the wooden floorboards beneath my feet unobstructed by carpet—probably a sort of back passage that servants would use, if we were in a different time and place.

It didn't take me long at all to find the prison—the last door on the left-hand side, right where the passage curved, was made of reinforced steel, and there was a glowing blue security pad there. Slowing to a stop, I slipped the keycard from my pocket and swiped it, then punched in the code I'd seen in my vision.

The locks disengaged with a series of echoing clicks, followed by a long, *loud* blare that made me wince. Stepping inside, I fumbled for a light switch on my right, and found one. Fluorescent bulbs glared, and animalistic hisses ensued as captives tried to shield themselves from light they were no longer used to seeing.

Eyes wide, I looked around the room. It was exactly as I'd seen it in my vision—rows and rows of iron cages stuffed with fae and other supernatural creatures. Now that the room was illuminated, I noticed a good deal of them were vampires, and my hand went instinctively to the vampire gun strapped to my side. But these weren't the bloodthirsty, evil beings I was used to gunning down on the dark streets of Chicago. These were sickly, listless, emaciated creatures, just as much of a victim as all the other supernaturals. Even the giant in the back, who must have been Maddock's employee who had gone missing, looked pathetic—he was curled up in a ball in his humongous cage, clearly trying to avoid the bars, and he looked like he hadn't eaten in a week even though he hadn't been gone that long.

Yes, I could waste time going around and killing all the vampires, but to what avail? My fight wasn't with them today. It was with the Onyx Order.

I crept down the rows of cages, sending up a silent *thanks* to the powers that be that the pain in my ankle was starting to ease. No permanent damage, then—at least not to me. I was sure the vampires here couldn't say the same.

I peered in each cage as I continued on, looking to see if Jason was amongst the prisoners. But when I caught no sign of him, my heart sank.

Don't despair, Brooke. He's not a supernatural. They're probably keeping him somewhere else.

But why? That was the burning question making the pit in my stomach grow no matter how much I tried to tell myself this was all going to work out somehow.

You can't afford to spend any more time here, I told myself as I walked around the room. The prisoners were all shouting for help now, those who weren't fae rattling the bars of their cages as they begged to be let out.

I warily eyed the vampires one last time, who were looking at me with a combination of hope and hunger, then ran my fingers over a metal switchboard set into the wall just to the left of the entrance.

A burly human stood in front of the switchboard, showing two witches how it operated. He flicked several of the switches, demonstrating the one that sent an electric charge through the cages, one that set off an alarm, and one that opened them all simultaneously.

The witches thanked him, and then one of them blasted him with a glowing red ball of energy that punched a hole straight through his chest. Gore splattered everywhere as the man fell to the floor.

"All right, all right," I muttered, pulling myself out of the vision as my gut roiled. Yeah, I'd seen death plenty of times, but there were still a few things that could make me queasy. "Let's get going here."

I took a deep breath, bracing myself, then flicked the appropriate switch. Another loud noise blared as the cage doors clanged open, and I was out the door, getting out of the way as fast as I could.

Unfortunately, I wasn't fast enough to get ahead of the desperate, angry, and scared horde of supernatural creatures, and pretty soon I was being jostled and buffeted against the walls as they overtook me. Fear hammered in my heart as a vampire turned toward me, red eyes glowing as his fangs flashed, but even though he was out of his mind with hunger, he didn't turn on me, nor did any of the others.

Maybe gratitude was a thing after all?

Either way, I wasn't going to wait for them to change their minds, or regain the energy to attack, or whatever it was that was saving my ass right now. But it wasn't like I'd had a lot of options, either. The witches pointed it out themselves—we were outnumbered.

Were being the operative word now. With the vamps lose—as long as they turned on the witches and not on Maddock or myself—the playing field was about to be leveled.

Grasping for the nearest door handle, I wrenched it open, then locked myself into a pitch black room. No, I hadn't checked the room for lurking enemies, but the alternative was staying on the other side where there was, for certain, a stampede of vampires who might kill me in their haste to escape. A dark, unknown room was a safer bet than certain trampling.

Heart hammering against my chest, I leaned against the door, then took slow, even breaths. My second-sight tingled like crazy, though, so I flipped on the light switch, wanting to know what magical thing was causing it to go off. But the room didn't seem out of the ordinary—it was a kind of sitting room, with low couches and tables and shelves filled with decorative knickknacks. A single casement window lay straight ahead, and I stepped toward it, drawn to the moonlight spilling through the pane.

As I approached the window, it shimmered, and suddenly it wasn't a window at all, but a painting of a woman sitting in a high backed chair in front of a window. Moonlight spilled over her, illuminating the dark hair she wore piled atop her head in an elaborate dressing, her pale-as-cream skin, and the high-collared black dress she wore with white lace ruffles. A beauty mark was the only thing that marred her otherwise flawless skin, and she would have been extraordinarily beautiful if not for the haughty, there's-shit-under-my-nose expression on her face.

"That's Simona Van Lucia." A familiar voice spoke softly, and I whirled to my left. The blonde witch from earlier stood in the shadows, a smile playing across her face as she leaned a hand on one of the arm chairs. "Our founder."

"Wait, what?" I leveled my gun at her, trying to ignore the way it trembled in my hand. "You're dead. I killed you!"

Blondie laughed, a tinkling sound that was completely at odds with the way she was behaving. "You killed most of us, I'll give you that," she said, taking a step toward me. "But I recharged enough that I was able to shield myself from the worst of your magic. An extraordinary talent you have," she added, her gaze crawling over me. "It's hardly any wonder that the Master wants you."

"What are you talking about?" I snapped, forcing myself not to back away as she closed the distance between us. "Who is your Master?"

"Dinnae talk to her," a hoarse voice ordered, and suddenly the shadows toward the back of the room lightened, revealing Maddock.

He was kneeling on the ground, his hands and feet bound by strange, glowing coils that I was willing to bet were made of pure energy. They seemed to be causing him extreme pain. Two witches flanked him on either side—Blondie's companions from the Main Hall—and the cruel, satisfied smiles told me all I needed to know.

"Maddock!" I lunged for him, but Blondie shoved me back, heedless of the gun in my hand.

"Now, now," she said lightly as I stumbled backward. "You see those restraints on Lord Tremaine's wrists? They have the ability to cause unimaginable pain. Even death. And my sisters are all too eager to put them to the test."

"If you hurt him, I'll kill you," I promised, my voice trembling with rage as I leveled the gun at Blondie's head. "I'll kill you, and then I'll feed you to the horde of prisoners stampeding through this godforsaken house right now. By the time they're done, there won't be enough left of you to bury in a box."

"Such violence!" Blondie exclaimed in mock-horror, pressing a hand to her buxom chest. "It's really not necessary, Detective Chandler. All you need to do is listen to what I have to say."

"And what is that?" I demanded.

She turned her attention back to the painting. "This portrait of Simona was painted nearly four-hundred years ago, just one year after the Onyx Order was founded. The crucifix around her neck was added later on, to remind us when we look upon her why we do what we do."

"And just why *is* it that you do what you do?" I sneered.

Blondie stepped back, a feline smile curving her lips as she gestured toward the painting again. "Why don't you find out for yourself?"

"No!" Maddock shouted again. "Brooke, *don't.*"

There was more emotion in that single last word than I'd heard from Maddock combined in all the time I'd known him. But as I looked upon the golden cross resting against Simona's chest, I was instantly drawn to it. Unable to heed his warning. I lifted a hand, brushing my fingers against the painted crucifix, and as I half-expected, a vision hit me.

Except it wasn't a vision, because I was watching myself standing in front of the same painting, in the same room, in the exact position that I stood now. The only difference was, a tall, sandy-haired man stood directly behind me.

As I looked at him through the perspective of the painting, the vision seemed to blur his face. That hardly mattered, though, because I instantly recognized the slight cant of his head, the way he stood with his weight shifted slightly onto his right leg—a quirk he'd developed to cope with an old knee injury—and those long, almost elegant fingers as they reached up to grab my shoulders.

"Tom?"

twenty five

I gasped as the vision broke, and the hand curling around my shoulder tightened. It was *real*.

I spun around, joy and disbelief warring for dominance in my heart as I looked up into his face. He was so familiar. So exactly the way I remembered him, with grey-green eyes that stared out of a long face with high, broad cheekbones and a prominent chin. Full lips that could curl into a sneer when interrogating a suspect or facing down a vampire, or curve into a smile, as they did now.

"Is it really you?" I asked, my voice a hushed, almost reverent whisper.

"It's really me," he said softly, his hands settling on my waist.

I framed his face with my own hands and kissed him long and hard, relief coursing through me so violently that I went weak in the knees. I kissed him so that I could block out every lip-lock I'd shared with Maddock over the past few days, and overwrite them with the man who truly deserved them. The man I *loved.*

"H-how are you here?" I whispered, pulling back.

I was acutely aware of eyes boring into me from across the room, and I even heard titters from the witches. I don't know what they thought was so funny about all this, and I didn't give a fuck. Tom was back—I knew it was him, because my second-sight wasn't going off. The man standing before me was flesh and blood, with no hint of illusion like the phoukas who had ambushed me in Maddock's home.

"I'll explain everything later." Tom gripped my shoulders and spun me around to face the painting again. "Right now, you need to go through that door and rescue your friend's son. He's being held there, on the other side."

"Door?" I asked, bewildered as I stared at the painting. Was this some kind of secret passageway?

But then I remembered we weren't alone, and I swung around to glare at Blondie. "Why are you just standing there? Why are you letting him help me?" Then I turned back to Tom. "How do you know about Shelley's son?" An alarm bell shrilled in my mind—something about this whole situation was very off. But there was so much going on right now that I couldn't zero in on what it was.

"Brooke," Maddock choked out, his voice alarmingly feeble. My stomach dropped as I looked over at him—his hair hung limp around his face, and his normally tanned skin was nearly as pale as a vampire's. "Ye cannae trust him. Dinnae go through."

"It's the fae you can't trust," Tom said, derision dripping from his voice. "He knew that I was alive, and yet he had no problem kissing you."

On the contrary, Maddock had all kinds of problems kissing

me, but my mind had latched onto a different part of Tom's statement.

"You knew Tom was alive!" I shouted at Maddock, heat rushing into my face. "And you didn't tell me?"

"It wasn't the right time." Maddock somehow managed to sound haughty despite being on the verge of death. "The deal was that I would help you find your fiancé if you helped me find the missing fae. A mutual goal that seems to have been met." He raked a scathing glare over Tom. "Now that we're all here, I suppose this is as good a time as any to tell ye—"

The witch on Maddock's right snapped her fingers, and an electrical charge crackled through him. Maddock's powerful neck snapped back beneath the force of it; his jaw worked, as if he were holding back a scream, but to his credit, he made no sound.

"Enough talk," Blondie snapped, her eyes cold. "It is time." She slapped her hand against the edge of the painting, and a mechanism engaged, gears and cogs creaking. A loud series of clicks followed, and the painting unhinged from the wall, revealing a flicker of torchlight from whatever lay beyond. "Go on."

Shaking my head, I held my ground, mind reeling as I tried to put the pieces of this impossible puzzle together. Why was Tom here? Why hadn't the witches killed him? If he'd been kept prisoner, why did he look so clean and unharmed? If he wasn't a prisoner, then where had he been all this time? Why hadn't he contacted me? My mind spat out possibilities, but none of them made any sense, and they all jumbled together incoherently.

"Brooke, you have to do this." Tom's voice was hard. "If you don't, Jason will die."

Jason will die.

The words echoed in my head, over and over, and I nodded. That was why I'd come here tonight, wasn't it? Not to rescue Tom—I'd thought he was dead—but to find Jason and return him safely to his mother. I'd promised, and no matter what else happened tonight, I had to keep that promise.

Resolved, I curled my fingers around the edge of the painting and pulled it aside. It swung forward, revealing the windowless room I'd seen earlier when I'd found Blondie's "borrowed" silver earring in the woods.

The single light bulb hung directly above the steel table, but the phoukas was crumpled in a corner of the room, and Jason was chained to the table instead. He'd been stripped down to a pair of red boxers with black bats on them, and anger lanced me as I took in the bruises and lacerations covering his pale skin.

He lifted his head, eyes stark with fear as they locked onto mine. His gaze was empty and detached, his lips dry as little more than a wheeze passed between them.

"H-help me…"

"I'm so glad you've finally arrived, Brooke." A man stepped forward from the shadows, and I gasped.

Father James?

And yet, it wasn't. The kindly, even genial, expression remained on his softened features, but he'd traded his pastor's outfit for a black, hooded robe. One that looked remarkably familiar.

"You!" I jabbed an accusing finger at him. "It was you who set fire to the motel room!"

He nodded approvingly. "Very good. Perhaps you aren't as stupid as I initially thought." He gestured with a silver blade in his hand toward Jason. "Although, the fact that you came here to rescue this stupid boy with only a single fae for backup doesn't exactly convince me of your intelligence, either."

I gritted my teeth. "You've been lying to me all along. Who the hell are you?"

"My true name is Vincent Van Lucia," he said as the witches filed in, dragging Maddock with them. "I'm a warlock—a direct descendent of Simona, and the current head of the Onyx Order. Yes, Father James Baxter is a lie, but an excellently fabricated one, wouldn't you agree?"

"A warlock?" I took a step back, my head spinning as I tried to reconcile this new piece of information with what I already knew. "Does that mean Detective Baxter is a warlock, too?"

"Guy?" Father James—no, *Vincent*— let out a scornful laugh. "I am his ancestor, as his line comes from my uncle, but the magic died out in his bloodline for some reason. It was simple enough for me to come into his life and addle his brain. After that, all it took was the right amount of paperwork to make him think I was his brother."

Addle his brain. Oh God.

"That's why he doesn't remember Tom," I said, more to myself. *Even though everyone else in the precinct does.*

Vincent nodded. "It was regrettable, but I had to erase all memory of Tom from Guy's mind. He had seen too much, and I couldn't kill him. The whole point of having him around was so I could have someone on the inside that my partner could use to get things done."

"But...but why?" I tried to piece the clues together, and kept coming up with explanations that couldn't be true. "Why would you erase Tom from Baxter's memory?"

"Because he would have exposed the truth—a truth you weren't ready to know yet."

"*What* truth?"

Father James—I just couldn't think of him as Vincent—sighed, as if this conversation was so tedious he could hardly bear it. "You know, I thought that our mutual hatred of vampires would make it easier for me to like you, but you're so insufferable that if I didn't need you, I would have killed you already."

"Is that why there were so many vampires trapped downstairs?" I asked. "Because you've got it in for them?"

"More than you can imagine." Father James's eyes blazed with such potent fury I nearly took a step back. "Many years ago, long before you were born into your current lifetime, vampires attacked me when I was driving home with my wife. I managed to survive, but they murdered her. The light of my life...so impossibly vibrant one moment, then gone the next." His eyes were downcast now, his voice reduced to a whisper, and if he didn't have Jason strapped to the table and Maddock bound up, I would have felt sorry for him.

"After that day," he continued, voice stronger now, "I gathered my brethren, and we traveled across the world, doing everything we could to extinguish the vermin who took my wife's life. But due to their filthy magic, vampires breed much faster than we could hope to extinguish them, so I realized we needed to come up with a better plan.

"I thought long and hard about this, seeking out supernaturals who were more powerful than I to gain glimpses into both past and future." His eyes lifted to mine, and a cruel smile curved his lips. "And that's how I discovered I needed you."

"Me?" The detective in me couldn't seem to stop asking questions, especially as Father James seemed to want me to know what was going on. Maybe if I got enough info from him, I could find a way out of this. "Why me? How the hell am I the key to wiping out vampires if I can't kill them any faster than you?"

"You're a shadow," Father James said simply. "A being born both witch and fae. Your ability to walk both worlds and hide your true nature in the shadows is one of the things that define you, and you, my dear, are one of the best. So much so, in fact, that even I had my doubts as to whether you were truly a shadow at all."

I shook my head vehemently, denying what he was saying with every fiber of my being even though a treacherous voice in my mind was nodding at how the explanation cleared up so many things. "I'm not a shadow—I'm not *anything*. There was nothing supernatural about my parents."

Father James arched an eyebrow. "From what I understand, you have no idea *who* your parents were."

I clenched my jaw—he was right, but I wasn't going to admit that to him. "I still don't believe you."

Father James shrugged. "Believe me or not, you're still here. And I couldn't have done it without my prodigy." He smiled over my shoulder.

My heart stopped, and I turned slowly. Last I checked, it'd been *Tom* standing behind me.

And there he was. The love of my life, standing behind me...pointing a gun at my head.

"No." My eyes pleaded with him as my heart tore to shreds in my chest. "No, Tom. Please. Put the gun down. Put it down and

walk away, and I'll forget this ever happened."

"No, you won't." Tom's face was a stony mask as he clicked off the safety. "Neither of us will."

"He's a convincing lover, isn't he?" Father James called from behind me just as my eyes began to well with tears. His scathing voice effectively dried my eyes, and I whirled around, glaring at him with as much hatred as I could possibly muster. "If not, you wouldn't be here right now. And then where would we be?"

"You sick bastard," I breathed, curling my trembling hands into fists. The realization was almost too much to bear. "You've been fucking with my head for years."

"All for a good cause, I assure you," Father James said pleasantly. "The world continues to rip itself apart with the procreation of vampires. Like this boy here." He flicked the ritual knife back toward Jason, who lay completely still on the table, frozen either by magic or fear. "I don't know what you kids see in vampires—" He sneered at the teenager. "—but you should be glad that I caught you before you made a mistake."

"Why should I be glad?" Jason's voice shook as he spoke for the first time, his dark eyes blazing. "What the fuck do I have to be glad about, when I'm strapped to this freezing table, about to be killed?"

Father James laughed. "Typical teenage boy, thinking the world revolves around you." He lowered the knife. "I'm not here to take your life, child. It means absolutely nothing to me, and I don't shed blood without a cause."

"He's bait," I said, feeling numb. "You kidnapped Jason to lure me here."

Father James scoffed. "*Everything* I've done was to lure you here, Brooke. To bring you to this very moment, so you could have the chance to make things right." His voice softened, and he took another step toward me. "You've always wanted to rid the world of vampires, right? Well, now you can. We can, together. Once and for all. I just had to make sure you were the right one before I brought you here."

He was crazy. Absolutely bat shit crazy. There was no other explanation.

"And just how the hell did you determine that?" I asked, wondering just how deep that crazy well went.

"By getting you to use magic." Father James smiled smugly. "That's why I sent the wraith to you—and it succeeded where Tom failed to do so."

When my eyebrows pulled together, Father James nearly rolled his eyes. "Must I spell it out for you?" He huffed. "Right. I sent the blasted man to confirm your powers. Normally, I prefer to handle such tasks myself, but you of course planted yourself right in the middle of the most vampire-infested city in the country. I'm sure that was no accident on Oscar's part."

My heart skipped a beat at Oscar's name. Would Father James discovering me make him a target, too? It slammed into me that maybe I'd been selfish about this whole thing. But I bit my tongue, not wanting to interrupt anything Father James said right now. He was my best shot at finding those answers, and I could keep him talking so long as I didn't send his fragile psychotic mind over the edge.

"So I sent Tom," Father James continued. "You know, because we can't have anything happening to me, else who would lead the coven? They would be too busy avenging my death to see the bigger picture. But with Tom there, we would have someone close to you—someone expendable. Someone who could get you to use magic so we could confirm your true nature once and for all."

For a long moment, we just stared at one another. I wasn't saying anything. Father James wouldn't let the conversation die just like that, so if I didn't speak, he would eventually start up again. And I was noting every fucking detail, piecing it all together. Searching for answers that could lead to stopping him and getting the fuck out of here.

True to my expectations, he continued. "You should be thankful we go through such measures to confirm these things," he said. "You could have been without a childhood, had we chosen to just take you without any assurances."

I swallowed, trying to bite back the words, but he'd found my Achilles heel. He'd touched on the thing I couldn't *not* respond to. "You knew since I was a child? How?"

"Your parents, of course. They fled their own coven to keep you safe. Not that running away worked, since they ended up dying by my hand—"

"You bastard!" I lunged forward, forgetting about the gun that Tom held to my head. But Father James simply raised his hand and shouted a spell, and I froze mid-strike.

"Now, now, Brooke. Your parents made their choice. I might not have liked them much for hiding you from us, but surely you take some solace in knowing they died protecting you, died refusing to give up your location? We didn't *want* to kill them, after all. We were just looking for you. A shadow, a child born of a witch and a fae. But of course they refused to give you up. Do you know we lost nearly a decade trying to find you after that?"

"Oh, I'm *so* sorry for the inconvenience." I tried to sound caustic, but my voice was trembling too much with rage. He'd left my vocal chords unfrozen for some reason. "You *sick* motherfucker."

"I have good taste, though," he said lightly. "And killer instincts. I didn't find you for another twelve years, but the moment I did, I was almost certain it was you. Even though Tom over here failed to get you to use magic in front of him, I knew you had it in you. I knew I could bring it out. And look—I did." Father James laughed, shaking his head. "You followed the breadcrumb trail I laid out perfectly. The offer from the chief of the Salem, P.D. to let you join them for a stint. The drug-dealing accountant fae that led you to the supernatural underbelly of Salem and showed you what was possible. The shade I coerced into attacking you in the alley. The wraith I sent to your apartment. All you needed was someone to lead you in the right direction, to challenge you so that your confidence and power would grow. And just look at you now! The second you connected with your power, you flourished."

He said this as if he was doing me a favor.

"Yeah, well, that's great and all, but what the hell do you want from me?" My voice was steady despite the rage still burning in my chest. "What's your big plan, now that you've got me where you want me?"

"It's a long story, to be honest, but let me give you the…Cliff's Notes?" He shrugged. "I've never understood you young people and your colloquialisms. In any case, hundreds of years of research have allowed me to unearth a spell that can erase the entire vampire gene pool from the Earth, but it's a spell that requires immense, almost god-like power. By offering yourself up as a willing sacrifice, I can perform a ritual that will allow me to acquire such power."

"Yer not serious!" Maddock exploded, speaking for the first time since he'd been dragged into the room. He struggled against his bonds, and one of the witches zapped him again. "The spell yer suggesting is—"

"Is what needs to be done," Father James said coldly. "And if you speak again, I'll have your tongue cut out." The witches zapped Maddock again, and his jaw clenched hard, cutting off whatever response he would have made.

"What the hell is Maddock talking about?" I demanded. "Just what kind of spell are you trying to perform that requires my *sacrifice*?"

"Don't concern yourself with the details," Father James snapped. "Focus on the boy's life—that's why you're here, isn't it? And don't think you're not expendable," he added with a glower. "If you don't cooperate, I'll kill you *and* the boy, and then I'll hunt down another shadow. You might be rare, maybe even more powerful than most, but you're not the only one who was born that way."

I stared at him. So this was it. Either I died, or I died. Those were my choices.

And if I didn't give myself up willingly, he would hunt down more of my…kind…and kill them, too, until one of them finally gave him what he wanted. Whatever that was.

"Well?" Father James demanded. He twirled the dagger in his right hand. "What's it going to be, Brooke?"

I ground my teeth together in frustration. None of the choices Father James gave me were acceptable, but I couldn't just come out and say that. I needed to buy a little more time, and I needed Father James' spell to loosen on me so that I could defend myself.

But first things first.

"The boy," I said, sounding resigned. "Let him go. You've already got me here at gunpoint. You've got nothing to lose by letting him go—think of it as an act of good faith."

Father James searched my gaze, and whatever he saw there must have satisfied him. "Fine. But you have to say the words first. You have to say, right here, right now, that you're giving yourself up willingly to me. And you have to do it properly too, with names. Like a legal document."

"No!" Maddock roared, but I refused to look at him. If I did, I was afraid I'd give into the desire to reassure him, and I couldn't do that. This had to look convincing.

"Shut up, Tremaine," I growled. *Please, for the love of whoever is up there listening,* trust me, *Maddock.* I took a deep breath, then said, "I, Brooke Chandler, willingly give myself up to Vincent Van Lucia of the Onyx Order."

"There now, that wasn't so hard, now was it?" A broad smile spread across Father James's features, lighting him up. He gestured to Blondie. "Release the boy."

Blondie lifted a hand and recited a spell. Jason screamed as the shackles flared, turning cherry hot, and he thrashed, trying to get away from the scalding heat. The shackles shattered abruptly, sending burning hot shrapnel flying, only narrowly missing where I stood. It happened so fast that Jason tumbled right off the table mid-thrash and cried out as he landed hard on the floor.

"Get up!" I shouted, and he struggled to his feet. "Get up, and get out of here!"

The kid gave me a wide-eyed look, full of guilt and fear. I glared at him fiercely, imparting threats of what would happen if he stayed without so much as opening my mouth, and he dashed out the door.

"Good riddance," Father James said, pulling out a gun from inside his robe. He leveled the barrel at me, and sharp panic stabbed me in the chest. "But I'm not letting you get off that easy, Brooke. You're going to suffer for all the trouble you put me through."

He fired, and I screamed, bracing myself for the slug. But the shot didn't hit me—instead it flew past me, and I heard a strange gurgling sound. Twisting my head around as best as the waning spell would allow me, I watched as Tom sank to his knees, clutching at the hole in his throat. Blood gushed from it, covering his clothes, his skin. And then he toppled face-first to the ground.

"No!" I shrieked, trying to get to him, but the spell held me fast, rooting me to the ground. Yes, Tom might have betrayed me, but I still loved him. Even the worst of betrayals couldn't undo years of emotion. I wasn't ready to let go of him yet, even if it was just the Tom I'd known then, and not the Tom he really was.

"You didn't think I was going to shoot you, I hope?" Father James asked, almost conversationally. "That would hardly fit the terms of the ritual. No, I figured shooting Tom would cause you the greatest pain in the shortest amount of time, and since I've already waited decades, I think I've been patient long enough. Besides, after all of his failures, he was a dead man anyway."

twenty six

"There now," Father James said soothingly as he lifted me onto the table. "Now that you've got nothing left to fight for, why don't you just relax? This will be over soon."

"I may have said the words willingly, but that doesn't mean I'm going to be relaxed," I snarled. I thrashed my head, tossing it this way and that as Father James began to remove my clothing, pulling off my blazer and unbuttoning my shirt. If I could move the rest of my body, I would have kicked his balls into his throat, but there was nothing for it.

"Stop this!" Maddock demanded, desperation and anger in his voice. "Father James...Vincent...whoever the bloody hell ye are. Stop this madness. Trade her for me!"

Father James's fingers paused on the third button of my blouse, and he looked up at Maddock with interest. "You, a powerful fae lord, would sacrifice yourself for this woman?"

"I have far more power than she does," Maddock said, and I was amazed at how much haughtiness he mustered into his words. "Surely ye can accomplish whatever spell yer trying to perform with me instead of her."

Father James laughed, a cold sound that sent a shiver vibrating along my spine. "You are powerful, Lord Tremaine, possibly the most powerful fae I've ever had here. And I will greatly enjoy siphoning every last drop of magic from you, which clearly I planned to do anyway. But the blood of these shadow folk is far more potent that any fae, which makes it invaluable—and in this case essential—in rituals requiring sacrificial magic. Ten fae as powerful as you could not replace her; if that were the case, we'd be done with this by now, yes, seeing the ease with which we've been collecting your kind? But you already knew that, didn't you? That's why you offered to trade your life for hers, because you knew it wouldn't work."

"You won't get away with this," Maddock growled, his brilliant green eyes glowing with hatred. "When the fae courts find out what you've done, they will come for you."

Father James laughed again. "By the time they find out, it will be too late. I will be far too powerful for them to stop. They will merely be lambs headed for the slaughter, making my job easier. Believe me, I welcome that day. I'll make sure to leave the door open."

Maddock's shoulders sagged, and my heart sank to my toes. Somehow, even though all sorts of horrible things had happened tonight, the sight of the mighty Maddock Tremaine slumping in defeat made me feel the worst. If he was reacting this way, then whatever Father James was about to do was unimaginably horrible.

And after I was gone, he was going to drain Maddock of his power, over and over and over again until greed pushed him into going too far and snuffing the very life from Maddock's body altogether. Just like the phoukas crumpled in the corner.

Drain him of his power.

The words echoed in my head, and an idea came to me. I had no idea if this would work, and I forced my face to be utterly blank, not wanting Father James to suspect my plan. There was a good chance this wouldn't work at all, especially considering that I'd never done anything like it in living memory. At this point, though, I had nothing left to lose. I needed to try.

Holding my breath, I sat perfectly still as Father James undressed me. He took his time with the buttons of my shirt, and I wanted to scream at the excruciatingly slow pace, but I forced myself to be patient. The shirt came off, leaving me in a support tank, and I didn't have to pretend a shiver at the lascivious gleam that entered Father James's eyes.

"It's too bad we're doing this under such circumstances, Brooke," he said softly as he slowly slid the fabric up my abdomen. Disgust crawled through my veins as his fingers traveled up my bare skin, but I forced myself to hold it together. "If I didn't have to kill you, I could spend some time enjoying you first." His eyes darkened as he pulled up my top, revealing my breasts. "Although I don't see why I can't take a few minutes anyway, since you've made me wait this long already. What's the harm? I'm in no rush, and you can't move."

Predictably, his hands clamped over my breasts, and that was my moment. I focused all my will at him, envisioning the power that pulsed within Father James's blackened soul, and wished with all my heart and soul for that power to be mine. A rope of energy snaked out of me and into him, and Father James stiffened as it latched onto the source of his magic.

"You bitch!" he croaked.

Mentally, I yanked with my inner power as hard as I could. His magical energy came spilling out of him, a bright red glow that enveloped us, and the witches cried out. Out of the corner of my eye, I saw them rush forward, trying to help their master, but their clothing and hair caught fire, and they fell back. They would be a problem, but I blocked them out, making sure my attention remained glued to Father James.

I locked my gaze with Father James's, absorbing the burning hatred and fear in his eyes as I absorbed his power. He was frozen in place, his hands still clamped on my breasts, and his fingers began to shrivel, gnarling up like the ancient man he really was. His face withered next, his skin becoming like paper, and his eyeballs shriveled away. Dried-up skin and flesh crumbled, and within minutes, even the bones of the hands that gripped my chest disintegrated, leaving me covered in a layer of absolutely revolting ash.

If the power Maddock had lent me before made me feel high, it was nothing compared to this. I felt like a goddess as pure energy radiated through my entire body, lighting up every single cell until I glowed, incandescent.

I rose from the table, the ash on my body evaporating, and took a single step toward the witches. They shrieked in horror, then turned tail and ran out of the room.

Flicking my hand in Maddock's direction, I flung a tendril of power at him. It latched onto his magical bindings, reducing them to nothing. Satisfied he would be fine, I took a step toward the door, intending to hunt down the rest of the witches.

But the more I moved, the hotter the power seemed to burn inside me, and suddenly, it was *too* hot. Pain engulfed me, and it was like the power was turning on me, attacking the very fibers of my being.

"Brooke!" Maddock shouted as I dropped to my knees.

I couldn't speak, couldn't see anything except a haze of red, and I knew with terrifying certainty that the power was about to devour me. Even in death, Father James was still trying to kill me.

"Brooke!" Long fingers dug into my shoulders, directing my attention to the man crouching in front of me. Maddock's leaf-green eyes bored into mine, anchoring me in the sea of pain, and I grabbed onto that lifeline and held on for all I was worth.

"Ye need to transfer some of your power to me!"

"Wh-what?" I croaked.

"Ye've taken in too much magic; it's burning ye up. Ye need to get rid of it! It's very similar to what ye did to Father James, ye just need to focus."

It took longer than it should have for his words to sink in, but when they did, I nodded. Just like with Father James, I tossed out a rope of power, latching it onto what I could only describe as Maddock's soul. But instead of pulling magic out of him, I pushed it *into* him.

Waves of energy flooded outward, and I pushed relentlessly, getting rid of as much as I could. It seemed like it took forever, but finally the pain began to abate, and the power sizzling through my veins returned to a more manageable level.

Panting, we both collapsed against the ground. I pulled my

shirt down, covering myself, and closed my eyes. The magic humming inside me was still many times greater than what Maddock had given me earlier, but it was no longer debilitating.

Tilting my head to the side, I watched Maddock. His gaze was latched onto the ceiling, chest rising and falling rapidly. A faint red glow enveloped his body—he was clearly still absorbing the magic I'd given him.

"So," I said when I'd gotten most of my breath back. "We're even now, right?"

Maddock turned to face me, his eyebrows raised. "What?"

"You've been mad at me for like, half a century, because I stole a bunch of your magic. But now I've just given you a bunch of magic—about two thirds of what I'd taken from Father James." And considering that I'd sensed magic from a variety of supernaturals within him, that was a lot. "So we're even now, right?"

To my surprise, Maddock gave me a lopsided grin. "We might be, Detective," he said quietly. "We might just be."

I smiled back—the first real smile I'd cracked all day. I wanted to hold onto this moment. To this one feel-good split-second in time.

But I had a feeling that killing Father James wasn't going to end my problems. If the memory Maddock had shown me was any indication, Past Life Me had thought things were going to go downhill from here. I needed to prepare for that eventuality.

I just hoped to hell that I was wrong.

twenty seven

After defeating Father James, clearing the rest of the house was a piece of cake. The witches were engaged in a full-out war with the other supernaturals, so Maddock simply used the ample power flowing through his veins to create a series of illusions that confused everyone and allowed the supernaturals to make a break for it. It pained me to watch so many vampires rush out into the night, wild and free, but there was no time to go after them—I needed to make sure Jason was safe.

"Go find the boy," Maddock growled, not looking at me. He'd herded the witches together into the main hall and was performing some kind of spell that would trap them in an alternate dimension. "The last thing I want to find out is that after all this, he was killed."

No kidding. Part of me wanted to stay and watch what Maddock was doing—the strange chanting and waving of his arms was changing the air, causing a variety of crisscrossing glowing blue lines to appear above us. But Maddock was right, so I tore my gaze away from the scene and left.

It didn't take me as long as I'd feared to find Jason. He was huddled in a closet only a few rooms down from the one where I'd had my final showdown with Father James. When I slid the closet open, he jumped, raising his forearms over his head to ward me off.

"Jesus," I muttered. He was still only dressed in that pair of boxers. I shrugged my blazer off, then held it out to him. "Come on, kid, let's get you covered up a little. It's freezing outside."

"I-I'm sorry I left you," he stammered, struggling to his feet. His dark, haunted eyes were full of shame, and he wouldn't meet my gaze even as he slipped my coat on. The fabric strained against shoulders that, even not fully grown, were almost too wide.

"Don't be. I told you to leave, and I meant it. You would have only been in the way." I winced at the way the words came out. "Sorry, I didn't mean it like that."

"No, I deserve that." Jason raked a hand through his black hair, turning his face away from me. "I deserve every mean thing you've got to say about me, so go ahead and let it loose. I fucked up. I treated my mom like shit, and my obsession with wanting to become a vampire led to this whole mess."

"Jason." I clapped a hand on his shoulder, and he flinched. "Jason. Look at me," I said, hardening my voice, and he slowly turned his gaze back to mine. "I could say all kinds of things to make you feel guilty, to make you think you're the worst scum on this earth for what you put your mother through and for all the stupid choices you've made that led you here."

He flinched, but didn't drop his gaze, and my estimation of him rose a little.

"But," I added, softening my voice now, "I'm not going to do that. I think this experience has been punishment enough, and I think you've learned your lesson. You're just a good kid who made some bad decisions. You know what you need to do now, though, don't you?"

Jason nodded slowly. "I need to apologize to my mother. And do whatever I can to set things right between us."

"That's right." I squeezed his shoulder again. "Look, this isn't going to be easy for you to hear, but you need me to say it, so I will." I paused, took a breath. "Whatever relationship you had between you and your father…that's never going to change. Whatever kind of man he was, he was your father, and there's no shame in missing him. But he's not here now, and your mother *is*. And so is your little brother, the only other piece left of your father aside from you."

"I know." Tears streamed from Jason's eyes now, and he swiped hastily at them. "It's just…I know what mom says about him, but he was my father."

"Yes. But you need to cherish what you have left, and stop holding onto what's already gone. That means you need to stop chasing after your father's ghost, and start taking care of your family. You're the man of the house now. They need you."

It was kind of healing giving that little speech, because it was just as much for him as it was for me. I knew how he felt about his father, because that's how I felt about Tom. The horrible truth couldn't erase years of conditioned emotions. But Jason and I both needed to let go of the ghosts of our pasts.

A feeble groan echoed from somewhere, and Jason and I froze.

"What the hell is that?" he whispered, terror in his voice.

"Stay here," I ordered. I grabbed my gun, then sidled out into the hall to see what was going on. Had Maddock missed one of the witches? But there was nothing to be seen. Just the empty corridor with its flickering candles and dusty portraits.

The groan came again, and I cautiously moved up the hall, heading in its direction. The hairs on the back of my neck rose as I realized it was coming from the hidden room where I'd defeated Father James. What the hell was going on? Was there a wraith in the room?

I entered, bracing myself to see the specter of Father James. Yeah, it sounded ridiculous, but after everything I'd seen in my life—and especially tonight—I wasn't about to discount the possibility.

But instead, I saw the phoukas, lying on the ground. I'd thought it was dead, had completely forgotten about it, but it was twitching, clearly trying to get to its feet.

As though the thing sensed my presence, it rolled to face me. Glassy eyes stared up at me, filled with a combination of hope and despair. My heart clenched as I realized it was hoping that I might kill it and put it out of its misery, and afraid that I would instead leave it here to suffer.

"Bloody hell!" Maddock swore, and I jumped.

Spinning around, I saw him standing just two feet to my right, behind me, his murderous glare latched onto the phoukas. Okay, so maybe the despair hadn't been directed at me after all.

Maddock growled. "I thought the damn thing was dead!"

"I'm guessing you finished imprisoning the witches?" I asked dryly.

"Damn right." Maddock advanced on the thing, and it curled up into a ball, retreating against the wall. "But it seems that my work here is not yet done."

"Stop." I put myself between Maddock's bulk and the pathetic creature shivering on the floor. "I'm not going to let you hurt him."

"Hurt *him*?" Maddock bellowed. "I'm not going to hurt *it*; I'm going to kill it! It's a fucking unseelie!"

"So what?" I shouted back. "You just let a horde of vampires go free into the night, and you're going to bitch at me because I'm willing to let this phoukas do the same? He's been tortured and drained for who knows how long, and he deserves to taste freedom now that we've killed his captors."

"Yer insane," Maddock said flatly.

"Bite me."

Ignoring Maddock, I turned away, then crouched down next to the phoukas. He trembled as I reached out with my hand, but with nowhere to go, the creature was forced to endure my touch. I placed my palm on its smooth, almost glass-like skin, then focused on tethering that rope. The phoukas's eyes widened as I forged the connection, and he began to glow faintly as I transferred power into him. Not nearly as much as I put into Maddock, but enough to breathe energy back into him.

Before my eyes, I watched the emaciated, beaten creature swell, its skin and muscle returning to its previous shape and luster. Long black hair, previously matted, turned into nearly downy-soft strands as he stood.

"Filthy vermin," Maddock grumbled from behind me, but I ignored him as I got to my feet as well.

"I feel...strong." The phoukas looked down at its hands in wonder, as if it couldn't believe they were real. "Stronger than I've felt in...I cannot even remember. I cannot even recall what I was like before I came here."

"How long have they held you?" I asked carefully. My heart swelled with a combination of happiness and sympathy for him. Perhaps unwise, since he was unseelie, but what could I do? I felt how I felt.

"I don't know." The phoukas's voice was hollow as he lifted his gaze to mine. "A century, perhaps? Maybe longer. But I am free now." He bowed, his long hair swinging forward with the motion. "I am in your debt, Brooke Chandler. If you ever have need of me, call my name, and I will come and grant you any single favor that is within my power to do so." His voice whispered in my head then, and somehow I knew he was telling me his name.

"Be well," he said, and then he launched himself past Maddock and out of the room.

I faced Maddock and arched an eyebrow at the look of utter disbelief on his face. "What are you looking at?"

"Ye just earned a favor from an unseelie." The shock in his voice told me this was an extremely rare event. "A no strings attached favor."

"Well, I guess that's what you get for doing good deeds," I said casually, not really interested in making a thing out of it. I had no idea what I wanted to do with this favor, and with everything that happened, I was desperate to put it out of my mind. I stepped past him, and my heart dropped into my shoes as my gaze latched onto Tom's body. The pool of blood that had spread beneath him was already starting to dry, and his fingers were curled stiffly at his sides, already well into rigor mortis.

"Stop." Maddock gently grabbed my arm as I moved toward Tom. "Ye dinnae want to see him like this."

I hesitated. Part of me thought that it would give me closure, to turn Tom's body over and see his dead face for myself. But after what he'd done to me, after the utter betrayal I'd suffered at his hands, I could hardly stand to look at him, never mind touch him. I didn't want the real Tom. I wanted my memory of him—of what we'd had. Seeing him would be too confusing for my emotions.

My hands dropped to my sides, and I sighed. "What are we going to do with him? We can't bring his body into the morgue. As far as everyone's concerned, he's already dead."

"Nothing." I swung my narrowed gaze toward Maddock, and he shrugged. "Nobody knows about this place. It's unlikely any human will ever stumble upon it. We can leave him here to rot. 'Twas what he was going to do with ye."

"I guess you're right." I shoved my hands into my pockets and ignored the little voice in my head that said Tom deserved a grave, regardless of what had gone down between us. That voice was full of guilt for something that wasn't my fault, and I wasn't going to listen to it. I'd wasted enough of my time already, trying to avenge a man who'd been serving my enemy this entire time. I wasn't going to waste any more.

"How did ye know that ye'd be able to kill Father James by siphoning his magic?" Maddock asked, drawing my attention away from my very dead ex-fiancé.

"I didn't," I admitted. "I just figured I could. I seem to be both an endless battery and an endless charger. Between that and the vision you showed me back at your cabin, it stood to reason that my ability to siphon magic might be stronger than that of a full-blooded witch, or a warlock like Father James."

"It is," Maddock confirmed. "That's why Father James wanted ye. I didna know ye were shadow born," Maddock added, as if he could read the thought right from my face. Perhaps living for centuries and having every recollection of it had that effect on people. Or maybe that was just the kind of person Maddock was. "I didna even know for certain if shadows were real. I thought they were a myth, or at best, a reality long extinct. But it may explain how ye can siphon power and reincarnate so quickly."

"Maybe those things are best left to people who don't know how to use it," I muttered, thinking of Father James' plan to take my ability for himself.

"If Father James had succeeded, nothing would have stopped him," Maddock said. "He would have had unfettered access to fae power, and could have used that power to do much more than simply annihilate the vampires. But," he added, leveling his gaze at me, "yer nothing like him."

"In more ways than one," I said, sliding my gaze back to Maddock. "But I don't see the point in all that trouble now that it's said and done. Wouldn't he have burned up with all that power, too?"

"The older ye are, the more magic yer able to tolerate at a single time," Maddock said. "As a centuries-old warlock, Father James's threshold would have been considerably higher than yers."

I raised an eyebrow. "Does that mean one day I'll be able to siphon off the amount of magic I did today without combusting into flames?"

"Aye," Maddock said. "And that, Detective, is exactly why yer so dangerous."

epilogue

"It's been a week now, and he still hasn't shown up."

I turned my head to look at Detective Baxter, who was leaning back in the driver's seat of his car. We were parked outside a possible suspect's door, once again doing reconnaissance work, but Guy clearly wasn't into it. Dark circles marred the skin beneath his eyes, and the expression in them was glassy and filled with worry.

"I'm sorry, Baxter," I said, and I really was. Father James might have been an evil bastard, but Detective Baxter only knew him as his brother, and he had every right to be worried about him. "I wish there was something I could do to help."

"You've helped plenty," Baxter said tiredly.

We'd put out BOLOs, questioned his congregation and staff, searched his apartment, retraced his steps in every way possible—well, except for the one way that would have led to the truth.

Because the truth was that Father James had been erased from the earth, had disintegrated completely. All that was left of him was the power that still hummed in my veins, waiting to be used again.

"I need to be doing more," Baxter said. "I need to be out there, looking for him."

"Are you sure he didn't just take off?" I asked, not for the first time. "You know, sometimes holy men have crises of faith. Maybe he needed time to re-evaluate himself, to examine his beliefs—"

"James wouldn't do that." Baxter's voice was quiet, but firm. "He was rock solid about his beliefs, and even if he wasn't, he wouldn't just up and leave without telling me." Anger seeped into his voice now. "He *wouldn't*."

The rest of the day passed like this, tension and resentment and anxiety bleeding off Baxter until I thought I would be sick with guilt. And not just because I felt guilty about killing off Father James, even if it had been the right thing to do. I'd been having intense nightmares the past couple of nights—nightmares that showed a thick darkness rolling over Salem. In several of them, Baxter was pointing a gun at my face and glaring at me with abject hatred.

When the day was over, I slammed into my Jeep, then pulled out my phone and called Maddock.

"What is it?" He answered on the first ring, and the butterflies in my stomach—which hadn't made an appearance since I'd last spoken to him—broke into a happy dance at the concern in his voice. Then again, that wasn't really surprising; we hadn't spoken in a week.

"Meet me at the mansion," I told him. "There's something we need to do."

I hung up the phone, then drove out there. Part of me was dreading the idea of going back to the Onyx Order's base—there were so many terrible memories within it, and I wasn't talking about my own. I'd caught glimpses of all kinds of horrific things when Maddock and I had cleared the place. But I needed to do something about Detective Baxter before I went insane with anxiety, and this was the best way to go about it.

"Are ye really going to refuse to let me teleport ye anywhere ever again?" Maddock demanded after I'd parked my car in the same lot as last time and hopped out of the vehicle.

"No," I admitted. "I just needed the drive to clear my head."

"Good. Then let's do it right now."

He wrapped his arms around my waist, and the next thing I knew, we were standing in the main hall inside the mansion. Nausea tickled the back of my throat, but it was much less severe than it had been the last time, and I wondered if the extra power residing in my body had anything to do with it.

"Now tell me what we're doing here."

I took a deep breath, then squared my shoulders and looked Maddock directly in the eye. "Detective Baxter is on a mission to find his brother. If we don't give him some kind of closure soon, he might very well end up coming here."

Maddock raised his eyebrows. "Here? To a place he won't be able to even see?"

"Here, to this general area that's just a bit too close to where things happened," I said quietly. "Here to where there might be traces of me in the surrounding areas as well as Father James. I know how you feel about law enforcement getting involved in the supernatural."

"Aye, ye do," Maddock murmured, looking me up and down. I scowled at him. "That's not what I meant."

"And just what do ye expect me to do, Detective?" Maddock asked. "We can't very well produce Father James's body. There is no trace of him in the mansion. Something which I believe was your doing," he added dryly.

I huffed. "I know that. But I was thinking that, since you're ancient and powerful and all, you might have something in your arsenal that could alter a body."

"And whose body do you plan on altering, exactly?" he asked softly.

I sucked in a deep breath. Stared Maddock straight in the eyes. Said the name that I'd hoped I would never have to speak again.

"Tom's."

Maddock threw back his head and laughed. The rich sound echoed in the empty space, filling me with a warmth that was entirely inappropriate for the situation. But I was thankful for the way it melted away the hurt that came with thinking about my ex-fiancé.

"Just when I think I have ye figured out, ye surprise me, Detective." Maddock's brilliant green eyes glimmered with humor, and possibly even a little admiration. "It's not going to be easy, but it's a good plan."

He wasn't kidding when he said it wasn't going to be easy. I gagged at the stench of rotting flesh as we entered the hidden chamber behind the painting where Maddock had left Tom. He was still face-down in the now dried puddle of blood, right where we left him. Maggots crawled over decaying flesh, the majority of his skin having deteriorated where the wriggly white worms devoured him.

"Ugh." I pressed my sleeve over my nose and mouth, resisting the urge to hurl. "I'm already starting to regret this."

"Too late now." Maddock's face twisted in an expression of disgust, but evidently he was made of stronger stuff than I, because he approached the body without the slightest bit of hesitation.

Crouching on the bare wooden floor, he allowed his hands to hover over the body. An orange glow emanated from them as he muttered strange words under his breath, and I watched as the maggots disintegrated.

Nice trick.

Maddock made a flicking motion with his wrists, and the body flipped over of its own accord. I flinched at the sight of Tom's mostly rotted face, but forced myself to look as Maddock worked his magic, transforming it. Before long, the corpse I was looking at no longer resembled Tom Garrison in any way. His clothes were changed to a dirty and torn pastor's robe, and what was left of his features and build were now Father James Baxter's.

"I'm guessing that if anyone runs a DNA test, they're going to find out it wasn't him?"

"Aye, but dinnae worry. I'll ensure it's taken care of." Maddock rose, eyeing the body with a mixture of satisfaction and revulsion. "We're already done with the hard part. Now we just need to find a place to dump him—a place where we can be sure he'll be found."

I let out a breath. "And then what?" I asked, turning to face him. "What do we do after that?"

Did we go on with our lives and pretend like this never happened?

"After that," Maddock said softly, his brilliant green gaze meeting mine. "We move on, and pray that Detective Baxter never finds out that ye murdered his brother."

The End

Want more? Join our insider's club at

http://shadowsofsalem.com/insiders-club/ for the latest

information on new releases and special events

MEET THE AUTHORS

Jasmine Walt is obsessed with books, chocolate, and sharp, pointy objects. Somehow, those three things melded together in her head and transformed into a desire to write. Usually fantastical stuff, with a healthy dose of action and romance. Her characters are a little (okay, a lot) on the snarky side, and they swear, but they mean well. Even the villains sometimes.

www.jasminewalt.com

USA Today bestselling author Rebecca Hamilton lives in Georgia with her husband and four kids, all of whom inspire her writing. Somewhere in between using magic to disappear booboos and sorcery to heal emotional wounds, she takes to her fictional worlds to see what perilous situations her characters will find themselves in next. Represented by Rossano Trentin of TZLA, Rebecca has been published internationally, in three languages. You can follow her on twitter @InkMuse

www.rebeccahamiltonbooks.com

CPSIA information can be obtained at www.ICGtesting.com
Printed in the USA
LVOW11s2107260916

506260LV00002B/432/P